ABOUT THE AUTHOR:

Born in Manchester, David Lightfoot is married with three daughters and eight grandchildren. He worked for over 30 years as a lecturer in a College of Further Education. Now retired, this is his second book. North Cornwall is an area that he is familiar with after spending many holidays there. He has always had an interest in ancient history and unexplained mysteries.

BY THE SAME AUTHOR:

───────────────

Sanctuary

Copyright © 2021 David J Lightfoot

The moral right of the author has been asserted.

Apart from any fair dealing for the purposes of research or private study, or criticism or review, as permitted under the Copyright, Designs and Patents Act 1988, this publication may only be reproduced, stored or transmitted, in any form or by any means, with the prior permission in writing of the publishers, or in the case of reprographic reproduction in accordance with the terms of licences issued by the Copyright Licensing Agency. Enquiries concerning reproduction outside those terms should be sent to the publishers.

Matador
9 Priory Business Park,
Wistow Road, Kibworth Beauchamp,
Leicestershire. LE8 0RX
Tel: 0116 279 2299
Email: books@troubador.co.uk
Web: www.troubador.co.uk/matador
Twitter: @matadorbooks

ISBN 978 1800464 230

British Library Cataloguing in Publication Data.
A catalogue record for this book is available from the British Library

Typeset in 10pt Minion Pro by Troubador Publishing Ltd, Leicester, UK

Matador is an imprint of Troubador Publishing Ltd

HIDDEN AGENDA

David J Lightfoot

To Carole Janet Lightfoot

Joy Penrose lived and worked on a farm in North Cornwall. One night she was wakened by a strange light and the sound of distressed animals. Together with the farmer she went to investigate. They both encountered what seemed to be an extra-terrestrial craft in the nearby woods. The craft flew off at speed, colliding with the blades of a wind turbine before disappearing in the night sky. The subsequent enquiry into this frightening incident generated the usual denials, misinformation and threats from officialdom.

It soon became apparent that there was something sinister taking place at a disused airfield nearby. Gradually a connection was uncovered between the unexplained sighting and the activities at the airfield. Research revealed a secret government program called 'The Transformer Project' was centred at the airfield.

By the conclusion of this mystery, all involved are forced to reflect on the origins of civilisation and to face the fact that we may not be alone in the Universe.

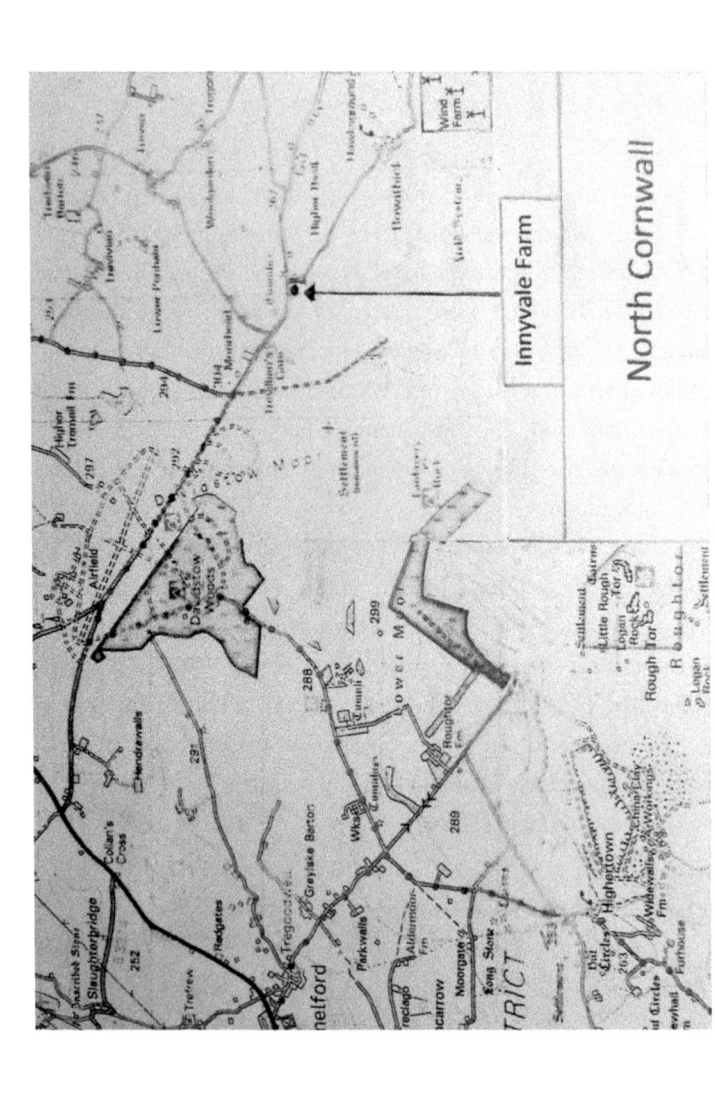

There is nothing hidden, that will not be revealed;
nor any secret that will not be known and come to light.

Luke 8:17

ONE

CLOSE ENCOUNTER

The sleeper awakes, but the nightmare continues.

In the shadow of the ancient granite masses known as Rough Tor and Brown Willy, on the edge of the bleak expanse of Bodmin Moor, stands Innyvale Farm. This small farm comprised about 20 acres, split between the cultivation of crops and the rearing of upland sheep. There are some places that are wild and some that are beautiful. Bodmin Moor is both wild and beautiful. It can be an inhospitable desolate wilderness when ravaged by the elements, but on a clear, calm day it is possible to climb to the summit of the Tors and view both the glistening waters of The Channel and the vast Atlantic Ocean. The remains of Stone Age enclosures litter the landscape, testament to the legacy of human habitation. Farming has survived in the fertile land that surrounds the moor, evidenced by the little collections of cottages, farmhouses and barns connected by narrow lanes. Nearby is the old Davidstow airfield, open windswept and abandoned. A few isolated concrete structures remain like tombstones in an ancient cemetery. They are reminders of a bygone age, but are now derelict and eroded by the weather. In this relatively remote area, people work hard to make a living in the same way that their ancestors always have. They are stoic and worldly, not prone to fanciful stories. However, in recent months a sense of unease has spread through the community. There have been reports of strange lights in the sky at night. Something has been spooking the animals. In guarded conversations some local people are talking about unidentified flying objects. Fear of the unknown is just below the surface and rumours of close encounters with aliens are no longer summarily dismissed.

It was in this environment that Joy Penrose got up for work at Innyvale Farm on a calm, spring morning. The clocks had just gone forward by one hour at the weekend and the prospect of longer days beckoned. She was conditioned to getting up early and today as she switched off her alarm at 6am she felt slightly more lethargic than usual having lost one hour's sleep. Early starts and late finishes were part of the routine on Innyvale Farm. At the start of that day Joy expected that it would be a routine Monday. She had no reason to anticipate that events later that day would transpire to make this day anything but routine.

After locking the door to her apartment, which she rented from the farmer, Joy reflected on how lucky she had been to secure her job on this local farm. She pushed back a strand of blonde hair that had fallen across her face and took a deep breath as she looked up into a cloudless blue sky. Even at this early hour, the warmth from the spring sunshine bathed her face bringing out the ruddy colour in her cheeks. It did not bother her that her jeans were muddy, and her jacket had worn patches on the elbow. Her first task was to assist the farmer with a sheep which had been having difficulty giving birth. It was the lambing season and there would be more arrivals in the next week or two. There was always something to do, mending fences, mucking out barns, driving the quad bike, cleaning equipment, checking dry stone walls, feeding livestock, grooming horses. It was never boring, but it was physically demanding. Certainly not the job for anyone worried about breaking a fingernail! After leaving Agricultural College two years ago with qualifications in animal husbandry, it was the job she had always wanted. Being outdoors helping the farmer with his flock and tending the crops were things that she always found rewarding. Joy had known the farmer, Bert Pennington, for many years. They had first become acquainted when her parents bought her a pony as a present on her tenth birthday. Bert had agreed to provide a stable for the pony and Joy became a regular visitor. As Bert and his wife did not have any children of their own, they had been pleased to offer help to this young local girl. Over time they had become fond of Joy and had developed a friendship with the Penrose family. Joy's ambition was to run her own farm. She had found suitable employment hard to find on her return to Cornwall. One day, on a visit to Innyvale Farm she received a proposition from Bert Pennington which she was pleased to accept. It was an invitation to work on his Farm. Bert had agreed to let her live in a self-contained apartment in a wing of the large farmhouse. He had convinced her that it would be good to gain experience before branching out on her own. The apartment had previously been used for guests holidaying in North Cornwall. Living there now formed a part of her package of remuneration and was close enough to allow her to make regular visits to her family home in Camelford. Working and living on the farm had enabled Joy, with Bert's permission, to develop a pony trekking activity. This venture had received good customer reviews on the tourist websites. It had gained an excellent reputation as an exciting outdoor pursuit location and the farm was now home to five ponies. Many customers returned season after season. This little enterprise provided enough income to support the cost of food and shelter for the ponies plus a little extra to supplement her farm wage. It gave Joy the confidence to imagine that one day she would run her own farm.

After a full day working on the farm, Joy made her final check on the ponies. The sun was dropping behind the trees of Davidstow Woods as she crossed the cobbled yard that led towards the farmhouse. She was looking forward to the prospect of a hot bath, good food and an early night. Across one of the fields she could see Bert with his checked shirt flapping over his camouflage trousers, his cap pulled low over his head checking that the sheep were settled and the gate to the field secured for the night. He was an affable employer with a strong belief that job satisfaction came from more than just the pay and conditions. In his view, it came from liking the work and performing tasks well. He did not stand for any nonsense but rewarded his employees fairly for their efforts. People knew where they stood when dealing with Bert Pennington. Joy liked him as a person and respected his skills in animal husbandry.

It may have been on the edge of the moor, but Innyvale Farm had convenient access. It had an entrance from a road which ran along the perimeter of the old Davidstow airfield before branching towards a village called Bowithick. Looking south, the low undulating hills of the moor, masked all but the summits of the craggy Tors. To the east was a wind farm. The large turbines rose from the ground like great white sentinels, sending out a low frequency hum. They may have been intended to save the environment, but they certainly spoilt the view. As Bert turned to walk back to the farmhouse, he could not help reflect that erecting turbines in the countryside created an eyesore. The front of the farmhouse faced west with open views towards the airfield perimeter and the dark coniferous trees of Davidstow Woods. It was the end of another hard day and Bert intended to spend a relaxing evening watching television. He was on his own this week.

His wife was nursing a strained ankle and had gone to stay with her sister in Exeter for a few days whilst she recovered.

As darkness closed in Joy had soaked in the bath for a while. The physical nature of the work that she did required stamina. Her thoughts wandered over the events of the day until the pangs of hunger reminded her that she still had some cooking to do. She had a healthy appetite and wasted no time preparing a hearty meal. Later, Joy indulged herself with a glass of wine whilst she washed up. She soon started to feel mellow from the effects of the wine and retired to her bedroom. Usually, she picked up a book and read for relaxation, but tonight she fell asleep almost as soon as her head touched the pillow. She suddenly started to dream about the farm being flooded by light, terrified animals stampeding around the farmyard. Then she was awake, or she thought she was. If this was reality, she could hear the agitated bleating of sheep outside. The flock sounded unusually noisy and restless. A white light flooded the bedroom throwing the shadow of the window frame onto the opposite wall even though the curtains were drawn. Not sure if she was still dreaming Joy picked up the bedside clock. The time showed that it was just after 11.30pm. It meant that she had only been asleep for an hour at most. She felt slightly disorientated and a little frightened. There was an unsettling, slightly surreal atmosphere. Familiar objects looked abnormal because of the light. The tranquillity of the night had become violated by discordant cries. Something was very wrong.

Curiosity trumped fear as Joy moved towards the window which faced west towards Davidstow airfield. She cautiously moved the corner of the curtain so that she could see outside. Her heart was beating quickly. The sheep were bathed in a high intensity beam of light which shone like a laser from a craft which was hovering above the farm. The startled animals were terrified, running in all directions in total panic. The scene was macabre. It was also hauntingly abnormal and alarming. Joy's first thoughts were that it was the police helicopter, but there was little audible sound, just a low-pitched hum. She could hear it and feel it resonating on the windowpane. It was like the sensation of sound vibration when standing too close to a bass speaker in a night club. Concerned for the safety of the animals she grabbed a torch from her bedside table and pulled on jeans and a tee shirt before staggering out through the front door. Not that she needed the torch because the craft continued to emit a vertical beam of light which swept up and down the field like a strobe at a concert. It appeared as though the craft was searching for something. It was shaped like a triangle and black. Suddenly, the light went out and the craft zoomed away at high speed, positioning itself above the distant trees at the edge of the airfield. Joy had never seen a helicopter or aircraft move so erratically and with such powerful acceleration. Again, the beam of light shot down and the craft descended into the woods. The animals were still making a discordant noise in the field behind the farmhouse. The glow from the craft pulsated eerily through the foliage as if from a small bonfire. For a moment Joy was transfixed by this weird phenomenon. Her pulse racing, her thoughts confused, she regained a measure of composure and realised that Bert Pennington was jogging back across the yard from the direction of the sheep field. Still dressed in his pyjamas his face was pallid and a deep frown wrinkled his brow.

"What on earth is it?" Joy remarked nervously.

Bert opened the door of his Land Rover which was parked in front of the farmhouse. He plucked a pair of binoculars from under the dashboard and turned towards her. He had a perplexed expression on his weathered features.

"I've no idea, but I'm going to find out." His voice was tense as he feverishly tried to focus the glasses.

He jumped into the driving seat and switched on the engine. His hand beckoned for Joy to follow. "Shut the front door and jump in if you want to come with me."

Fortunately, Joy had left her boots just outside the front door and her fleece was in the hall. By the time she had put these items on Bert was impatiently moving off and she had to run down the yard to catch the departing Land Rover.

The Land Rover lurched over the cobbled farmyard and headed towards the woods which were about a mile away. "So much for an early night," Bert grumbled. "I have lived on the farm for thirty years and in that time I have never seen anything like this. I'll be making a complaint in the morning about the disturbance if this turns out to be some military exercise."

If he had not felt so absorbed by events Bert would have been slightly embarrassed to be sitting next to an attractive young woman whilst dressed in his pyjamas. He was trying to think of some rational explanation for what he had seen. "Something very odd is happening. The animals are clearly spooked by it too. Did they tell you at college that animals have a deeper sense than us in detecting danger? I have a bad feeling that this is going to be something very sinister so if you prefer to stay in the vehicle it will probably be safer."

"Well I have to admit that I feel scared, but I want to know what this is as much as you do," Joy replied.

They parked the vehicle at the edge of the woods near to some grassy humps on the edge of the airfield that had once been bunkers used to store ammunition. Bert collected a torch from his toolbox and hung the binoculars around his thick neck.

The sight of Bert dressed in pyjamas with binoculars draped around his neck like a necklace, his bald head reflecting the light emanating from the woods, reminded Joy of a scene from a horror film. Even though fearful of entering the wood, she could not prevent a nervous smile from invading her face at the sight of her companion.

Conscious of the unwanted attention, Bert barked abruptly. "Don't stand there grinning. Grab the camera from the glove compartment and follow me." His anxiety was making him uncharacteristically rude.

The dark shapes of the trees were starkly silhouetted by the brightness of the light as they picked their way through the undergrowth in the general direction of the glow. In places the undergrowth was thick and brambles clawed against their legs. The damp grass was beginning to grow longer now that spring had arrived and the sticky buds on low branches left tacky smears on their clothing. As they got nearer, they could see a triangular shaped craft parked in a section of the wood which had been cleared of trees to form a firebreak. It was a clear night, making the woods cold and damp, but neither of them noticed as adrenaline coursed through their bodies. As they got closer, they felt an invisible suppression impeding the way forward, as though they were walking through deep water. Their vision had become impaired making the scene ahead blurry. Stumbling through the last clumps of damp bracken they were now only yards away. Movement and vision were now fully restored.

The craft was silent, but they could feel electricity in the air and on their clothing. A white glowing light rotated on the lower section of the structure. Joy pressed the shutter and the camera responded with a flash which reflected off the black, smooth surface of the frame. Bert moved forward a few yards and put his hands on the glasslike surface of the craft. It was hot to the touch and so he quickly removed his hands from contact. It was a small object, no bigger than a double decker bus. The black side panels seemed to join each other seamlessly with little evidence of rivets or bolts. There were symbols moulded on one side where two small panels joined to cover what appeared to be some kind of hatch. Joy was about to photograph these when the object suddenly took off vertically and hovered above the treetops. A laser of white light suddenly shone down lighting up the clearing as brightly as daylight. Seconds later the laser retracted and the object flew away so quickly that almost instantaneously it was gone. There was absolute silence. No engine noise, no bird or animal sounds. The transition was so abrupt it reminded Joy of a spotlight turning off. As they stood there among the tall dark shadows of the conifers, the pair were temporarily immobilised by a mixture of fear and wonder. Joy could not hide the tremor in her voice as she spoke. Her senses sharpened as adrenaline surged through her body.

"I never really believed in flying saucers, but I have just changed my mind. It is a horrible thought, like having a nightmare only to realise that it is real."

"Whatever that was it was definitely under intelligent control," Bert responded. "Did you see the way it navigated clear of the tree trunks before shooting off at a sharp angle? This is no dream. Look at the grass in the clearing."

There were scorch marks below where the craft had been parked and the undergrowth was flattened. On all sides of the clearing leaves and debris had been swept back as if a whirlwind had descended into the confines of the wood. Joy took a series of photos showing the effects on the vegetation. The camera flashed momentarily illuminating the scene. Now that the glow from the craft had gone the woods were pitched into total darkness. The only light came from the pinpricks of stars showing in the sky in gaps between the trees. The couple felt the unwelcome embrace of the cold dark isolation of the deserted forest. This was not a place to linger, so they concentrated on establishing their composure as the need to retrace their steps became a priority.

"Let's get back to the Rover before we freeze," suggested Bert. He was shivering and desperate to cloak himself in the thick blanket which he always left to cover the back seat of the vehicle.

Joy looked at Bert and laughed nervously, "Well you will come out in the woods wearing your pyjamas!"

It was time consuming threading their way back through the woods with such poor visibility, but using the light from the torch they emerged near to where they had parked.

The road that led back to the farm was narrow. It was fortunate that Bert knew the route so well. They had just passed the road junction near a place called Trevillian's Gate, which gave access to Bodmin Moor, when the headlights suddenly dimmed and the engine cut out. Hovering over the road just ahead they were shocked to see that the triangular shaped craft had reappeared. Bert took out his mobile to photograph the object, but the battery appeared to be dead. The same sensation of pervading static electricity encompassed the environment. They both cautiously got out of the vehicle and stood motionlessly in awe. The craft appeared to be marking time. They could feel the energy exuding from it and see the glow from a pulsing light reflecting on the damp surface of the road. Without warning or any sound from a propulsion system, the craft flew away at speed in a north easterly direction. Suddenly, a tremendous flash, as bright as sheet lightning, illuminated the sky accompanied by a deep metallic groan.

"It's the turbines. I think it has collided with one of the wind turbines," gasped Bert.

As he spoke the craft snaked away across the moorland and then disappeared somewhere to the south west of their position. Seated back in the Land Rover Bert pressed the start button. The engine burst into life without any problem. It had not broken down. It had been temporarily immobilised.

"We had better check that nobody has been hurt up by the wind farm," Joy suggested.

The unmanned wind farm was less than a mile away. It was a bleak location just on the edge of the moorland. Bert pulled up by the wind farm which appeared to be deserted. Only the constant low hum of the working turbines resonated over the moorland. Joy took a spare torch from the Land Rover's toolbox before they both separated to cover different sections of the site dwarfed by the huge, towering structures. The night sky was inky black and Joy looked up to admire the stars. She wondered if the strange craft could have come from one of them. Bert's voice echoed from a position at the far end of the site summoning her to join him.

She trudged over the uneven surface of the moor towards where she could see the beam from Bert's torch. The ground was soft underfoot, but as Joy got closer to Bert's position, she trod on something hard. It was a flat piece of black metal which had pivoted upwards from the scrub narrowly missing her ankle. The metallic panel measured about a half a metre square. Joy shone her torch on the panel as she bent down to pick it up. It felt strangely light weight for its size. It looked as if a giant claw had scraped across the smooth, glassy surface leaving one edge torn and jagged. Still visible was a symbol etched into the material similar in appearance to an Egyptian hieroglyph. Joy hurried over to show Bert who was viewing a damaged turbine blade. It had been constructed facing towards the prevailing south westerly winds on an elevated part of the land at the edge of the wind farm. Standing close to the turbine the couple felt insignificant as the main structure soared one hundred metres above them. It was now silent, stark, stationary. It had originally housed three twenty metre blades. Two of the blades hung limply, twisted and inoperable. White smoke drifted lazily out of the motor unit at the top of the wounded turbine.

"Whatever has impacted with this structure must surely have suffered some damage," Bert speculated as he panned his torch over the ground. "It has mangled two blades as if they were plastic."

Joy held out the panel that she had trodden on. "I found this on my way over."

Bert shone his torch onto the panel and Joy could tell from his expression that he was excited.

"This is a wonderful piece of solid evidence. It may hold clues as to its origin both from its composition and that symbol. We need to take this back to the farm immediately. The military are likely to have been alerted if this incident has shown up on radar. We will decide whether they can have this piece of debris after we have had time to look at it more thoroughly."

As Joy walked back to the vehicle Bert made a final scan of the area surrounding the damaged turbine. He was about to leave when he noticed a black object half embedded in a tuft of grass. Its shiny surface reflected the light from the torch. Bert tugged the object energetically and it emerged from the grass quite easily. It was obviously another section of debris from the unidentified craft, about the same size as the part that Joy had trodden on. Bert tugged the piece of debris out of the ground and carried it back to the vehicle. Joy was already in the passenger seat and Bert was able to discretely stow this second piece of debris in the boot covering it with a cloth. He suspected that there would be a visit from the military investigation team in the morning and his instinct told him it would be wise to retain some of the physical evidence of the collision. There had been cases of people who had cooperated with the military later being discredited and unable to prove the reality of what they had seen. He was sorry that he could not bring himself to reveal his discovery to Joy, but he reasoned that it would be in both their best interests in the long term if she did not know. He intended to hide the second panel in a part of the farm well away from the panel that Joy had found.

As they approached the farm Bert caught sight of headlights approaching from the direction of the airfield. After turning into the cobbled yard in front of the farm Bert extinguished the vehicle's lights and motioned for Joy to stay in her seat. Looking into the rear-view mirror Bert watched a small fleet of military vehicles surging up the road heading in the direction of the turbines. Within seconds the convoy passed and the farm was returned to darkness. They both walked towards the farmhouse and Joy looked at her watch. It was just after one o'clock in the morning.

"That's odd," Joy exclaimed. "I would have thought that it would be much later considering our walk in the woods and the excursion to the turbines."

"Surprising how fast the time goes when you are enjoying yourself," joked Bert. "We had better get some sleep. Another busy day is in front of us and I expect we will get interrupted by visitors from the defence ministry."

That night Bert had a vivid dream. He was floating through the heavens being drawn towards a star which was brighter than all the others. A series of shapes appeared in his field of vision like the electronic head up display projected on a windscreen. It was a dream that Bert found hard to get out of his mind the next day.

Sleep was something that did not come readily to Joy. After she climbed back into bed, she picked up the clock to set the alarm and was surprised to see that the display was registering ten past two. Looking at her watch again it showed the time as one fifteen. So somewhere during the evening about one hour was unaccounted for. She remembered putting the watch forward an hour at the weekend and checking that it was correctly adjusted to British Summer Time. Joy reasoned that her watch must have stopped just like the car engine during the encounter with the alien craft.

This thought and the memories of the night's events kept her awake for a long time. Perhaps, other people living in the area had seen the lights. Exhausted, both mentally and physically, Joy fell into a shallow sleep.

When she awoke Joy could tell it was a sunny morning as little patches of light that had escaped the curtains were making patterns on the wall. In the distance a church bell was chiming. Joy dragged herself out of bed. Every bone in her body screamed for her to rest. The allure of sleep was hard to resist. She knew immediately that it was going to be a hard day. She ate some toast and drank hot tea before venturing outside. Evidence of the visitation during the night could not be ignored. A dead sheep was skewered on the blades of a plough parked at the rear of the farmhouse. Its eyes were wide open and its tongue draped limply from its mouth. Extreme exertion at the time of death had left the poor animal's mouth open, frozen, like a sinkhole in snow. The desperate animal looked as if it had taken its final breath at the end of a terrifying stampede. Bert was attempting to extract the animal, beads of sweat dripping from his bald head even though the temperature outside was still relatively cool. Joy walked over to help him.

"I don't expect that we will be able to claim compensation for the loss of this animal," gasped Bert as he pulled and tugged at the carcass. "This is what happens when panic takes hold. Can you fetch the quad bike round with the small trailer and we will take the animal for burial at the bottom end of the field?"

While he waited for Joy to return Bert took out his mobile and searched for the local news reports. There was a short item carrying a report of a fireball in a quarry near Rough Tor. Bert was not surprised to read that the area had been sealed off to the public. When Joy returned with the quad bike Bert showed her the news item on his phone. He made no mention of his dream, but something about it troubled him.

"Sounds like it could be that damaged craft. I wouldn't be surprised if it crashed after the impact with the turbine," Joy speculated.

"That's exactly what I thought," replied Bert as he lugged the carcass onto the trailer. "It is in the direction where we last saw the craft heading. There is no point in trying to check because the military will have secured the whole area. From what I have read about similar cases, they quickly seal the area, remove all evidence and then send out rumours diverting attention away from what was really found." They classify their own reports as 'Top Secret'. The public is lucky if they receive a redacted copy many years later in response to requests under the Freedom of Information Act. Why they think that the public will not be able to cope with the facts is beyond me."

After making sure that the dead animal was secure on the trailer, Joy searched her phone for the online section of 'The Cornish Gazette'. It was the local paper and could usually be relied upon to give updates on breaking news stories. Sure enough there was an item reporting that strange lights had been seen in the sky. Apparently, the newspaper had been flooded with reports from members of the public who thought that they had seen a UFO. She felt frustrated that after what they had witnessed during the night the whole matter could be suppressed by faceless bureaucrats. How could they be so manipulative? Surely it was better to be stricken by the truth than soothed by a pack of lies. As she punched the telephone number of 'The Cornish Gazette' into her mobile she decided that she was not going to keep this incident to herself.

TWO

REPORT OF A NIGHT VISITOR

The facts are always less than what actually happens.
Nadine Gordimer

The road that borders the old Davidstow airfield is straight and flat. As Chris Arbor drove his red Honda Civic along the long, narrow ribbon of tarmac, his thoughts turned to the job he was now assigned to. The words of Winston Churchill resounded in his head as he mulled over the report he had been sent to investigate. 'There are a terrible lot of lies going around the world and the worst of it is half of them are true.' Just now these words seemed hauntingly poignant.

Chris had been working as a journalist for 'The Cornish Gazette' for the last five years. After leaving Exeter University with an English Degree he had spent several years learning his trade at a weekly magazine in Bournemouth, but had taken this job at 'The Cornish Gazette' because it meant he could return to the family home in Cornwall. It was one of those occasions when it seemed the right thing to do. After his long-term relationship with a girl he had met at University ended, life did not seem the same. Together they had enjoyed some good times, but the places they frequented were all around and constantly reminded Chris of a once happy relationship. The girl had found someone new so there was no point on dwelling on the past. At this time in his life Chris thought a change of environment would help his social rehabilitation. He was an optimistic person and he tried to maintain a positive outlook. Good humoured, and with a willingness to empathise when people told their stories, he was generally able to dig into the heart of the issues he was assigned to report on. Having an easy rapport with people was often an asset when trying to gain their trust. In his work, people reported stories that were sometimes unusual, often dramatic and occasionally tragic. Chris was never sure what his next assignment would contain.

North Cornwall was an area he knew and loved. Since the death of his mother Chris's father had found life difficult. When he moved back to share the house with his father it helped them both. Domestically, this arrangement had worked quite well over the years, but had meant that Chris had not been as occupationally mobile as otherwise would have been the case. Not that he minded that much as he had never been overly ambitious. He had lots of friends nearby and enjoyed the flexibility that working on a small newspaper gave him. Being one of the more experienced journalists he had the opportunity to research topics selected by the editor and had gained a reputation as a feature writer on local issues.

During the last few days, the newspaper had been receiving a flood of information about UFO sightings. Most of the reports were of little interest as they could not be substantiated and there were always some people who thought it amusing to create a hoax. Occasionally, there would be a report that had a ring of authenticity. It was one of these that had been received from someone called Joy Penrose. Apparently, Joy had contacted the newspaper because something unusual had happened the previous night on the farm where she lived.

The editor of 'The Cornish Gazette' was not a tolerant person. Some people would describe him as rude. He tended to be a bit dismissive, especially if he perceived that his time was being wasted. People reporting UFO sightings often fell into the time-wasting category. This time, the report from Joy Penrose, was different. It was not just the sincerity in her voice that had been convincing, but the rarity of an incident of this sort that involved physical evidence. The details that Joy gave were very specific and from her description and the passion with which she related the story he decided that if it was fake news Joy deserved an Oscar. This was a close encounter of the convincing kind and it prompted him to dispatch his star journalist to the farm.

"Just see what this is all about," the editor had said to Chris more in hope than expectation. "It may be that there is just something newsworthy in it. If you need to dig into the event a bit more so be it, but you will have to be sharp to meet today's deadline. Best to keep an open mind as there could be a perfectly rational explanation. However, the respondent did not sound like a run of the mill fantasist." Chris picked up the address and keyed the postcode into his satnav.

The Honda shuddered as it passed over the bars of a cattle grid. On one side of the road Brown Willy and Rough Tor towered up majestically from the bleak, flat marshland that formed this northern end of Bodmin Moor. To his left Chris could see the vast flat plain of the old Davidstow airfield. It had been a vital World War Two base for RAF bomber command. Flights had left here on antisubmarine patrols over the Bay of Biscay helping to protect the North Atlantic shipping routes. Cracked in places and with clumps of grass growing between the joints, the concrete slab runways could still be clearly seen. Neglected and in decay were the remains of buildings where aircrew had trained, where bombs had been stored and where men had been billeted. These were places where the memories of long-gone service personnel were trapped. On this vast exposed plateau of relics, where the thunder of powerful engines had once predominated, there was now only silence. It was a haunting place to traverse especially when thinking about Unidentified Flying Objects. On the western perimeter of the airfield was a large forest of conifers known as Davidstow Woods. Dark and dense, only punctuated by the occasional firebreak, the woods bordered the length of the airfield.

Chris had investigated many UFO reports and frankly he was bored by the subject. There were so many reports, but never any conclusive evidence. Not one alien body had been found. There was not a single piece of wreckage from an alien craft to pick up and examine. Thousands of photographs, hours of video footage and YouTube clips were easy to access. Most of these were mischievous hoaxes, or mistaken identifications. To read the myriad of case reports collected by BUFORA you would expect to see a UFO every time you went to the dustbin. Yet, on reflection, there were too many incidents to dismiss them all as hoaxes. Amongst the attention seeking fraudsters, the fantasists, cranks, and the mentally unstable, there were pilots, policemen, servicemen and people with reputations at stake. They were adamant that they had sighted things in the sky that they could not explain. Some people must have genuinely seen things that they could not identify. However, this did not necessarily mean they were seeing alien aircraft. Governments across the world had not helped by deliberately debunking reports with fallacious stories about hot air balloons, meteor showers, and lighthouse beams. This official disinformation is why Chris remembered the words of Churchill and it is why he did not dismiss every report out of hand. To try to take a balanced view of Unidentified Flying

Objects amongst the fog of hysteria and misinformation was not easy. Surely NASA would not be funding the SETI programme (Search for Extra Terrestrial Intelligence) if they did not think it was possible that other life forms existed in the universe. Not a single signal or recurring pulse had been detected by SETI in response to years of outgoing signals announcing the presence of life on earth. We had flashed our presence to the galaxy, but so far, the galaxy had not responded. There was a great silence.

Between 2007 and 2012 The Pentagon had financed a project named the Advanced Aviation Threat Identification Programme. Videos in 2017 released from the cockpits of US Navy jets purporting to show unidentified craft being chased off the West Coast of America were blurred and inconclusive. This may have been an attempt to reassure the public that the authorities were aware of the presence of unidentified craft, but not to worry, they had the problem under control. If they had clearer images, they were certainly not publishing them. It was rumoured that the funding for the AATIP programme had been extended beyond 2014 which pointed to the fact that The Pentagon must have thought there was more to find out.

Then there were the UFO reports corroborated by more than one person and where radar had detected objects. These could not be easily dismissed as delusions. Chris had read the results of a review of these types of case. Analysis of the locations of the sightings over long time periods showed that many were along the trajectory of Ley lines. One such line ran from St Michaels' Mount in Cornwall through Glastonbury, Stonehenge and as far north as Lindisfarne. It was suggested by some investigators that these lines were not just coincidental lines joining famous places, but lines describing routes of magnetic activity on the surface of the Earth. Chris wondered if it could be possible that alien craft were using these lines as navigation aids in a similar way to those famous geometrical designs on the desert plateau near to the town of Nazca in Peru?

As Chris clattered across another cattle grid that marked the edge of the moor, he glanced in his mirror to see the airfield receding behind him. Ahead he could see the top of a group of wind turbines. He glanced at the satnav which showed that he was approaching his destination at Innyvale Farm. Looking up from the screen he had to swerve violently to the left as a military vehicle carrying an object covered by a black tarpaulin loomed round a bend just ahead. The thought occurred to him that it was more dangerous driving on these narrow roads than any threat posed by aliens.

There had been many reports of strange lights in the sky the previous night and the editor had in recent months received a glut of e-mails about UFO activity over Bodmin Moor. He had singled out this report from a person called Joy Penrose because she was claiming that there was physical evidence of damage caused by what she described as an unidentified craft. It sounded like that this was something verifiable. It could be a 'hot' topic. Chris was hoping that Joy's story would not only be credible, but also backed up by irrefutable proof of a visitation from space. He remained sceptical as he neared the entrance to the farm.

The driveway approach to Innyvale Farm was not very long, but involved a sharp turn off the road between two granite pillars. Chris had to get out of the car to open a large, galvanised metal gate, which had been closed to prevent sheep wandering onto the highway. A cool breeze ruffled his short brown hair as he bent to undo the latch. The pungent smell of manure drifted in the air announcing the proximity of livestock. Chris was not very tall and had to lean heavily on the gate to start it moving. Straightening his back after pushing the heavy gate open, he looked up the drive to see the grey stone façade of the farmhouse. Just beyond was a yard where horses were stabled. A flock of sheep with a red letter 'I' stamped on their fleeces were grazing in the adjoining fields. Chris parked the car and was met by the farmer, a bald, robust fellow with the bronzed complexion common to those who worked on the land. He was obviously busy and welcomed Chris with the news that he did not have much time for visitors that day.

"I had to bury a sheep this morning. Something terrified the poor creatures causing utter panic. Anyway, what do you want?" enquired Bert with undisguised irritability.

"I have arranged to meet someone called Joy Penrose," Chris replied. "I am from 'The Cornish Gazette'. Joy called the newspaper because she wanted to tell a story about an encounter with a mysterious craft."

It did not seem to be a good time to have a discussion with Bert although it sounded as though he would be an equally good witness.

Bert was rather taken aback by this information. He had not realised that Joy was intending to publicly disclose their nocturnal experiences. On the other hand, there was no reason why the facts needed to be hidden. He resented the thought that by keeping quiet he would be assisting in a cover up.

"Well, you're welcome to talk to Joy. That's her over there." He pointed towards the stable yard. "All I can tell you is that whatever it was, spooked the livestock, damaged a turbine and resulted in an interruption to our valuable sleep," he moaned.

"There were many reports of strange lights in the sky over the moors last night. It's always helpful to get another account of events," said Chris diplomatically.

The farmer gave a weary shrug of his shoulders before escorting Chris into the farmhouse. "If you can excuse me for a minute, I will tell Joy that you are here."

As Bert left the room he stopped in the doorway. His face was pale, his expression serious and sincere. "I can assure you that whatever landed near here last night was not from this earth."

Joy was preoccupied grooming the horses in the stables and was surprised to hear Bert's voice. He felt a little indignant that Joy had not consulted him before contacting the press.

"The journalist that you contacted is waiting in the farmhouse. Why didn't you tell me he was coming?"

"I'm sorry Bert. It was when you passed me the newspaper this morning and told me that there would be a cover up. It annoyed me to think that people would never know the truth unless we spoke out."

"Well, we agree on that, but it's too late to discuss it now. Does he know about the debris we found at the turbine?"

"I don't think I mentioned anything about that," replied Joy. "I do think we should show the panel as proof that we haven't imagined the whole thing."

Bert nodded "Alright, if you go to chat with the journalist now, I will join you in a few minutes. There is something I need to do first," said Bert.

He watched as Joy made her way to the farmhouse and disappeared inside. Then he walked over to the parked Land Rover and removed the piece of debris that he had found by the turbine. The metal panel was still carefully wrapped in a cloth. Bert sealed the whole package inside a plastic dustbin bag. Moving to a mound of manure next to the barn he buried the bag under the stinking pile. Bert had a feeling that they were going to need some future insurance should things turn unpleasant when they received the inevitable visit from the Ministry of Defence. The fact that Joy knew nothing about this second piece of debris would protect her from bearing responsibility against accusations of withholding evidence should events turn nasty.

Bert hurried back to the farmhouse and took a seat at the living room table next to Joy. They faced the journalist who formally introduced himself as Chris Arbor. There was an awkward silence for a few seconds broken only when Joy offered to make a drink. Not wanting to waste time Bert came straight to the point.

"We can tell you what happened here last night. Whether you will want to write about it in your paper is up to you. I am not deluded and do not seek publicity."

Chris sighed. The farmer's lack of enthusiasm was not a good omen. He was beginning to suspect that this meeting was going to be difficult.

"There have been reports from other people about strange lights in the sky. Some reports are saying that some, yet unidentified craft, crashed into the old china clay quarry near to Rough Tor. I thought it important to hear your story in case it fits with this pattern of events."

Joy returned to the table with three cups of coffee on a tray and looked at Bert who was sitting upright with his arms folded across his chest. This was a posture that she recognised as indicating that Bert might be argumentative.

"Shall I tell the story, or you?" she asked, looking straight at Bert.

Bert picked up his drink and took a long gulp before standing up to leave. He was a knowledgeable farmer, but lacked cultural elegance around the table.

"There's no point in two of us losing good working time. I trust that Joy will tell you everything. She experienced everything that I did last night."

He squeezed Joy's shoulder gently and whispered in her ear. "Just miss out the bit about my pyjamas!" Joy smiled at the memory and Bert left to continue his work on the farm.

It was obvious that Joy was nervous about discussing her experience the previous night with a complete stranger. She talked about horses, her trekking business, the weather conditions, anything except for UFO's. Chris responded by asking questions and slowly Joy relaxed. He wanted to get an idea of her character to assess her reliability as a witness. They continued to talk about Joy's work on the farm and it quickly became apparent that she was a hard-working person with little time or inclination to make up fanciful stories. Chris quickly warmed to Joy's unpretentious portrayal of the growth in her pony trekking business. He liked her unsophisticated personality and rural earthy charm. She was not wearing any trace of makeup, but her fresh complexion and sun-tanned appearance made her attractive in a natural sort of way.

Joy had felt frustrated that people might be dismissive about what she had seen. Even her short phone conversation with her parents had been an anti-climax. They had told her to keep a low profile, but this did not seem appropriate in these sensational circumstances. Surely, she thought, it would be better to share the events in case others had something to add. Contacting the newspaper had been her reaction against obfuscation. She was conscious that she could be ridiculed as a crank. On the other hand, she knew what she had seen was not an illusion. She had decided that on balance it was better to go public than remain anonymous. Anyway, she had passed the point of no return after she had phoned the newspaper.

Eventually, Joy began to describe the events of the previous night. She started to talk slowly, but as she recounted what she had seen she became increasingly animated. It was clear that this was no hoax. There was excitement in her eyes as she relived the sequence of events which had interrupted her sleep during what should have been a tranquil Monday night.

"Have you any idea of how big the craft was?" asked Chris. "I don't suppose that you have a photo?"

"It is hard to say what the exact size was, except that when we saw it from close up in the forest it was fairly small. I would say that it was about the size of a double decker bus, triangular and a glossy black colour. I could not see a window or a canopy. We were so close that Bert put his hand on it and it was hot to the touch."

Joy continued to relate the series of events. Her memories were fresh as she clearly revisited the encounter in the forest, the re-appearance of the craft on the road home, the collision with the turbine and finally the discovery of the debris. Suddenly, Joy remembered that she had taken a photograph on Bert's camera.

"Excuse me for a moment while I collect my camera from the car."

Chris waited. It was an absorbing story and he was convinced that something very unusual had happened. He had interviewed many people and he prided himself on assessing the veracity of what they told him. He did not know whether Joy had seen an alien craft, but he was certain that he had been given the facts as perceived.

A few minutes later Joy returned with Bert's camera and a metal panel loosely wrapped in a dustsheet. Feverishly, she tracked through the images on the camera searching for the shot she knew she had taken of the craft in the forest. Chris looked expectantly at the dustsheet. Disappointingly, there was just an overexposed white blur where the photo should have been. If Joy had communicated more fully with Bert, she would have learned that he had photographed the panel and deleted the image before sending it to his desktop computer. He had also printed the image before deleting the computer file. Bert anticipated a visit from the authorities and had taken precautions against possible infringements to his privacy. He was not interested in the content.

"It is probably the effects of the electrical atmosphere we felt when we were close to the craft," Joy explained. "When we drove near to the craft on the road all the electrics cut out. I think it must have been giving off some sort of electrical field which caused interference."

"Can you draw a sketch of what you saw?" asked Chris.

Feeling that this failure could undermine her story, Joy quickly drew a picture of what she saw. The sketch looked childish, lacking scale and detail.

Chris tried to help. "From the ground to the top of the object how high was it compared to the surrounding conifer trees?"

Joy added a full-grown conifer to the side of her sketch of the object and checked the scale. "I estimate that it was only about a third of the height of the tree."

They both laughed at the thought of this sketch being embedded into the newspaper article. "I am not sure that we need to include that sketch!"

"No, but you may want to consider including this." Joy hurriedly extracted the black metal panel from within the dustsheet. Chris picked it up and examined it closely. He noticed immediately how light it felt. Running his finger over the glassy black surface he was able to rub off the superficial dirt marks, but there were etched scrapes made by the turbine blade that could not be removed.

"This material must be extremely strong and resilient to withstand an impact of the magnitude to be expected from the blade of a wind turbine," he said thoughtfully. "The scrape marks are from the blades. There does not seem to be serious scouring across the surface. The weakness is in the joint of the panel to the main structure. I can't see any rivet holes or bolts, but there does seem to be a resin on the edges where the panel was fixed to a chassis."

Joy touched the resin and it had a sticky feel, dark coloured like treacle although there was no discernible smell.

"What do you think of the shapes on the surface?" asked Joy pointing to what appeared to be symbols moulded into the structure of the panel.

Chris touched the contours of the symbols and scratched his head. "It is hard to say with only part of the symbols showing. Maybe if we had the panel next to this it would make more sense. The shapes do appear to be markings of some type. One shape could be a section of a pyramid next to a profile of a tall building."

"Is that a star and a tiny cloud adjacent to the building?" Joy speculated. "They remind me of the symbols that you see on the walls of Egyptian pyramids."

"Do you mind if I photograph the exhibit?" Chris asked.

"Go ahead. I hope that your photograph turns out better than the one I took in the woods."

This lucky find could be incredibly significant. For once there was a piece of hard evidence that could be analysed in a laboratory. Something physical had obviously impacted with the turbine blade. Somewhere a triangular shaped craft was flying with a bit missing. Chris wondered if the damage had caused the craft to crash. The reports from the quarry were surely more than just a coincidence.

"Have you time to show me the turbine, I would like to take a few pictures before I leave. We can use my car," said Chris gently.

Joy knew that Bert would not be happy about her leaving the farm during the working day, but he reluctantly agreed knowing that the turbine was literally a couple of minutes away.

"Please make sure you bring her back here straight away. We have work to do," he shouted to the pair as he made his way back into the barn.

As they approached the damaged turbine Joy repeated that she had felt the need to contact the press as she feared the facts would never be released by the authorities. "I know what I saw was real because the farmer also saw it and the turbine hasn't damaged itself. When you write your article please try to avoid making me sound stupid. I don't want people to think I'm a crank," implored Joy.

"There is no need for you to worry," said Chris. "You may get a few people coming up here to see for themselves though. Perversely, the publicity may enhance your business; put you on the map so to speak. I have found your story compelling and I will not be exaggerating or sensationalising any of it. One thing to keep in mind though, is that what you saw has not yet been identified, so it may not necessarily be anything to do with aliens. All you can say is that you saw an unidentified flying object."

"If it wasn't an alien craft then what else could it have been?" asked Joy inquisitively.

"That's something that needs further investigation," Chris replied. "There are aircraft flying about that are part of secret government development programmes. They may not be manned in the conventional way. These drones are not just from this country. This is always in the Top Secret category and details are few and far between."

"I don't think a drone could move so quickly and erratically. It made right angled turns and shot into the distance within seconds." Joy went quiet as they passed the spot on the road where the craft had appeared the night before.

As the road neared the site of the turbines, they became aware of a strong security presence. Soldiers in military fatigues were patrolling the perimeter of the field and red and white tape with the words 'crime scene' printed on it fluttered in the breeze. The broken turbine blades had been removed leaving the turbine tower standing forlorn with its one remaining blade. Chris pulled to the side of the road and took out his camera.

"Would you object to being on a photo showing the turbine in the background? If we are quick, we may just get away without anyone noticing."

Joy felt reassured by Chris's calm presence. He had been patient and given serious consideration to what must have seemed a fantastic story. She had hesitated about publicising the whole episode, especially when she had talked to her parents who had advised caution. Alright, she thought to herself, the cost may be ridicule from some people, but the publicity could help raise the profile of the business. She had already talked to the press. A photograph was not going to make much difference.

"Just a minute while I straighten my hair," she called to Chris as she brushed her hand across her face.

Chris may have appeared outwardly calm, but his heart was beating faster. Already, he could see one of the soldiers walking towards the road. There was just time to take one shot on his mobile phone, before they had to jump back into the car. Chris quickly reversed into a gateway and spun the car back in the direction of the farm. In his mirror he saw the soldier on his cell phone. He hoped that he would be able to clear the area before his car was intercepted.

Back at the farm Chris quickly explained that he would like to arrange to have the metal part subjected to laboratory analysis.

"I don't want to take the part with me now because I suspect that I might be stopped and searched by the military on my way back to the office. One of the soldiers at the turbine site may have seen me take that photo and phoned ahead. They have a habit of quickly setting up roadblocks. Can you meet me after work tonight and deliver the panel to me?"

"I am visiting my mum in Camelford this evening," said Joy. "If it is convenient for you to call at their address around eight o'clock, I could hand the panel to you." Joy scribbled the address details on a scrap of paper.

Privately Chris was glad to have an excuse to contact Joy again. He liked her and had found her friendly and articulate. She was quite attractive too, in a plain sort of way. He would certainly make sure that he kept her in touch with developments.

"See you at eight," he called from the car as he turned towards the road.

Once on the straight section of road that traversed the whole length of the Davidstow airfield Chris was beginning to relax. The dark green conifers of the woods stretched out on his left and he reflected on the courage that the farmer and his assistant had shown in searching this exposed area after dark, knowing that an unidentified object was hidden somewhere between the trees. Peering ahead Chris noticed that a dark green Land Rover was parked across the road. Instinctively, he braked and swerved into the next flat grassy area at the side of the road. Quickly, he selected the image of the panel and deleted it. There was no time to remove the picture of the turbine site. Trying to remain calm and impassive he continued towards the roadblock where he was beckoned to stop by a soldier in uniform.

"Please park over there," instructed the soldier pointing to a space at the roadside. Chris got out of the vehicle and the voice commanded, "Place your hands on the roof of the car."

Obediently, Chris did as instructed. Hands frisked his body and removed the mobile phone from his pocket.

"I have been alerted by my team that you have taken a photograph in a restricted area. Photography is forbidden in that place until clearance is given by the Ministry. I have to tell you that your phone may now be confiscated and sent for analysis."

Chris did not want to be without his phone. It was an essential device that he needed for the many communications he made every day. All his contact addresses, telephone numbers, email address details and messages were stored in there. When he was allowed to turn around, he decided to admit his mistake. Sometimes humility was rewarded by compassion.

"I am sorry that I infringed your rules. I did not realise that wind turbines were classified objects. It was just an impulse to photograph my friend with the words 'crime scene' fluttering on the tape next to her. Anyway, I only took one picture and I am not sure that it has been recorded. The battery must be extremely low as I have not had chance to charge it today.

The soldier checked the battery level which was indeed low. He instructed one of his team to search the car. Meanwhile, he scrolled through the photographs recorded on the phone. The picture of the turbine appeared on the screen and the soldier immediately deleted it. Chris stood patiently at the side of the road conscious of the many eyes surveying his predicament as traffic was waved past unimpeded.

A voice shouted from the direction of the car. "The vehicle is clean Sir!"

The soldier who appeared to be in charge gave Chris a long and penetrating stare. There was a pause while he made up his mind about the creature that stood before him. This naive civilian surely could not be a threat to security. Much to Chris's relief he tossed the phone through the open window of the car and it landed with a thump on the driver's seat.

"You need to be more careful where you point your camera in future, or you stand to lose more than your phone. Keep well clear of restricted areas." The soldier gestured for the roadblock to be moved. His final words were spoken as a command not an option, "On your way buddy."

There was no point in further conversation. Chris nodded and drove back to the office feeling a strong sense of relief. Sitting at his desk, he feverishly wrote his newspaper report. He knew that it was always best to write while the events were still fresh in the mind. He was also eager not to miss the looming deadline. Under the headline 'MOORLAND ENCOUNTER' the Wednesday editions of 'The Cornish Gazette' were distributed to newsagents throughout the region. It was a faithful report of his meeting and showed the small handwritten sketch that Joy had scribbled earlier showing the alien craft in the forest. It was crude, but Joy was not claiming to be an artist. What Chris did not mention in his report or to his editor was the small metal panel that had been found. More urgent was the need to search for somewhere with facilities capable of analysing the part he had arranged to collect from Joy at her Camelford address.

An internet search revealed that the nearest place with a suitable laboratory was The New Technologies Centre located near to St Mawgan about thirty miles away. After a call on his mobile he arranged to meet a metallurgist at two o'clock the following afternoon. Meanwhile, the office was buzzing with rumours about the crash at the quarry near Rough Tor. The whole area around the quarry had been isolated and there was a strong military presence around the site. Local people had reported a low loader navigating through the narrow country roads. It carried a cargo which appeared larger at the base than at the top and was covered by a large green sheet. Police outriders had been observed, escorting the load, as it slowly headed south down the Atlantic Highway in the direction of Newquay Airport.

THREE

THE TRANSFORMER PROJECT

Our little systems have their day.
They have their day and cease to be.
Alfred Lord Tennyson

It promised to be another routine working day for Henry Penrose as he cruised along the Atlantic Highway between his home in Camelford and his place of employment, Precision Castings (Wadebridge) Limited. He enjoyed the drive to work as it allowed him to implode into his own world. His car was a private capsule, enclosed and discrete. The road gently wound its way through heavily wooded areas before rising slightly into open farmland as it approached Wadebridge. As he commuted along this route which he was so familiar with, his thoughts kept returning to his wife Alice who he knew would be spending her last week in her job as a sport and fitness instructor at the Camelot Leisure Centre in Camelford. The Centre was a place special to them both because it was where they had met. He knew that this coming Friday would be a pivotal moment in her life and he hoped that she would not find the wrench of leaving her job too emotionally draining. Henry was aware of how stressed Alice had become in recent months. She was returning from work tired and listless, sometimes falling asleep on the sofa just after tea. What good was a large joint income if there was a continuing deterioration to the quality of their life? It had made Henry sad to see his wife so fatigued at the end of a working day with her head in her hands and her golden brown hair hanging untidily across her face. They had talked at length about various options before they both eventually agreed that if a voluntary redundancy offer became available then Alice should take it.

In Alice's head was an ambition that she had quietly harboured for some time. As the onerous nature of her job had weighed more and more on her shoulders, the dream of running her own activity centre had become increasingly attractive. She was not afraid of hard work and running her own venture would involve the skills that she already had. Although she knew that self-employment would not be without problems, Alice wanted a change. The challenge of starting a business in a way that harnessed her skills excited her. She had talked about her ideas with Henry, but he always advised caution. He was an engineer and had a good job. Alice was fully aware that he worried about their future financial security if she left her job. Their finances meant that they could afford repayments on a larger mortgage and they had been searching for property that had the potential for use as an outdoor pursuits centre.

The previous evening when their daughter Joy had visited, she had been involved in the discussions about her mother's proposal. Henry was proud to see her making such a success of her trekking business on Bodmin Moor. Joy was Henry and Alice's only child. Since she was a young girl, she had loved horses and for years she had kept a pony at Innyvale Farm. She had learned to ride there and Henry was grateful that Bert Pennington had not only offered his daughter a job, but had made an apartment available near the stables. He was surprised when Joy had offered to join the proposed new venture. She had suggested the transfer of her pony trekking resources to enrich the activities. If Alice's new venture got started it really would be a family affair.

Henry had not reacted with as much enthusiasm when Joy told him about the recent events at Innyvale Farm. He was not interested in the subject of UFO's classifying it as something that only weird people discussed. When Joy had been insistent that there had been an unexplained visitation at the farm, he had advised her to keep it to herself. Yet he could tell from the earnest look in her eyes that she was serious and disturbed by the incident.

"We can talk about it when we meet at the weekend," he remembered hearing himself saying in an attempt to stall the conversation.

Henry pulled into the company's car park and found his usual space near the front entrance. All staff entered the manufacturing plant through the front reception which was light and clean to create a good impression for visitors. There was another doorway further down the building which was mainly used for deliveries of goods to the storeroom. Henry glanced across at the receptionist who seemed so engrossed in a newspaper that she had not noticed him.

"I wouldn't believe everything it says in 'The Cornish Gazette.'" Henry joked as he passed through reception.

The receptionist looked up. As she responded to his comment, Henry could tell that she was excited. "It's a story about that UFO near Davidstow airfield the other night. There is an account of the whole drama witnessed by your daughter, Joy Penrose. Apparently, a strange craft frightened horses, sheep and other animals on Innyvale Farm. Your daughter says that it damaged a wind turbine," chirped the receptionist with a wry smile as she held out the newspaper for Henry to read.

Now he wished he had taken the whole thing more seriously. He felt embarrassed that he was associated with this story. Joy was not a fanciful person and Henry knew that she would never make a frivolous report, but what was she thinking – talking to a newspaper? It was out of character and he was beginning to worry about whether her imagination had got the better of her.

Holding up his hand in a gesture of resignation, Henry returned the newspaper to the receptionist. "I will have to read that article more fully later." He tried to conceal his embarrassment, but there was no evading the fact that his daughter had filed this controversial report. To support her he said solemnly, "Joy says she saw something which she could not explain and she is perfectly at liberty to report the matter."

The receptionist smiled at Henry and returned her attention to the newspaper. She obviously thought it odd that Henry could be so disinterested in such an extraordinary event, especially when it was reported by his own daughter. He had a reputation for being focussed and not easily distracted from his work. If he thought starting work was more interesting than reading that his daughter had seen an alien craft, it seemed a bit sad.

Henry entered the production area of the manufacturing plant through a heavy door at the rear of reception. The photograph of his daughter in the newspaper kept returning to him. He could imagine what people would be thinking when they read the newspaper, but he had work to do. He did not think his daughter was in danger and decided he would phone later to check that she was alright.

Mercifully, he felt the veil of attention lift as soon as the door shut behind him. It was like entering a different world, one with which he was familiar and felt at home in. The wood veneers, the smell of polish, the spotless furniture and climatic control was replaced by rows of machines, the musky odour of metal, hot wax and the shimmering heat of the foundry. A shrill, piercing screech emanated from the far end of the factory where work had already started fettling metal burrs from castings. Henry progressed along a corridor between two red lines which Health and Safety had designated a route of safe passage and eventually reached a small, partitioned office, with the sign 'Works Manager' on the door.

His first job after leaving school had been at this manufacturing company and he had not looked back since. School had not suited him very well. He was a practical person who preferred making things rather than academic work. The company made small, precision engineered metal parts, through a method called the lost wax process. He had started as a clerk in the buying department and had come to the notice of the Production Director as a person with potential. After serving time learning how to read technical drawings, he joined the marketing team calculating quotations from drawings sent in by potential customers. He had always been fascinated by the work of the toolmakers in the production department and had served time learning this skill. His extensive knowledge of the company and engineering expertise meant that he was now employed as the Works Manager. He was temporarily reverting to his old job using his skills as a toolmaker to cover for a colleague who was away on holiday.

The parts the company manufactured were usually quite small, like the mechanism to insert coins into a slot machine or a section of a windscreen wiper. Occasionally special types of metal had to be used for a specific application such as a ball joint for an artificial limb. Customers would submit detailed drawings of the finished part with their order. The job of a toolmaker in this company was to create an aluminium mould to the exact dimensions as specified by the drawings. He would cut a block of aluminium in half and excavate a cavity in each half so that when the top and bottom sections of the aluminium were married together there would be an interior cavity to the exact size and shape of the finished metal casting. This aluminium mould had to be injected with a special wax under high pressure. When the wax solidified, the aluminium halves of the mould were separated and the wax pattern extracted. Although it was only made of wax, this moulded wax shape was an exact replica of the metal part required by the customer. The wax pattern now represented the finished product, although it had to go through many more stages in the production process. Making the aluminium mould was skilled, precision work that required careful use of a cutting tool. It was the first crucial stage of the precision casting process.

Henry had not been at the bench in the workshop area awfully long that morning when the land line phone rang. He was carefully crafting a shape in a block of aluminium and was annoyed that his concentration was being interrupted. He removed the tool, switched off the power supply and strode across to answer the phone which was attached to the wall.

"Henry Penrose here," snapped Henry. His voice betrayed his irritation at this intrusion.

"Henry! It's Bob Mortimer here. You have not forgotten about that 3D printer trial that we talked about last week, have you? It is due to start at 2 o'clock so we need to think about leaving within the next half hour."

Henry looked at his watch. It was midday. He remembered that Mortimer had made them both an appointment to visit The New Technologies Centre where they would be able to observe a 3D printer in operation. Henry was not convinced that the printer would be of much use as an application to the production of precision castings and he had relegated the matter to the back of his mind. However, Mortimer was the Managing Director and he had already acquainted himself with the process and was excited about the potential for their business.

"I'll be right there," Henry replied feeling guilty at the need to be reminded. There was something about the phone call that made Henry a little uneasy. At first, he could not think what it was and then he realised it was the word 'trial'. He was sure that in previous conversations about the 3D printer the word demonstration had been used. Had something in the true nature of this meeting changed during the week that had passed since it was last mentioned?

The New Technologies Centre was located in a converted hangar on the edge of Newquay airport. It was hardly an imposing building. Single storey, with grey painted breeze block walls covered by curved corrugated sheets for the roof. Since 2008 Newquay Airport had been taken over by the local council following a government strategic defence review. There was a long wide runway which could accommodate large commercial airliners. The RAF still retained a presence at the far side of the airfield, where they trained staff and produced parts for helicopters within an old, converted hangar. They used the runway occasionally for test flights of pilotless aircraft which needed the discrete open spaces of the Atlantic. Apart from developing the commercial passenger terminal of Newquay Airport, the council were keen to develop a small enterprise zone. They hoped to compensate for the jobs lost after RAF operational activities had been downgraded. The New Technologies Centre was the first venture to have become established at the site.

The letters NTC were written boldly on a big sign at the entrance to the car park. Mortimer's new Jaguar XJS turned off the road and stopped behind an old, red Honda Civic. The driver was involved in a heated discussion with a member of the security staff who was manning a red and white striped barrier. The Jag's electric window opened letting in a welcome blast of fresh sea air as Bob leaned out to check how long they were going to be kept waiting. He was not the most patient of people. The security guard's radio crackled into life interrupting their conversation. The call confirmed that the Honda driver did in fact have an appointment. Giving the driver a penetrating look he raised the barrier. Chris Arbor raised his eyes to show displeasure at the delay. His patience stretched to the limit by having to deal with what he considered to be a security jobsworth. Bob Mortimer's Jaguar now slowly moved into the space vacated by the Honda.

"Bob Mortimer and Henry Penrose from Precision Castings (Wadebridge) Limited," shouted Bob over the sound of the wind. "We have an appointment to see Dennis Torrance."

Apologising for the delay the guard confirmed their identity whilst delivering his opinion about time wasting journalists. Henry noticed a remote-controlled camera perched on the top of a high pole. It looked like a vulture from where he was sitting. Slowly, the camera turned in their direction, its zoom lens focusing on their registration plate.

The barrier slowly raised itself and the visitors searched for a vacant parking space on the concrete apron in front of the Centre. It did not seem a very friendly welcome. Aware that they were being scrutinised by hidden cameras, the pair walked purposefully towards the main door where they were met by a tall man with a shaven head. His muscular physique and formal demeanour gave Henry the impression that he had served in the armed forces. Holding out his hand to Bob he introduced himself as Dennis Torrance.

Until recently, Dennis Torrance had been away on tours of duty in Iraq and Afghanistan. His involvement in these inhospitable war zones had been one of the reasons why he had elected to become involved in the production of parts using new techniques. There had been too many instances where vehicles, helicopters and other machines of war had been rendered inoperative due to delays in the supply of spare parts. Missions had been compromised by lack of serviceable equipment, a scenario which Dennis found very annoying. He was now permanently based in the UK responsible for procurement and logistics. He was frustrated by the length of time it took for parts to arrive in the supply chain. Ideally, it would have been better to have had a production facility on site within the base. Shortages played on his conscience because he knew that his comrades could only do their jobs efficiently given the necessary resources. He did not want to be the cause of anyone getting killed or injured because of deficiencies in equipment.

On one occasion Dennis had been aboard a helicopter on a mission to rescue soldiers injured during a firefight with the Taliban. Whilst taking off under hostile fire, the helicopter had been raked with bullets fired from the ground. Only the skill of the pilot had enabled them to return to base. The incident focussed Dennis's mind on the perils that military personnel faced day after day in theatres of war. The greatest loss was never really the equipment, it was the people. The equipment could be repaired or replaced given efficient methods of production, sufficient time and money. Technology could provide a way to expose the machines to danger whilst people stayed safe. In this context unmanned drones were of special interest to both Dennis and his military colleagues.

Dennis had now become involved with a military task force on a special project called 'The Transformer Project'. This project was financed by the Defence Ministry who constantly liaised with the task force. It concerned the development of a new generation of remotely controlled aircraft and these were currently being tested and assessed. These drones would be stealthy, modular craft, capable of breaking apart and attacking multiple targets before docking together post attack. They would have to be as light as possible to increase range and save aviation fuel. They would need to be capable of flying at high altitude with the lowest possible radar signature. The use of flat surfaces, sharp edges and special paint would be used to help deflect radar signals. Needless to say, 'The Transformer Project' was designated Top Secret and knowledge of it was confined to very few people.

One of the problems with the development of unmanned drones was the issue of weight. The lighter the craft the less fuel would be needed and the greater the payload that the drone could carry. Dennis was investigating the use of new techniques which could produce strong, lightweight parts. Instead of the traditional metal casting process Dennis was interested in the deployment of 3D printers to make some of the parts. His views were respected by his senior officers and that is why he had been appointed as a Technology Development Officer within the task force.

This afternoon, Dennis felt that he had an opportunity to make progress in his quest to harness new technology. Today's meeting could be the start of a new phase in his plans. Wearing a grey, polo neck sweater he stroked his carefully manicured beard as the two visitors approached. He was a tall man and stood erect, arms held tightly to his side, as if he were on parade.

"Dennis, this is my colleague Henry Penrose," said Mortimer by way of introduction.

Dennis smiled and looked down towards Henry. As they shook hands Dennis's mobile rang and Henry caught a glimpse of a tattoo on his wrist as he lifted the phone to his ear. The design of the tattoo looked like a military insignia of some kind.

"Excuse me for a moment," said Dennis. He did not try to conceal his displeasure at being called at this inconvenient time. The brutality of the wars in the Middle East had reduced his threshold of tolerance and he had to employ anger management strategies to control his temper. Dennis took a deep breath and strode to one side away from earshot. The call was from the chief metallurgist who was scheduled to join the demonstration of the printer.

"What is it?" asked Dennis abruptly.

"I'm sorry, but I have inadvertently doubled booked my appointments this afternoon," explained the metallurgist. "There is a journalist in reception who phoned me yesterday. He reckons that he has recovered a part from whatever collided with that wind turbine on the moor. He wants the part subjected to a full examination in the laboratory."

"Well if that's what he wants then he will have to wait," snapped Dennis. He was fully aware who the journalist was. He had read the newspaper article twice, but was surprised to learn that a metal part had been found.

"Tell him that to fully test the part will take at least half a day. Get the part off him and give him a receipt. Secure the part in the strong room inside a container which will not generate undue interest. Explain that you will call him as soon as you have the results of the tests. I would like to be with you when those tests take place. In the meantime, come and join us without delay."

A few minutes later the harassed metallurgist entered the room looking stressed. A bead of sweat trickled down from his brow before he quickly wiped it away with his handkerchief. Dennis introduced him and explained that he would be showing them examples of items produced by the 3D process using various metal alloys.

"I suppose that you are wondering what relevance my IT devices have to your work," said Dennis inquisitively as they all entered a room where a 3D printer had been set up. His precise language, formal demeanour and posture were reminiscent of a person used to discipline, structure and logic. The Ministry of Defence had strict protocols regarding who had a need to know and about what they needed to know. Dennis allocated tasks on a compartmentalised basis so that workers on one task had no idea who or what their contribution was in relationship to the program as a whole. In this way Dennis hoped to maintain secrecy and minimise the risk of leaks to the public at large.

Henry looked at the 3D printer and then at the computer equipment attached to it before looking back at Dennis.

"It is certainly different to the equipment that I am familiar with," he said diplomatically. He had read about 3D printers, but had never seen one in operation and considered then to be expensive, slow machines that produced inferior products. Colleagues had told him that the process of 3D printing was so slow that mushrooms grew faster than the 3D printer grew parts.

The metallurgist picked up a small metal object from the table. It looked like a piece of chain mail. The object was about 5cm long with two parallel metal sections joined by a lattice weave of thin metal strips. He handed it to Henry who was surprised at how light, but rigid in construction the object was.

"What is it?" Henry enquired.

"It is a part for use inside aircraft engines," explained the metallurgist. "By using metal powder and designing the part not as a solid object, but as a hollow latticed structure there is a tremendous weight saving with commensurate fuel efficiency savings for the aircraft. Please have a look at the other examples that are displayed on the table. Some are bronze, some aluminium, some titanium. We can adjust the mix to suit whatever the proposed use of the part." The metallurgist seemed more at ease now that he was talking about metals.

"The military task force that I represent are very interested in this process of production for the manufacture of parts for future generations of aircraft," said Dennis.

The implications of this new process were starting to dawn on Henry and he was beginning to feel a little uneasy. If these objects could be produced in metal by a printer there would be no need to make wax patterns from aluminium moulds. The whole process of casting by the lost wax process could be made redundant.

As if reading his mind Mortimer intervened. "At the moment I am just considering a small trial of this equipment to see how it compares with our traditional methods of production. I want you to work in partnership with Dennis to evaluate whether the process has a potential for us." He nodded to Dennis to start his presentation.

Looking towards Henry, Dennis thought it expedient to introduce his presentation with a basic reassurance.

"I have to say that I do not expect that this technology will replace the traditional casting method overnight. It may complement it. It may supplement it. Mr Mortimer and I have discussed the potential for a joint venture where we bring the expertise for production of parts through the 3D printing technique and you evaluate against production of the same part through your usual casting method."

This information was news to Henry, but he showed no surprise. What he did need to clarify was how the evaluation process would work.

"I can see that you want our company to produce intricate parts using our conventional casting process and compare it with the same parts produced on your equipment. Can you tell me what factors the evaluation will be based on?" asked Henry.

"We will be comparing the quality, the weight, the production times for various volumes and the relative costs," Dennis replied. "If we find that certain parts can be better produced using the 3D printing process your company will be in a favourable position to receive our future orders. I think that we are on the verge of a new era in production."

At this point Bob Mortimer joined in. "I am hoping that you will be able to learn how to operate the 3D process so that in the future our company will have the incentive to set up a new production facility in Wadebridge with you as manager."

"So just to help me to clarify matters," said Henry. "I will be meeting Dennis at The New Technologies Centre on a regular basis and together we will evaluate parts produced by our separate processes using the same original drawings. During my visits he will be training me in the operation of the 3D process so that eventually our company can run a special facility," stated Henry boldly.

"Broadly, that is the plan," Dennis replied. "I will sometimes come to your factory and sometimes you will come to The New Technologies Centre. As time goes on the potential for our joint venture should become clearer and we can consider adapting our plans."

"So, this is a long-term project?" ventured Henry.

"Let's say we will be working together very closely over the next twelve months," replied Dennis unequivocally. "Obviously, as a contractor to the military you will be expected to sign the Official Secrets Act. Your security screening has already been cleared, but I am a little concerned that your daughter's involvement in the incident at Innyvale Farm could lead to a conflict of interest for you."

"I can't see what you mean," said Henry with an air of indignation. "My daughter is an adult in her own right and she makes her own decisions. What has that got to do with my work?"

Although Henry would have preferred Joy to have kept her experience out of the public domain and felt embarrassed by the publicity, he respected her right to exercise free speech.

Both Henry and Bob were unaware that elsewhere in the same building a journalist by the name of Chris Arbor had called in to deposit a mysterious metal part. On the other hand, Dennis was now fully aware of the purpose of the journalist's visit. He was dismayed with the newspaper reports that had been posted about the incident at Innyvale Farm. He was unhappy that attention was being drawn to an area that he saw as his experimental domain. The last thing he needed was a public spotlight falling on the area around the airfield. The Russians already harboured suspicions as to what type of projects were being developed at St Mawgan and radar tracings of their aircraft movements off the coast were becoming more frequent.

"If you are working on special projects you don't want the press being attracted to your door because a close family member is associated with stories about aliens." Dennis snapped back.

"I can assure you that nothing that my daughter does or says will impinge on my work." Henry was annoyed at the implied suggestion that he could not be trusted with national security because of his relationship with his daughter.

Dennis held up his hand and signalled for the metallurgist to begin the demonstration. "I think enough has been said. It is time to watch and learn."

Over the next 40 minutes Bob Mortimer and Henry Penrose were to witness the full potential of this new technology.

When their meeting had concluded Dennis and the metallurgist accompanied Henry and Bob to the front entrance where they said goodbye. Dennis walked with the metallurgist to the laboratory where the metal panel left earlier by Chris Arbor resided in the secure room. The metallurgist opened the access door and indicated a box to which was attached a white sticky label. The contact details of the reporter at 'The Cornish Gazette' had been written on a label in black, felt tipped pen. Dennis wanted to get possession of this panel for two reasons. Firstly, to gain control of any unwanted publicity that could be generated and secondly to satisfy his own curiosity. He decided to try a gentle diplomatic approach with the metallurgist.

"If it would save you time, I can take this part to the military laboratory for analysis," suggested Dennis as he picked up the object. As if confirming his intention to remove the object he continued, "I am sure that you have more pressing things to attend to."

The metallurgist had suffered encounters with Dennis before. He knew that he could be short tempered and did not want to pick a battle about what he thought was an item of little scientific interest.

"Ok, replied the metallurgist. "You take the part, but it will be up to your team to disseminate the data. I told the journalist that he could expect a report in the next day or two."

Dennis gave no reply. He strode out of the building and made for the car park where his grey transit van was parked. The journalist would get a report, but its content would be what Dennis decided he would like the outside world to hear.

Long before Henry and Bob Mortimer had left, Chris Arbor had returned to his car feeling that his visit had been a bit of an anti-climax. He had become convinced that he was holding something special, perhaps even unique. The metallurgist had not given any indication that the part was exceptional in any way. Chris was disappointed when told that the tests could not be carried out there and then. The laboratory had promised to contact him with the results within the next few days and so he would just have to be patient. As he drove towards the exit of The New Technologies Centre his head was full of thoughts about the story he could write for his newspaper whatever the results of the tests were.

Quietly, methodically and efficiently Dennis ensured that the official security machinery of government slipped into gear. Contacts in the shadowy areas of government were activated. People who were not on any payroll, but operated in the quasi world of restricted information responded to coded protocols. Their existence could be denied by officialdom. Their anonymity used to facilitate duplicity, prevarication and disinformation whilst leaving those with their hands on the levers of power immune. They were sometimes described as the 'self-employed of nefarious protocols'. They were also commonly referred to as 'The Men in Black'. In line with their brief, they were about to interrupt the working day at Innyvale Farm.

In the late afternoon of that busy Wednesday, just when a semblance of normality was being restored to the business, a large car pulled up in the yard of Innyvale Farm. Inside were two men, immaculately dressed in black suits, wearing white shirts and black ties. They looked like funeral directors. One of the men leaned casually against the car whilst the other went to round up their human targets. Joy had seen the car arrive and had already gone to find out who the visitors were. They stated their determination to question Bert and Joy about their UFO sighting. A few minutes later Bert arrived having been accosted by the other visitor. He was clearly displeased with the interruption to his work and was not holding back from expressing his views. A blotchy, red rash had appeared on his wrists over the last twenty-four hours and they were both itching. His sleep had been troubled by a dream featuring a bright star which was becoming more vivid each time it recurred. These discomforts were not helping to extend his patience.

"It would have been more courteous of you if you had made an appointment," he complained.

Bert's moaning about the inconvenience fell on deaf ears. These two impassive characters were not interested in arguments. The men briefly flashed cards which showed identification numbers beneath the symbol of a portcullis.

It was obvious that they were a team, because even though they did not say much to each other, they conducted a synchronised interrogation. Even their movements were choreographed. They were the ones who were in control and they demanded answers.

It was with a shrug of resignation that Bert recounted the events of Sunday night. One of the men asked the questions while the other stood blocking the door. Joy repeated the whole saga again from her perspective. The only fact that was not revealed was the second damaged panel that remained hidden under the pile of manure. The men listened carefully, but they did not offer any opinions or register surprise. They asked to see where the photographs had been hidden and were shown the camera with the spoiled exposures. Eventually, Bert stood up to bid the pair goodbye. He was told to sit down. One of the men pulled a sheet of paper from his pocket and placed it on the table. Smoothing the surface of the paper with one hand, the man offered a pen to Bert with the other.

"Sign at the bottom," the man commanded. "This is where you agree to say nothing to the public and keep what you saw to yourselves. If you are asked questions by anyone you will disclaim any knowledge of what you saw. It is a matter of national security."

"You want me to sign this pathetic disclaimer?" shouted Bert indignantly. "You can't censor us in this way."

The man leaned forward and Bert could smell his hot, spearmint flavoured breath. "If you value keeping this farm then I suggest you sign. It would be a shame if your sources of credit suddenly dried up."

"That's blatant intimidation," gasped Bert angrily.

"It's your choice. Sign or suffer the consequences."

Bert signed and the pen was passed to Joy.

"Your turn, if you want to avoid attending a clinic to assess your mental condition."

Joy's mouth opened in protest. "My mental condition is fine thank you. What about yours?" She knew it was a facetious response, but she did not like the men and had no intention of hiding her distaste for their methods.

"Anyone making reports about aliens to local newspapers can be certified as mentally unstable. A psychological profile to judge your suitability to work with the public could be made essential should you ever want to apply for any sort of licencing."

Flushed with indignation Joy wanted to say that she would be complaining to their boss, but the threats were real and made her think better of it. Better to give them what they want and live to fight another day. She glared at the man across the table as she scrawled her signature on the document.

Bert stood up and faced the men. "The facts aren't going to change because you are too arrogant to face up to them."

"Ignorance of some facts can be a comfort. It is not a question of arrogance, but expediency," snapped the man.

Their mission complete, the two men left as unceremoniously as they had arrived. The disclaimer spread snugly inside a yellow folder placed centrally on the rear seat of the car.

"Were they from the government?" asked Joy incredulously. "I want to complain about their behaviour to their superiors."

"Bastards from the Ministry of Defence I think," said Bert with distaste. "If I were you, I would keep quiet. What is the point in demanding human rights from faceless people who place themselves above the normal laws? You will end up chasing shadows, going round in circles, being passed from one department to another. You will face procrastination, disinformation and dirty tricks. I suggest that it will be more productive to concentrate on our work here. Let's get back to it or we won't have a farm left to lose."

FOUR

MYSTERIOUS DEPARTURE

> Doubt is not a pleasant condition,
> but certainty is an absurd one.
> *Voltaire.*

Sport was something that Alice Penrose had always enjoyed. Even though she was not very tall she had a good sense of balance and her physique was robust enough to compensate for her lack of height in racquet games. In the pool she was a proficient swimmer and enjoyed giving swimming and life-saving lessons. As a teenager she had won many swimming gala events and her collection of trophies festooned the display cabinet in her lounge. In her work at the Leisure Centre she had enjoyed interacting with people young and old, getting satisfaction from contributing to their improved fitness and overseeing the development of new skills. However, this Friday was a special day. It was to be the last time that she would be leaving the building as an employee.

Alice had worked for the last ten years at the Camelot Leisure Centre operated by the local council. During the recent recession, the council had carried out an evaluation exercise at the Leisure Centre aimed at improving productivity. The aim had been to provide the same services with fewer staff. As part of this evaluation process all the Camelot Leisure Centre's employees had been required to reapply for their jobs. Alice had been presented with a new 'improved' job description. A voluntary redundancy scheme was linked to the proposals for anyone who wanted to opt out. The procedure was for the individual member of staff to apply for voluntary redundancy under the scheme. The council would ultimately decide on each application after considering each case on its merits.

Unfortunately, the new job involved additional tasks without any commensurate salary enhancement. Already feeling fully stretched by the tasks on her existing contract, increasingly disillusioned by late nights, volumes of paperwork, and convoluted procedures, she knew in her heart that it was time for a change. Most importantly she knew that she would be liberated from the stress that had been making her depressed. Now that she had passed her fifty fifth birthday, it felt the time had come to be decisive. If she did not move on and try something new, she probably never would.

Alice and Henry Penrose had discussed these matters with their daughter Joy who they were proud to see making such a success of the trekking business on Bodmin Moor. She had offered to help supplement the outdoor activities that could be offered by her mother's new venture. Knowing that she had the support of her family gave Alice the confidence to submit her application for voluntary redundancy to the council. She wondered what their reaction would be in view of the length of her service. When she was told that her application had been successful, she felt mixed emotions. Human Resources eulogised her contributions to the work of the Camelot Leisure Centre and told her how sorry they were to lose her services. Ultimately, they would save the high salary that Alice had received as part of her incremental pay scale. This was the reality in an organisation that was faced with budget restraints. She was not indispensable whatever service she had given. On the one hand was the sad realisation that she was expendable. On the other, freedom from stress plus the £30,000 severance money which was her entitlement within the terms of the redundancy package. She had decided to risk leaving the security of her job at the Leisure Centre in exchange for immediate money in the bank and the hopeful ambition to become self-employed.

Alice knew lots of people at the Camelot Leisure Centre and some had become good friends as well as colleagues. Saying goodbye to them all on her final day at the Leisure Centre had been sad, but Alice knew that she had made her choice and there could be no going back. Many people had expressed the idea of meeting up in the future, but Alice knew that she would not see most of them again. Ten years ago, she had sat down at her brand new desk. Today she noticed the empty space usually covered by day to day paperwork. It had been a busy workstation, but now it looked tarnished and worn. As she left the building that last evening Alice felt a sense of liberation. Holding a large bunch of flowers in one hand she brushed her hair back away from her face with her other hand and took in a deep breath. With each step she felt the burden of her chores lifting from her shoulders. The fresh Cornish air flooded into her lungs as she looked up towards the heavens. It had been a lovely day and the evening sky was clear except for a white vapour trail emanating from a silver dot. Walking across the car park towards her car Alice read a poster inside a large outdoor display cabinet which read 'Cornwall – Outdoor Activities for all Seasons'. She started to think about her idea for setting up her own centre, but her thoughts were suddenly and brutally interrupted by a loud pulsating boom. The deep, thunderous explosion of sound could not have been louder if the gates of hell had been slammed shut. The glass in the advertising display flexed and rattled as a shock wave resonated its invisible path over the landscape. Alice stood frozen and stunned as did every other person in the vicinity. For a moment there was an unnatural silence. Not even the sound of a bird singing. Then gradually the birdsong restarted and everyone turned to stare at each other, displaying mystified, worried expressions. What on earth could have caused such a dramatic disturbance? High above, the silver dot of the passing aircraft had gone. Instead of one white trail across the cloudless sky there were now three and one of them had formed a very odd pattern. Instead of the usual straight line it had formed into a series of white doughnut shaped rings. Someone expressed the view that it had been an aircraft going through the sound barrier. A man in a cowboy hat was holding his mobile to his ear. Alice could hear that he was speaking to someone at the nearby airbase. He had wasted no time trying to get an explanation. From his agitated body language Alice presumed that he was getting the usual military response to this sort of enquiry. She had read somewhere that their default was to refuse to disclose the movements of aircraft or give any other information on the grounds of national security. The man returned his phone to his pocket and swore in frustration. It was an unsettling incident, but as the shock subsided, people shrugged their shoulders and continued on their way.

Alice drove home with her bouquet carefully packed in the boot. The incident in the car park had left her feeling uneasy. She intended to check if there was anything about this event on the news. There was nothing on the television, but the next morning all the local newspapers carried reports of a loud explosion over North Cornwall. None of the authorities including the Ministry of Defence were able to add anything new other than to point out that there had been a meteor shower at about that time. Alice began to wonder if what she had heard was in any way connected to the UFO that her daughter had reported previously. She was not the only one unconvinced by the stories about a meteor shower. That same morning radio bulletins started to carry reports of two long distance Russian TU-95MS 'Bear' strategic bombers that had mysteriously strayed into British airspace just off the North Cornish coast. Civilian observers reported seeing Typhoon jets screaming low across the coast near Treyarnon. Later reports confirmed that fighter aircraft had been scrambled to intercept two large Russian reconnaissance planes.

On the Friday afternoon shortly before Alice had been leaving her job for the last time, an airline captain called Brian Cowley had just taken off from Birmingham airport on a flight to the Canary Islands. His Airbus A320 had a full contingent of passengers who were in high spirits, on route to their holiday destination. It was routine procedure to fly west towards the coast of South West Wales before making a turn south to follow the Cornish Coast and then out across the Atlantic Ocean. It was a clear, fine evening as the plane passed over Lundy Island with only a few white fair weather clouds drifting across the Bristol Channel. The Captain had just been in radio contact with air traffic control. They had wished the crew a good flight and authorised the turn towards Cornwall. The aircraft was slowly climbing and had reached 17000 feet when without warning a black and green triangular shaped craft appeared, closing rapidly from the south west at a height of 20,000 feet. Both the pilot and co-pilot watched the large craft cruise across the sky, leaving two distinct vapour trails in its wake. There could be no mistake that the object was solid as the sun glinted over its surface as it banked. Alarmed that he could no longer see the intruder craft, Captain Cowley immediately reported a near miss to Air Traffic Control. They were unable to confirm any trace of any other aircraft in his vicinity. Out of the cockpit window the co-pilot looked down and could clearly see Hartland Point off the Devon Coast. He also noticed that flying below them, no more than 200 yards below their port wing tip was a small triangular shaped craft. It was much smaller than the craft that the pilots had seen earlier, but it was painted in the same distinctive black and green colours. After tracking the A320 for a few minutes the unidentified craft banked and shot away at tremendous speed disappearing in a sudden flash of light. The trajectory of this smaller craft and its controlled behaviour persuaded the pilots that it must have been under intelligent guidance. It certainly was not a hot air balloon or a meteorite. Neither was it an aircraft type that they had ever seen before. The senior air hostess reported that several passengers had witnessed the strange craft and that they were feeling nervous about the closeness of the encounter. One or two passengers had taken photos on their mobiles and there was an excited buss of conversation as they showed the footage to fellow passengers. Captain Cowley quickly made an announcement to everyone on board that the crew were aware of the unidentified craft and reassured the passengers that their flight was safely on course for arrival in Gran Canaria as scheduled. Nevertheless, he felt anxious by what he had seen and intended to file an official report on the incident after his plane landed.

The news reports in Cornwall all mentioned that an explosion had taken place at high altitude just south of Bude. The resultant shock wave had shaken buildings, causing damage to windows and glass houses. There were lots of stories about Russian reconnaissance planes intruding into the area. It was not clear that any of these events were related, but on reading these reports less than a week after his visit to The New Technologies Centre, it was a turning point for Chris Arbor. Something, he thought, was odd. There were too many coincidences, too many people reporting lights in the sky, too much evidence to ignore. He felt a thrill as the thought of initiating a research project into these events took shape in his head. This was an issue that he intended to resolve.

Chris remembered how excited he had felt when taking his sample metal part into The New Technologies Centre and how deflated he had been on his way home. On a more cheerful note it was Saturday morning and he was shopping in a supermarket a few miles from home. Tonight a few friends were calling round and he wanted to make sure that he had a stock of refreshments. His thoughts were interrupted by a call on his mobile. It was someone who he had never spoken to before calling from a laboratory. Chris did not catch the full name as the call coincided with an announcement on the supermarket public address system. There was a tone of urgency in the caller's voice who was insisting that they meet at his home address in Bodmin immediately. It was about the sample that he had left for analysis. The voice on the mobile stressed that any delay could adversely affect Chris's health.

Chris felt perplexed. The call left him slightly bewildered and he was finding it difficult to concentrate on his shopping list. When he had called into The New Technologies Centre nobody was interested in him. Now they were calling him on a Saturday asking for an urgent meeting. Initially, he thought about taking his time to finish his shopping, but he remembered that his father was at home and he was not always confident when dealing with strangers. He quickly filled his basket with some essential items, paid at the checkout and hurried across the vast open plateau of tarmac to where he had left his car.

As Chris turned into his driveway, he saw that parked outside his house was a large dark blue Lexus with smoked glass windows. He locked his car and entered the house with his bag of shopping. It was an ordinary three bedroomed post war semi-detached situated on an elevated site overlooking the town of Bodmin. The house had been in the family for years and was owned by his father who now spent a lot of time indoors because of his failing health. Property in Bodmin had always been cheaper to buy than in the nearby town of Wadebridge. Chris had hoped to have warned his father about the arrival of visitors, but glancing through the window he heard the twin clump of car doors as two men emerged from the dark coloured saloon. At first glance they could only be differentiated by the fact that one of them was wearing sunglasses which seemed odd as it was a dull day. They were both impeccably dressed in black suits. They did not have the look of technicians. They had the demeanour of military personnel dressed in civilian clothes. For one fleeting moment Chris was engulfed by an ominous feeling of impending trouble. Were these men wolves dressed as sheep? There was a sharp knock on the front door which he hurried to open.

The man with the sunglasses filled the doorway. He spoke with a slight West Country accent and was so tall that Chris felt like a midget in comparison. "Mister Christopher Arbor?"

Chris nodded and the man fleetingly displayed some sort of identification card.

"We need to talk to you about the matter of your recent visit to The New Technologies Centre," the man said curtly.

Chris directed the men to enter and led them to the kitchen where they sat down around an oak dining table. He checked that his father was aware that they had visitors. He was watching television in the lounge and after being reassured that all was well returned his attention to the programme. Chris joined the visitors in the kitchen.

There was to be no small talk and for a few seconds there was an awkward silence. Raising his glasses to rest on his forehead the tall man who seemed to be the spokesmen of the duo spoke first. He had cold, grey eyes which seemed in stark contrast to his white pallor. "After you physically handled the metal panel that you delivered to The New Technologies Centre, have you experienced any side effects such as feeling sickly? Have you noticed any rashes anywhere on your body?" he asked directly.

"Of course, I haven't. Why do you ask?" enquired Chris indignantly. "If I had been ill, I wouldn't have been at work."

"Your journalistic work could be the cause of your illness," replied the man sharply. "You have reported an incident concerning a UFO." The man was not asking, he was asserting it as a fact.

Chris found himself baffled by this comment, but before he could reply the mysterious visitor continued.

"The sample that you collected at the site of the damaged wind turbine has been referred to our laboratories. It was found to emit higher than normal levels of radiation. We need to check that you are not contaminated. If you wouldn't mind standing near the door my colleague will test to see if you are clear."

"Well I do mind," said Chris angrily. "You can't come in here virtually unannounced and start to make medical tests. I've not even had a clear view of your identification."

"We can take you to our base, if you prefer," retorted the visitor presenting his identification card. "Or we can return with a search warrant. We have to make sure that the community is protected."

This time Chris made sure he read the details in full. The card verified that the man was an official from the Ministry of Defence. The other man remained silent. He was much smaller and plumper than his colleague with a sullen demeanour. Chris did not like his disrespectful attitude. Grudgingly, this thuggish man extracted his card for Chris to check. He gave the impression that he did not care whether Chris knew who he was or not.

There did not seem to be any point in continuing to object. It would just result in heightened aggravation. There was a slight air of intimidation in the command to stand by the door which Chris did not like. It was his house they were in after all. He should be the one giving instructions. In the end, Chris took a deep breath and with a shrug of his shoulders, stalked over towards the door. As directed, he stood legs apart and with his arms outstretched as the rotund thug ran a Geiger counter over his entire body. The man showed his colleague the reading and Chris returned to the table.

"Looks like you are in the clear after all," said the tall man with dark glasses. "Where did you store the metal part before you brought it in?"

"It was in the boot of my car," Chris replied.

"If you pass your keys to my colleague, he will check the car whilst I update you on the laboratory report." As if mesmerised by this unorthodox interview Chris meekly handed over his keys and sat arms folded in resignation. He just wanted to hear the facts and for the men to leave.

The tall man continued, "The panel that you recovered was not from any identifiable aircraft operating in UK airspace. The results from our preliminary analysis show that it was made from what we call 'metamaterials'. These are not metal alloys, but synthetic materials with composite structures that exhibit properties not found naturally. Our technicians have concluded that these materials have not been manufactured locally. You could even say they are unique in composition. They are extraordinarily strong, light, and yet malleable. We found that the material you delivered could be dented and twisted, but was very resilient at withstanding any sort of impact. That is why the part you recovered formed a complete section, just like a piece of Lego is a complete part of a whole model. When the craft hit the turbine, it was able to continue flying for a short time without that part. However, the panel was radioactive suggesting that it had been near to a reactor based propulsion system."

"Are you confirming that the part is from an alien spacecraft?" Chris asked impatiently.

"We are keeping an open mind as to its origins. Who knows what developments are being made by other countries. There is a technological arms race and we may not be winning it. However, we do not think that there is any immediate threat being posed to our national security. Further tests will need to be made. It will be some time before definitive conclusions can be drawn." The man stood up and moved towards the front door. The interview was ending. Obviously, nothing more was being given away by these unwelcome visitors.

"What have you done with the metal part?" Chris enquired. "I would like it back."

"It's safely enclosed in a vacuum sealed container," said the man in a matter of fact voice as he left the house.

"Any problems with the car," he said as he met his colleague on the driveway. The man shook his head and the pair moved as if to leave. The man with the sunglasses bent forward is if to speak directly into Chris's ear. His breath smelled of spearmint.

"A word of advice," he whispered into Chris's ear. "If you value your health it is not a good idea to involve yourself in matters that you do not understand."

Chris considered this remark to be so stupid that he almost laughed. "I am a journalist. My job is to investigate issues that are not fully understood so that the public is kept informed."

Still dispassionate, the man replied. "I repeat that you are advised to leave these matters with the authorities. The public do not need to be alarmed by rumours. There must be no more newspaper stories about this incident. It would be a pity if you became suspected of assisting enemies of the United Kingdom."

The man turned and threw Chris's car keys to him as he left. He walked straight to his car which then accelerated away at speed. Chris was left standing alone and stunned on his driveway. He had received a warning and that frightened him a bit. He also knew that the efficacy of any research project can be measured by the amount of interest shown by security forces. He felt intrigued that there was something being hidden and he decided that he would not be deterred from finding the truth. Feeling slightly exhilarated Chris returned to the house and put the kettle on. He was joined by his father who had wandered into the kitchen having viewed the end of his television programme.

"Who were those people?" asked his father.

"They were just checking a story I was involved with at work," Chris replied solemnly. "I doubt we will be hearing from them again."

What Chris did not know was that from now on a small tracking device fitted below the spare wheel in the boot of his car would be feeding back his whereabouts to a special section within the Ministry of Defence. His every move could be monitored by unseen bureaucrats. Chris's investigation was going to be made much harder.

FIVE

GRENAH MANOR

Henry Penrose was sitting at his desk looking through the office window which revealed a view encompassing a large section of the factory floor. He did not see the machine operators injecting wax into the moulds and he did not hear the music which played continuously from speakers on the factory walls. He was reflecting on matters in his private life. At first, he started to think about his wife. Alice had seemed more relaxed and content even though it was only a few days since she had left her job. Henry was concerned about their future. He was aware that Alice would need to find another activity to occupy her time and he agreed that operating an outdoor pursuits centre would fit her skill set. The problem was going to be in finding a base for this venture at a price that they could afford. Then the worry about his role in The Transformer Project and his daughter's involvement with the UFO issue kept resurfacing. He was suddenly jerked back to attention by the sound of someone noisily entering the office. The old metal office door grated on the concrete floor every time it opened. It was something that Henry had been meaning to report to maintenance, but kept forgetting as there were always more pressing matters to deal with.

There was an old swivel chair in the corner of the office and Bob Mortimer unceremoniously lowered himself onto the faded green synthetic leather surface. There was a low squeak as Bob rotated the chair so that he could face Henry. He knew that Henry was less than enthusiastic about the company's involvement in The Transformer Project, but after a long association as a colleague he sensed that there was something distracting his Works Manager's attention. He had decided to speak to Henry directly to see if he could help to resolve any problems.

"Look Henry, I am not going to pretend that this is a casual visit. I have noticed that you have not been yourself recently and I wondered if I could help. I know that you are not exactly ecstatic about our involvement in The Transformer Project. Can I do more to reassure you about that? I know it involves a big change and we may need to fine tune your schedule."

A slight sense of shock and surprise enveloped Henry. He had no idea that his demeanour had changed so much as to be noticeable by others, let alone the Managing Director.

"Well, I must admit that the new project will be challenging, but I intend to give it my full attention," said Henry defensively.

"I am not here to question your commitment. It is just that you have been giving the impression that you are going through the motions, even though your mind is somewhere else. When I opened the door just now you were lost in thought. I don't want to pry or embarrass you, but we have a long association and I can't help notice a change in you."

Henry gave a deep sigh. He knew it was true that his mind had not been fully on the job in recent days. As Bob was a trusted colleague, he decided to confide some of his problems. What harm could it do?

"I realise that I was distracted as you came in. If it were just the new project, I could overcome my misgivings without too much trouble. There are some major family issues which have arisen recently. Alice has left her job and wants to start a venture of her own operating an outdoor pursuits centre. I worry that we may not have sufficient resources to start a venture of this type and we have no place to operate from. I need to help her get this sorted out before she becomes despondent."

Bob scratched his head. He knew Alice could be very single minded from previous discussions with Henry. The changes that Henry was describing would be a challenge for the whole family. Henry was about to speak again, but Bob held up his hand.

"No need to say another word. We may be able to help each other in solving this problem. I am a shareholder and Board member of a property development company. We are currently involved in the refurbishment of an old Grade11 listed building called Grenah Manor. Our plans include converting rooms in the old Manor House to become self-catering accommodation for holiday guests. When the conversion is complete there will be a common meeting area, kitchen and dining area. At the rear of the Manor House is a semi derelict coach house and stables. Work is well under way on the coach house where eight apartments will cater for up to eighteen guests. Forgive the pun, but the stables building is still a shambles at the moment. The company is considering renting the coach house and stables to a suitable party. Someone who has an acceptable business plan for the use of the premises and who has experience of the leisure industry would be ideal."

Bob never usually talked about his business interests outside Precision Castings, so Henry was a bit taken aback. He doubted that the rent that would be demanded by the property company would be within the budget that he had talked about with Alice.

"Where is Grenah Manor?" Henry asked.

"It's situated on the edge of Bodmin Moor, next to the Camel Valley. Just the place to use as a base for an outdoor pursuits centre! I could take you and Alice for a look round after work tomorrow if you like. Then you can see for yourself if the place is suitable."

Henry rubbed his chin thoughtfully. "Well that's very generous of you. I will talk to Alice about it. There's nothing to be lost in checking to see if the place would suit us, but from what you have said I fear that it may be too expensive for us."

"Don't worry about money just now. Let us see if the property would suit your business plan. We will address the financial side of it later if you want to follow through with a deal." Bob smiled as he hauled himself out of the chair and headed for the door. "Hope to meet you and Alice tomorrow evening then."

The following day Henry and Alice felt apprehensive as they sat in the back of Bob's Jaguar car. They were not used to being chauffeured about, but Bob had insisted that he wanted to take them to the site personally. The car turned off the main road and passed through two stone pillars. Ahead was a long, narrow driveway, bordered by bushes and a variety of mature trees. Through gaps in the foliage sheep could be seen grazing in fields on either side. The tarmac driveway was only wide enough for one vehicle although the acreage owned by the landowner was big. It was an impressive approach to the Manor House and Alice was reminded about the disparities between the rich and the poor.

"This is the access road in," said Bob. "All traffic leaves along an exit road at the rear of the property which connects back about half a mile further down the main road. This should prevent congestion."

As the vehicle rounded a bend in the driveway, they got their first glimpse of the Manor House. The exterior elevations of the building were festooned in scaffolding, but it was obvious that this was going to be an impressive building when the work was complete. All the windows had been replaced, the granite stonework sand blasted and the metal studied entrance door stripped and revarnished. Most of the workforce had dispersed as it was the end of the working day, but a man in a yellow helmet looked down from the scaffolding as the car approached. Bob parked and waved to the man who immediately started to descend a ladder which was secured to the scaffold poles.

As Bob reached into the boot of the car for helmets and 'high visibility' vests he nodded towards the approaching figure. "Here comes the foreman. I will ask him to show us round the inside of the building. We will have to wear these hard hats and yellow vests to comply with safety regulations."

They entered through an arched stone porch housing the oak door with the metal studs. Once inside it was clear that the main construction work had been completed. The smell of new paint filled the air. Chairs and tables were stacked in the centre of what would be the dining area. One wall of the dining area had a double door that led into a room with a large granite fireplace. The rear wall of the dining room had a door that linked to a large storage area with access to the kitchen. Another door gave access to the garden outside. The double doors in the dining room were wide open and Henry walked through to view the impressive granite fireplace in the communal area. This is where he presumed the guests could meet to relax after their meals. A curving, wooden staircase, swept up from the communal area to an open landing which ran the length of the building. There was a fire escape door at one end of the landing. All other doors provided access to guest apartments.

"It's been quite a job," said the foreman lifting his helmet and wiping his brow with his sleeve. "Should have all the work on this building finished by the end of next week. Although, there are some interior fittings for the guest rooms due for delivery in the next day or two."

After a swift look around one of the guest rooms it was clear that this building had character. It would be an appealing, comfortable place to stay. Bob explained to the foreman that his associates were particularly interested in the coach house and stables. The foreman held out his hand to indicate the route that they should take and started to walk purposefully in the direction of the coach house. They all rounded the corner of the Manor House before passing through a brick arch and entered a small walled garden. Presumably, it had, at some time in the past, provided produce for the kitchens. As the group progressed through the gardens, Bob provided a brief commentary, like a tour guide at a holiday destination.

"The property was originally built in the seventeenth century by a family made rich from the proceeds of a local China Clay quarry. After the quarry became exhausted the owners diversified into agriculture. The Manor has changed hands more often than would have been expected for a property of this stature and grace. The problem has been that the running costs of the estate have been greater than the income generated from the farming produce. The company that I represent bought the whole thirty-acre estate which had fallen into disrepair. We have set up a subsidiary company with the object of providing leisure accommodation for holiday makers. In the future there will be a swimming pool and a pitch and putt golf course. Local people will be able to book sessions although guests will have priority.

Situated more than seven miles from the coast, the trees in the grounds of Grenah Manor still showed the influence of the powerful south westerly winds that sometimes roared from the Atlantic Ocean. The branches grew strongly on one side and the trunks were bent away from the prevailing wind making them appear like shredded umbrellas. The orchard that had once adorned the grounds of the Manor House was still there, but the quantity of windswept rotting apples strewn amongst the trees bore testament to neglect. Alice thought that they must have been there since last autumn. Beyond the orchard was a cobbled yard which fronted the coach house. The building was in the midst of conversion to apartments. It was a stone building which sported a retiled roof and replacement double glazed windows. The foreman took them through the front door into a small hallway from which stairs led to the first-floor apartments. Straight in front was a corridor with a door to each apartment. At the far end of the corridor was an emergency exit door. With a flourish of his hand, the foreman brought their attention to a large plan pinned to the wall. The whole place smelled of timber and new plaster.

"As you can see on this plan, we have four apartments on the ground floor and four apartments on the first floor. All apartments will have en-suite facilities," he said proudly. There is full compliance to regulations including a first-floor fire escape to the garden."

Alice was impressed with the building, but she was worried about the sleeping arrangements if there were a mixture of unattached male and female guests booked onto her courses.

"We could furnish each of the apartments with two single beds. That would give us a total capacity for sixteen people" said Alice thoughtfully. "I anticipate interest from schools, colleges, commercial businesses as well as various clubs and holiday companies. It will not always be couples who need accommodation."

Bob could see the concern on Alice's face so he spoke to reassure her "Each apartment could be furnished with two single beds. Each bed can be pushed together to make a double if required or the room can be shared with the single beds parted. This would help to attain flexibility. Another option would be to furnish some rooms with a set of bunk beds plus a single bed. You would have to decide on total numbers to book when you had full information about the composition of your groups. Remember though, that the regulations do not allow more than a maximum of eighteen people in the building. Have you any thoughts about your group sizes?"

"Until we gain some experience, I would think a maximum would be sixteen people. We cannot really cope with more because of the supervision and equipment needed. The rooms will be fine, although I am wondering whether you would be able to offer our guests catering and space for presentations or meetings in the Manor House?" Alice was thinking about groups of students on residential outings.

"If you think the accommodation would be suitable, I am certain that we will be able to come to an arrangement," said Bob reassuringly. "You will be marketing to a different client group which will have different requirements to our holiday makers."

After a few moments thought Bob devised a possible solution. "The large storeroom at the back of the dining room in the Manor House could easily be divided with a partition. This would give enough space to accommodate the catering needs of your groups. It links to the kitchen and by reorganising the furniture you could also use it for your meetings. By working together, we can maximise the use of the kitchen facilities and staff."

Alice felt reassured by these comments and a surge of enthusiasm flowed through her as she contemplated the potential of this site. This location would be ideal for outdoor pursuits and the coach house accommodation whilst basic would be comfortable for the type of customers expected.

The group exited the coach house and formed a huddle on the cobbled yard from where the semi derelict stable building was visible in its dilapidated state. It had a gaping hole in the front, presumably to give access to a cart. Open to the elements, lichen and sprigs of grass clung to the brickwork. The doors had long since disintegrated as had all the windows. Adjoining this was a workshop and stables for four horses. Above on the first floor was a large hay loft. The building was a shell, forlorn and neglected with its rafters exposed like the rib cage of a rotting carcass. Alice thought that it would be easier to demolish and rebuild rather than renovate.

"As you can see," explained the foreman, "there is a need for extensive refurbishment to this old stable block. We have permission in our rebuild plan to include a two bedroomed apartment in the roof area above the stables."

"I think this place would be ideal for a riding centre being close to the moor and the river," said Bob in a surge of positivity. "Given reasonable weather all the building work should be completed in time for opening during the summer."

"It looks impressive, but we need to know how much you will be charging," said Henry. "We will have to check that the costs are consistent with our business plan."

"Well, I appreciate that you need to know the facts so that you can check your budget. I can offer a token rental at a rate significantly less than the market rate for the coach house accommodation and the stable block. In return you would make a lump sum contribution of £25,000 to the cost of renovating the stable block. Once your business starts to make profits, we would expect to receive 2.5% of your net profit." Bob escorted the couple to a bench under an old apple tree.

The foreman walked off in the direction of the Manor House. "Thanks for your time," Bob called over to him.

"What will be the length of the lease?" Henry had always known that it would require a large investment to get this business running, but it was the thought that he would be paying for buildings that he would never own.

"It would be a twenty-year lease in the first place. There would be an option to renew for a further ten years after a review of how your business was progressing. Take this information away and think about the proposal. I will confirm the contractual details of the lease in writing and if you could give me an answer by the end of next week we can move forward," said Bob.

Evaluation of Bob's proposal preoccupied Alice and Henry in the days following their visit to Grenah Manor. They revisited their business plan and recalculated the financial aspects. Alice had her redundancy money, but they would need to obtain a bank loan to cover furnishing and essential equipment. There were a lot of associated costs such as insurance and maintenance to consider. They would have to ensure that they quoted realistic prices to cover these. Henry slowly became convinced that providing they could generate sufficient custom, there was the prospect for a healthy profit. The potential for the business to be used by different types of groups all year round would help occupancy levels. They knew that there may be demand from commercial businesses during the summer months and schools and college groups during the winter season. Henry had complete faith in Alice's abilities in delivering professional programmes. In some ways he was reassured by the project. He had talked to Alice about his changing role at Precision Castings and about how he had misgivings regarding the changing methods of casting manufacture. He thought that having another business running might be a future safety net should he become too disaffected with his job or be faced with redundancy in the future.

Although Alice had floated the idea of the outdoor pursuits centre with her daughter on many previous occasions, she now met with Joy to explain the latest developments. Merging Joy's pony trekking activity into the new business would be ideal as it would enrich the program and boost the overall income. When Joy heard that a concrete proposal was on the table it focussed her mind. She was happy to join the family business in principle. She felt sad that she would have to leave her job at Innyvale Farm. Bert Pennington had been good to her and she was worried about letting him down. It would also be a risk leaving her present job in case the family business failed. Alice took Joy for a look around Grenah Manor so that she could see for herself the facilities. Alice knew that together they could make this venture thrive. It would mean that Joy could reduce her own rental costs by consolidating her business at Grenah Manor. There would be a new stable block for her ponies and an apartment to live in on site.

The pair of fledgling entrepreneurs started to compile a list of priority jobs that needed to be done when Joy received a call on her mobile. It was the journalist Chris Arbor. He explained that he had news about the test results on the metal sample recovered from the site of the wind turbine near Innyvale Farm. Joy was pleased that Chris had taken the trouble to contact her again although he had sounded a little pessimistic about the result of the tests. He wanted to talk to Joy about the events surrounding the UFO sighting and asked if she was free to have lunch the following day. To her surprise Joy felt pleased at the prospect of meeting Chris again. She had been impressed with his patient and sympathetic approach to her report about her UFO encounter. He seemed like a considerate person and she was impressed with his diligence in following up her version of events. After quickly checking her phone's diary she happily accepted his invitation. She felt excited to be meeting Chris again and it was not just to hear the test results.

Turning to her mother who had raised an inquisitive eyebrow she tried to remain dispassionate. "I have just been invited out for lunch tomorrow, which will be a nice change. It's that journalist who called about my story. Do you remember him?"

She was careful not to elaborate about the circumstances as she knew that her mother would be concerned about her getting involved with anything to do with UFO's.

"He seemed a pleasant young man, but I would be careful about getting involved with any more stories about strange sightings," said Alice as the two women returned to their car. "I hope you have a good weekend. I have an appointment with the bank manager in the morning and can now say that the pony trekking will be part of our activities."

"Will you be going on your own?" Joy enquired.

"Your dad has been given time off work to join me. It is in Bob Mortimer's interests that we present a convincing proposal and it will create the impression that we are united in our request," Alice replied.

On the last day of April Henry, Alice and Joy met with Bob Mortimer and agreed the terms for the lease for the coach house and stables. Both parties employed their own solicitors to draft the contract. A milestone in their lives had been reached.

SIX
ROMANTIC LIAISON

———————

Joy had left Grenah Manor feeling content. Her enthusiasm for what she saw as a new chapter in her life was not diminished the next day as she travelled to meet Chris Arbor. The Lazy Fox was a restaurant attached to a hotel situated in an elevated position overlooking the Camel Estuary. Chris had selected a table in a quiet corner of the restaurant with a view of the river as it wound its final few miles through green, undulating fields, towards Padstow and the Atlantic. He knew from previous visits that people did not like this table because it was a gloomy part of the restaurant. There were two photographs on the walls near to the table. One showed the old stone bridge across the River Camel, which had been there for centuries and the other the new bridge built recently to form part of the town's bypass route. Joy approached the table accompanied by a waiter who lit a little candle inside a glass bowl. The light flickered creating a cosy glow. He then asked whether the couple required drinks prior to ordering food. As Joy sat down, the shimmering light from the candle enhanced her tanned complexion, highlighting her blonde hair. Joy was wearing an emerald green dress which revealed her curvaceous figure. Chris thought she looked stunning.

It seemed an appropriate moment to complement her. "You look nice," he said warmly. "I am really pleased that we have been able to meet again. I hope that you can excuse my dishevelled state. I had a puncture on the way here and had to change the wheel. It's my second puncture in a week; unbelievable!"

"Sounds like you need some new tyres," Joy replied unsympathetically. "I'm glad you managed to get here though, because so many things have happened since we last met."

"Probably need a new car," Chris reflected. "It is odd though, because of all the years I have owned this car most of the problems have been in the last week or two. The car passed its MOT only about a month ago and there was no report of any excessive tyre wear."

"Sometimes you can just be unlucky. They say these things come in threes, so better be careful on the way home!" Joy said as she glanced through the menu.

As they waited for their meal to arrive Chris asked about Joy's work on the farm. She started to explain what she had done since leaving school.

"I wasn't sure what I wanted to do. I knew that I did not want to work in an office. Outdoor work appealed to me much more as I have always liked animals and have owned a pony since the age of ten. Bert Pennington let me keep the pony on his farm and I sometimes provided him with an extra pair of hands. When I finished my college course Bert offered me a job so that I could gain more experience of farming. Recently, my mum left her job and she was offered the chance to run an outdoor pursuits centre from what was an old Manor House. The buildings included stables for my ponies so when she asked me about joining her new venture, I could not resist the opportunity. It is going to be a new era in my life."

"So, you will have to leave your job on the farm. Bert Pennington is going to miss you," Chris remarked.

"Yes. I am not looking forward to telling him, but I think he will understand. He always knew that I was ambitious to strike out on my own. Besides, there are plenty of other people to fill my shoes."

"From where I'm sitting, I can't think of anyone better than you to fill your shoes." Joy felt her face colour slightly at Chris's compliment.

After the food arrived Chris summarised the events which had happened since they had last met. He explained about his less than enthusiastic reception at The New Technologies Centre and the visitors who came to his house. Joy listened carefully, becoming increasingly sceptical as the story unfolded. She was not an assertive person, but could not resist the chance to articulate her thoughts.

"Do you believe what those men told you because I certainly don't? It sounds like they were the same men who came to the farm. They made threats and wanted to hide recent events from general disclosure. In your case, it is as though they were trying to divert your attention from something they do not want making public. Perhaps they were spreading disinformation in an effort to mask reality."

"I agree that they were evasive," Chris replied. "They wouldn't confirm where they thought the metal panel had come from, except to say that it had certain unusual qualities and that national security wasn't threatened. When I thought about what they said there were inconsistencies. If the metal was as strong as they said why did a piece shear off on impact with the turbine? If there were radiation emissions why were they so ambivalent? They were not even wearing protective clothing themselves. The Russians seem to be more concerned than our own security forces, sending their reconnaissance aircraft to the area. Of course, I realise that one particular incident may be just a coincidence."

They both ate quietly for a while enjoying the food accompanied by a glass of wine. Joy had time to reflect on the sightings at Innyvale Farm. Wine inevitably had the effect of making her relax. It also loosened her tongue. She began to feel less and less inhibited and by the time the meal was finished she spoke candidly.

"I know what I saw that night. There have been too many other sightings, too many coincidences and too many anomalies to dismiss this as nothing special. I think someone knows a lot more than is being disclosed and wants to deter proper investigation."

"I fear that you may be right," said Chris. "There is the smell of a cover-up and we have both been subjected to some intimidation. I noticed it first at the time of the incident in the car park when I visited The New Technologies Centre. Then there followed the intrusion of the men at my home and the visit to you and Bert at the farm. It is conceivable that there is something that we are unaware of that the authorities want to keep out of the public domain. It could be something even more important to them than alien spacecraft."

Joy felt comfortable with Chris as they sat at their little secluded table. It seemed like a world temporarily isolated from the reality outside. Chris's hand was resting on the table and it was obvious that he was troubled. Joy leaned forward and gave his hand a gentle squeeze.

"I would like to help you get to the bottom of this murky business. Perhaps, I can help with some research of my own?" she suggested politely. Joy felt angry that the authorities did not seem to care how she felt after the traumatic encounter at the farm. Even worse, they were trying to discredit the validity of her story. Unexpectedly, Chris took hold of her hand and held it firmly. Joy was thrilled to feel the physical contact. His hand felt warm and his grip reassuring. He looked across the table and spoke quietly, but earnestly.

"Over the years I have had to investigate lots of stories, which may give you the impression that my job is exciting. Many of the investigations have been about trivial matters which could be resolved quickly. This case could be a long and hazardous investigation," Chris stated cautiously. "If we work together on an informal basis it will make it much more appealing though."

"Was it a surprise to get my call about events on Innyvale Farm?" Joy asked.

"To be honest we had been receiving lots of calls about encounters with UFO's. At first, I was very sceptical about your call, thinking it would be a waste of time. That changed when I met you at the farm and I realised that something very unusual had happened. If you are serious about forming some sort of research partnership, I would like that, but you aren't going to have a lot of spare time with your new venture starting."

"I'm sure that I will be able to make time to help you find the truth behind whatever agenda is being hidden away. It will give me time to get to know you better too."

"There isn't that much to know about me," Chris said modestly. "I studied English at Exeter University and during that time I had a long-term relationship with a girl on my course. That relationship broke down after I started working on a magazine in Bournemouth. The hours were long and sometimes I did not get home until late. Her job involved travelling away and we just slowly seemed to drift apart. After we decided to part, I wanted to make a fresh start, so when the chance of a job nearer to home became available I had no hesitation in applying. I have no regrets about working for 'The Cornish Gazette'."

"Do you live on your own now that you have moved back?" Joy asked cautiously.

"I live with my dad in Bodmin. Mum died a few years back and dad was finding life on his own difficult. It was another reason that I came back to work here. Anyway, enough about me, you haven't told me much about your relationships."

"Well I had lived in Cornwall all my life and so it was a bit of a wrench going to Agricultural College in Cheshire. I soon made lots of new friends and have kept in touch with some of them. We survived the rigours of the course and shared the ups and downs of student life, but I did not have a serious relationship with anyone. My roots were down here in Cornwall and I was lucky to know Bert Pennington who offered me the job on his farm. Since then I have been too busy to think about a relationship with anyone."

"So, we both came back to Cornwall and have been brought together by that fateful encounter you had in the woods one dark night," said Chris philosophically.

Joy was impressed with this journalist, who she had only met so recently. What he said was true. If she had not had the encounter with the alien craft, she would probably never have met him. He seemed intelligent and well informed. Fate may have played a part, but crucially, they shared a common interest. In her case the interest was recently generated, but nevertheless profound. As they enjoyed their dessert the conversation moved to a discussion about the existence of aliens.

"If it became known that intelligent alien life exists outside our planet would you be shocked?" asked Chris.

"I think I would be more worried than shocked", Joy replied. "In many ways it would be more surprising if we were alone considering the size of the Universe. It is the thought that they must be more technically advanced having the ability for inter planetary travel. We could be at risk of being colonised by them, just like we colonised the American Indians. Invaders are usually more concerned with exploitation than benevolence."

"That is a valid point that you have made, but remember scientists have recently discovered hundreds of Earth like planets orbiting stars within our own galaxy. They are planets about the same size as the Earth and in a position not too near or too far from their star. It is a beneficial position they call 'The Goldilocks Zone'. If we go back millions of years when the Earth cooled and oceans formed, the first cells evolved from this primeval soup. Eventually, these cells joined to form more complex organisms and the evolutionary process started. If physics and chemistry turned into biology under these conditions, then there is no reason to expect that given the same conditions, there would not be the same results," explained Chris. The excitement in his voice betrayed the deep interest that he held for this subject.

"Yes, but I don't understand how it is possible for physics and chemistry to create biology," said Joy.

"I agree that this is unknown at the moment," Chris replied. "All that can be said is that in a laboratory experiment the conditions that existed at the time when the Earth was formed were simulated. The result was the creation of a cell. What I am saying is that although we don't know how this happens, it happened here and so it could happen anywhere else in the physical universe given the same conditions."

Joy thought about this for a minute and felt uneasy. She found herself worrying that her orthodox Christian beliefs were being undermined. She was not a particularly religious person, but surprisingly the implications of mankind not being unique troubled her.

Speaking defensively Joy said, "If some of these hundreds of planets in 'The Goldilocks Zone' are likely to have the same conditions as when life evolved on Earth why have we never had contact with the lifeforms which inhabited them?"

"You ask profound questions and I am no expert," said Chris.

"However, there are a number of reasons why this may be so. Firstly, there is the distance. The nearest stars in our own galaxy are millions of light years away. Secondly, as civilizations become more advanced, they tend to disappear. Some self-destruct through nuclear warfare and some become infected with diseases like Ebola which wipe them out."

"There is something about this in a magazine article I read recently," added Joy. "It was along the line that as civilizations become more and more advanced, they pass through various stages. They develop from subsistence and agriculture, to industrial and mechanical, before entering the advanced technological and electronic age. At this late, mature, stage of advancement robots are created with artificial intelligence. The robots were said to be capable of learning and reproducing themselves. They were not prone to biological diseases and could repair and reform themselves like in that film."

"You mean like what happened in the film 'Predator'? Chris asked.

Joy thought for a moment. "Yes, it reminded me of that film. The robots would not need food or drink and they would never die so it would be practical for them to travel huge distances over long periods of time. They would be the legacy of a previous civilisation."

"Alien craft could be like drones with robots as pilots," said Chris thoughtfully. "Well it is possible that a machine of that type could have damaged the turbine. It would certainly prove that even robots aren't infallible."

They both reflected at the thought of fallible robots. Chris noticed a mischievous twinkle in Joy's blue eyes as she continued with an air of flippancy in her voice. "Of course, it might have been some secret drone sent by the military to spy on Innyvale Farm. There are rumours that under the land are rich deposits of China Clay!"

"Many a true word has been spoken in jest," said Chris. "Actually, I have my suspicions about what is going on over at Newquay Airport."

"What do you mean?" Joy enquired.

In a hushed voice Chris confided his thoughts about the UFO incident. "There is something odd about the way the authorities have been so determined to keep hold of that metal part. They were keen for me to drop any further investigation, threatening me to leave well alone if I valued my health. I thought they meant that the radiation would be a danger, but when I think back, I am not too sure. They seemed too ready to allow me to conclude that there had in fact been a UFO incident. Usually, they devise some obscure reason why it must have been mistaken identity. I suspect that they are hiding something else. Someone does seem determined to divert attention away from the report of what you saw and they may be associated with The New Technologies Centre at Newquay airport."

"Is there any way we can find out more about what is going on?" asked Joy. Then she remembered overhearing a conversation between her parents. She could not be sure, but she thought it was to do with her father's work on some special project being carried out at The New Technologies Centre. The realisation that her father may be connected to this mysterious centre sent a shudder through her body. She decided to keep this information to herself as she did not want to cause problems for her father.

"No need to wrack your brains too much just at the moment." Chris interjected to break the pause in their conversation. "There is someone that I have arranged to meet next Wednesday who may be able to help with research into these matters and I wondered if you would like to come with me."

Joy brushed back a lock of hair that had strayed over her face. "You mean as your personal research assistant?"

"I mean as my friend. I would value your company," said Chris sincerely.

Joy felt flattered by these remarks. Helping Chris with research would mean seeing him more often. "I would be pleased to help you. I need to show that I am not some naive person whose imagination gets the better of them. When you see something, physically feel it and see collateral damage caused by it, you know that it is real. What I saw is making me feel determined to find out more."

Chris raised Joy's hand from the table and kissed it gallantly. "No one will accuse you of naivety while I'm around," he smiled. "I think you will find the person we are going to meet interesting because he is an airline pilot who is absolutely convinced that he has seen a UFO. He read my report and wants to discuss the details. I have arranged to meet him in Newquay Airport lounge on Wednesday at midday. He will only be there for an hour or so. He is on a return flight to Manchester with a full load of holidaymakers."

"I suppose it is a popular flight if it will save a long 8 hour drive down the motorways," said Joy.

As they left the restaurant, they both felt content after their meal. It was satisfying to have relaxed in each other's company. They had learned things about each other and hopefully, could research UFO's with a more vigorous teamwork approach. Leaning on Joy's car the couple enjoyed a warm embrace before leaving in separate directions. What they did not know was that they were being monitored and their watchers were tracking their every step. Powerful influences wanted to make sure that it was they and not some interfering civilians who remained in control. The truth may have been out there, but it was going to be remarkable elusive to pin down.

SEVEN

A PILOT'S TALE

The editor of The Cornish Gazette was a fairly tolerant individual, but he had limits. As he approached Chris Arbor's desk on that fateful morning he was flushed with anger because he considered that his trust had been abused. He beckoned to the glass door of his office and directed Chris to follow. Once inside the editor quickly shut the door and immediately launched into the source of his annoyance.

"You wrote that article about the UFO sighting at Innyvale Farm without disclosing to me that you had collected a piece of physical debris from the site. Furthermore, you have been privately seeking to test the metal part that you recovered at The New Technologies Centre. Why did you not tell me about it and why no mention of it in your report?" ranted the editor.

"I did not want to spread alarm," Chris replied calmly. "I thought it would be best to check the facts before disclosure."

"Well you have succeeded in spreading alarm with me," snorted the editor indignantly. "I have received a call from a member of The Defence Press and Broadcasting Advisory Committee threatening to serve this newspaper with a Defence Advisory Notice. I had to explain that I knew nothing about a piece of physical evidence."

"I am sorry that it has caused you embarrassment," said Chris defensively. "That was not my intension. You know that there have been lots of UFO reports lately and I thought it would protect our integrity if we only reported the facts which could be verified."

"It sounds to me as though you want to run this newspaper. I thought I was the person who made editorial decisions," the editor snapped.

There was a quiet moment as both protagonists considered their positions before Chris spoke again.

"This has not turned out as I expected. I had no idea that UFO reports could cause such agitation amongst the establishment. They have sent people around to my house and frankly I am getting rather disillusioned with the whole business."

The editor put his head in his hands before raising his ruddy face to speak. "This has got to stop," he raged. "You must drop any further investigation into that Innyvale Farm incident immediately. You have ruffled the feathers of some powerful people and I can't risk jeopardising the future of this newspaper."

"So, we are bowing to censorship pressures?" Chris stated provocatively.

The editor responded quietly. His initial anger had subsided to be replaced with a more measured, slightly malevolent attitude. His tone was sombre, his voice menacing and his message unequivocal.

"If you continue with this investigation you risk compromising your own safety and the future of this newspaper. People have worked hard to establish the Gazette and I do not want its long-term survival endangered by a story about Unidentified Flying Objects. Now is there anything else that you want to tell me before we leave this issue?"

Chris remembered the photograph he had taken of the damaged panel. In hindsight, he was glad that he had deleted it at the military checkpoint. The meeting with the pilot next week was another matter. This meeting would be during office hours. It had been his initiative to contact the pilot and so he felt morally bound to notify the editor about this.

"As it is the Innyvale Farm incident that seems to be causing offence, this does not preclude any further reports on the UFO subject in general does it? I have a meeting scheduled with the pilot of a plane who reported a near miss with an unidentified craft whilst passing over our part of Cornwall. There is a lot of public interest in the subject of Unidentified Flying Objects and it will help to boost the paper's circulation if we provide articles from time to time," said Chris cautiously.

"Your job is to continue to report on matters of public interest and Unidentified Flying Objects are not a taboo subject for this newspaper. However, before you submit any UFO story, I want to read the article first," stated the editor. "The Innyvale Farm incident is closed though, is that clear?"

It was with a sense of relief that Chris left the heated atmosphere of the newspaper office knowing that his editor was fully aware of his meeting with the pilot on Wednesday. He felt regret that he had been chastised by his editor, but rather than being deterred from investigating these matters he was determined to carry on. The difference now would be that all the data would need to be filtered, so as not to upset the sensitivity of his editor, or cause problems for his future employment.

The meeting with Captain Cowley took place as arranged at Newquay Airport. Chris put his arm around Joy's waist as they made their way to the observation lounge. The airport information screens were showing that the aircraft was 'on approach'. They felt like a couple who were awaiting the return of a long absent relative. Although the sky was overcast the internal holiday flight from Manchester suddenly emerged out of the grey cloud cover. Approaching from over the sea, as a little black dot, it rapidly morphed into a plane and made a perfect landing on the long ribbon of tarmac that formed the UK's longest runway. The captain had already told Chris that this was not the usual route that he serviced. He was filling in because of staff shortages on the domestic routes. Realistically, he would have a couple of hours to spend with them as the ground crew turned the aircraft round for the return flight to Manchester. As a priority user of the executive lounge at Newquay he had organised priority passes for two guests. They could meet and talk in comfort without attracting unwanted attention. As the aircraft taxied to a halt Chris and Joy collected their passes for the executive lounge from the information desk. It was not long before they were joined by the captain.

Dressed in his uniform the captain looked very professional. After they had all introduced themselves, he took off his jacket and laid it carefully on the adjoining seat. His navy-blue pullover, white shirt and tie made his appearance a little formal, but Joy thought he was handsome for a middle-aged man. He had thick black hair neatly groomed and his eyes peered knowingly from beneath dark bushy eyebrows. He spoke clearly with no trace of an accent as he explained that he had worked for a commercial airline for a few years before transferring to passenger planes. Until his recent encounter with the strange triangular craft over the South West Peninsular he told them that he had never seen anything like it before.

After ordering a round of drinks, there was no mistaking his sincerity as he calmly recalled what he had seen.

"Everything had been routine until my co-pilot alerted me to the presence of another aircraft. I was surprised and more than a little alarmed to see a triangular shaped craft in such close proximity.

When the craft started to move erratically, I began to fear for the safety of the aircraft. One minute the craft would be tracking us on our port side. Then it would momentarily disappear, before emerging on our starboard side. I did not recognise the craft as a design I had ever seen before and its movements were abnormally fast. Without warning the intruder shot away at tremendous speed and disappeared. Later, I checked with air traffic control. They were unequivocal that there had been no known civilian or military aircraft in the vicinity at the time and there was no trace on the radar recordings. As other members of the passengers and crew had also seen the craft and confirmed the sighting, it could not have been a trick of my eye or an aberration of light."

"Wow!" Joy exclaimed. "You must have been shocked knowing that your plane was put in jeopardy by this craft."

"I was incredulous that following my report of this encounter, subsequent investigations failed to explain the incident. It takes courage for airline pilots to report an encounter with a UFO. There is always the risk of being assessed as unstable or deluded. Careers can be at risk if this sort of thing finds its way into your personal record. I was frustrated by the negativity and misinformation circulated by the authorities after my reports were shelved. It was a serious passenger safety issue at the end of the day. I felt moved to protect my professional reputation by conducting my own private investigations. I knew what I had seen was real and had become convinced that Unidentified Flying Objects existed. What I was not sure about was whether the craft were alien or terrestrial in origin."

Undaunted, the captain had felt duty bound to report this incident and remained convinced that unexplained objects inhabited the skies. He confirmed that he had been spending a lot of his spare time researching the UFO phenomena. He had heard about the current series of UFO reports in Cornwall and was keen to respond after Chris had contacted him.

"I am pleased that we were able to arrange to meet today," said the captain as he slowly sipped from his glass of orange juice. "Your report about Innyvale Farm contained references to a damaged wind turbine. This aspect is unusual and I wondered if you could add any more details so that I can update my general knowledge on this subject?" He was a perceptive man who suspected that there was probably more to the report than had appeared in the press.

Chris rested his pint of ale on the table and turned to ask Joy if she would recount her experience regarding that dark and eventful Sunday night at Innyvale Farm. She readily agreed to tell the story first-hand, but when she got to the part about the damaged turbine Chris realised that he had not yet told her about the reporting restrictions at the newspaper. He had been too distracted by the pleasure of her company. The unpleasantness in the newspaper office had slipped to the back of his mind. Too late now, as Joy described finding the metal part.

A feeling of panic ran through him as he addressed the captain. Trying to keep the pleading out of his voice he said, "Sorry to interrupt, but I have to ask that you keep this to yourself. There are reporting restrictions at my newspaper. I don't want to be linked to publicity about Innyvale Farm and I don't want Joy to be subject to harassment by the authorities."

Captain Crowley looked across the table at Joy and his sharp eyes seemed to lock onto her with unusual intensity. He was obviously passionate about this subject. "Don't worry about publicity. I am not interested in discussing these affairs with any of the media. Your story is of interest to me only as supplementing my research. I have no intension of naming you or publishing your story. It is just that the date of my encounter coincided with the date of your report. I thought there may be a connection. I am finding the details of what you are telling me valuable in aiding my research. It is a pleasure to talk to both of you completely off the record."

Time was passing very quickly as the captain continued to explain his observations with real enthusiasm. "Your initial description fits into the typical pattern as reported by many other people. These unidentified objects often approach at tremendous speed, have huge powers of acceleration and can move at unbelievable angles before suddenly disappearing. Many sober observers have said that they were involved in everyday activities with no thought or interest in the UFO phenomenon. Many described a strange feeling, almost like a sixth sense that resulted in them needing to turn and look. This phenomenon is often referred to as the 'Oz Factor'. It was like they felt that they were being watched and had a compulsion to turn. What they saw they always tried to rationalise in everyday terms. If the object was in the sky, they initially thought it must be an aircraft only to discard this seconds later when realising that the behaviour of the object did not conform in any way to that of an aircraft. Your reactions to the sighting at the farm were perfectly normal and I hope that it helps to know that other people have shared your experience."

"It is reassuring to talk to you about this," Joy replied. "Even my parents have felt embarrassed to hear of my encounter. Yet, there is something different in my case. Physical evidence remained after the incident. It is proof that I did not just imagine the whole event."

"I am intrigued to hear about the physical evidence," said the captain. "Can you tell me more about it? Was there anything distinctive that might help towards further research?"

Joy described how near she had been to the craft and how it had affected the electrical system on the car during the encounter on the road.

"Just by chance I trod on this metal panel when I was at the site of the collision with the turbine. Chris took it away to be tested."

"I took a photograph, but had to delete it from the camera on my way back from the farm," said Chris wistfully. "Just visible on the panel there was something engraved on the surface. It appeared to be part of a letter or symbol embossed into the structure of the panel. It was not a painted symbol of the sort that would appear on the tail of an aircraft. It looked like a building next to a small star. I remember that there was what looked like part of a triangle too."

The captain replied enthusiastically. "That is fascinating. It is rare to recover a panel and even rarer to see a symbol. The authorities are usually first on the scene and that is the last you hear of it. To make sense of it we would really need to see all the symbols. If it was possible to read the full marking it might give a clue as to the origin of the craft."

Little did the participants at this meeting know that a second panel was residing under a pile of dung within the confines of Innyvale Farm. Bert was keeping it as 'insurance' in case it would be needed at some future date. He was more bothered about the earthly problems that could occur as a result of their encounter. These authorities within the Ministry of Defence scared him more than aliens. If they had recovered the damaged craft, they would know that there was still a part missing and would be searching.

Chris started to tell the story about his attempts to organise analysis of the recovered metal panel. At this point, he felt his anxiety levels rise as the stress of his discussion with his editor returned, but he knew that he would have to give an account of his own experiences. After all it was he who had produced the written report of the sighting at the farm. This discussion had passed the point of no return. He wanted to tell the captain the full story. There was no point in meeting if the truth was incomplete, so he described the visit from the two men after he had left the metal panel for examination. This was something which had always struck him as odd. Their latent hostility had been palpable. He had not been deterred by their visit, in fact he felt surprised that they had seemed so disinterested in the face of what amounted to a rare piece of hard evidence. Surely, if there was conclusive evidence that British airspace was being intruded by alien craft this would be a pivotal moment in addressing possible threats. The silence from the authorities was deafening as they continued to debunk reports of lights in the sky with their usual vacuous explanations. He had a continuing suspicion that there was more happening in the background than he was aware of and this had maintained his interest. Many reports of UFO's had continued to flow in and as an investigative journalist he continued to sense that buried in all these reports was something of an untold story. Facts do not cease to exist simply because they are ignored.

As she listened to the details of Chris's problems with the metal part, something significant that she had read jogged Joy's memory.

"Do you think that the authorities are testing some secret aircraft and are using UFO reports as a cover story?" she asked nervously. "It's just that one day I was browsing the internet and I came across a story published by 'The New York Times'. I am not sure of the exact date, but it was sometime around December, 2017. Apparently, the same story was picked up by 'The Washington Post'. As I read the articles it became apparent that large sums of money were being allocated to a private firm and the funds had been approved by Congress. I started to think that there could be more to the UFO stories than I had suspected."

A frown contoured the captain's face. "Until the mid-1960's the American Central Intelligence Agency (CIA) maintained three lines of thought on UFO sightings. They were (1) experimental aircraft (2) delusions of the mind or (3) a campaign by the Soviet Union to sow the seeds of doubt in government. Since 1966 they added a fourth aspect, that Unidentified Flying Objects were craft from outer space."

Joy was confused. "Why did they suddenly decide to add that fourth category?"

"From what I have read the Americans found out that the Soviets were taking the phenomenon seriously and so not to appear uninformed they established their own investigation unit. I suppose the Americans did not want to be at a disadvantage in the unlikely event that there was contact in the future with aliens! However, to return to your thoughts about the stories you read on the internet. I would not be surprised to hear that they refer to a company called Bigelow Aerospace. You know that Hangar 18 in Area 51, located in the Nevada desert, is rumoured to house the remnants of the craft that crashed at Roswell in 1947. Far less reported is the giant hangar on the edge of Las Vegas which is headquarters of Bigelow Aerospace. Recently the hangar doors have remained closed. The only staff left there are armed guards who patrol this deserted 50 acre site. Apparently, the company has been paid by the USA Department of Defence to use the site to store parts from crashed alien craft. The materials in storage are said to be peculiar alloys that defy scientific analysis and physically affect people who encounter them. The Pentagon has now enforced a complete information blackout."

Joy could not keep the excitement out of her voice, "Yes, I remember that company's name now you mention it. Perhaps there is an official cover up!"

The captain smiled. His eyes seemed to peep from under his bushy brows exploring Joy's reaction as he asked. "I must ask if you have heard of The Transformer Project?"

"No, I have never heard of it," Joy replied immediately. She felt that she was getting out of her comfort zone and she glanced nervously towards Chris for reassurance.

"I have to tell you that when I read your report in' The Cornish Gazette' I immediately suspected a link to this project." said the captain. "From the little information that I have, I know that the Transformer Project is concerned with the development of a drone. It is top secret so few details have filtered out, but rumour has it that there is an unmanned aircraft being developed which is virtually invisible to radar, can move at tremendous speed and can be programmed to hit multiple targets during a single flight."

"Is it being tested in Cornwall?" asked Chris.

"No one knows for sure, but the circumstantial evidence makes me suspect that this is the source of some of the UFO reports that you have been receiving," stated the captain. "There are rumours that a prototype aircraft has been built and I have heard that it is triangular. The same shape that you reported at the farm."

"How do you know all this?" asked Chris.

"There is nothing official. I have just been reading between the lines. As a pilot I go to meetings about aircraft development, about countering terrorism, about partnership with the military and other health and safety issues. We must constantly update our training to keep our pilot's licence. Sometimes there are representatives from the manufacturing plants. I piece together bits of data and try not to make two plus two equal five," said the captain.

Some of what the captain had said was of comfort because Chris had begun to think that he was suffering from paranoia. Other aspects confirmed what Chris already knew. There had been various attempts to explain away these unexplained anomalies by the authorities. Sometimes it would be weather balloons, tricks of light, lasers on low cloud and even the beams of lighthouses.

"That's interesting. Could all these people be so mistaken?" asked Chris.

The captain did not think so. "I have no interest in conspiracy theories. I have formed a hypothesis and I am now trying to validate it by my research."

They had been talking for over an hour and the captain was conscious that his departure slot for the return trip to Manchester was approaching. "I must return this aircraft to Manchester and so I will have to go now. I have to run the pre-flight checks," he said whilst checking his watch.

Before parting he left a photograph handed to him by one of the passengers on the A320 flight. Although taken by the camera on a smart phone it clearly showed a black and green triangular shaped metallic craft. There was no doubt that it was a genuine photograph as the A320 wing tip, white clouds, and the Cornish coast were clearly visible in the background. There did not appear to be any windows or cockpit. The shape of the craft reminded Chris of a visit to The Sea Life Centre in Newquay, where he had seen a Ray swim above his field of vision.

"Looking at that photo now, it does have the appearance of a drone," reflected the captain. "If you continue to investigate it would be worth checking the dates of the UFO reports occurring during the last couple of months in this area and the locations. You may find a pattern. If so, why not use this information to make some strategic observations? It may be possible to obtain some photographic evidence. Then let me know and we can compare notes again. I must warn you not to use e-mail to send photos as I am under surveillance. Please just text that you would like to visit the Doom Bar. I will know then to contact you discretely. Remember that when you intrude, physically or theoretically into matters where access is forbidden, you may be subjected to intimidation and threats. The nearer you get to forbidden truth, the more interest will be shown in your activities by security forces and esoteric groups. On the other hand, the orthodox scientific community will feign no interest. You will need to be brave and persistent to continue your enquiries through the fog of misinformation. There will always be overt and covert threats to your safety."

As the captain prepared to leave, he advised them both to be careful because he knew that the authorities would be ruthless in hiding secret projects from public attention. "My own home has been ransacked and bugged. My telephone has been tapped. I have been followed and my mail interfered with."

He put his jacket back on and straightened his tie before shaking their hands. Then he passed his business card to Chris before making his way to the departure area. As he disappeared around a corner it suddenly felt lonely. Like when you have said goodbye to a friend who might never return. The captain's final words resonated in Chris's memory. "In the search for the truth, what you find may not be the same as what you can share."

Obviously, the captain was an experienced pilot and it was hard to see that he would be prone to illusions, distractions, or exaggerated imagination. During each flight he was busy in the cockpit and conscious that the lives of passengers rested with his training and professionalism. The meeting had been productive, not just about the incident with the A320, but in how to approach a thorough and systematic investigation. It had been a useful and revealing meeting, but it did leave the two investigators feeling vulnerable. They were novices in these matters and crossing forbidden boundaries would be dangerous.

Chris felt emboldened by the exchange of information with the captain. He could see a way forward towards developing a systematic way of examining the UFO data. The prospect of ongoing research excited his journalistic tendencies. For her part, Joy was far more cautious. She did not mind helping with research, but she had the pony trekking business to consider. There would be limited time to devote to the UFO studies especially if she were to join in the new venture with her mother. Then there were the potential risks of interference from the authorities, and the danger to other members of her family if she antagonised those who wanted to keep their secrets behind closed doors.

Ultimately, it was the personal relationship between the couple which facilitated teamwork and that relationship was developing fast. As they kissed before leaving the airport Joy could not shake off a feeling of disquiet. Every time The New Technologies Centre had been mentioned she thought about the work that her father was doing. She had not wanted to pry into her father's work or cause him any difficulty with her investigations. It was a growing suspicion that he could be a contributor to the development of this secret drone which she and her boyfriend were trying to expose. Sooner or later this conflict of interests could return to test her loyalties.

EIGHT
GRAND OPENING

It had been a lovely summer. Not only had the weather been good, but so had the time shared between Joy and the man she had grown attached to. She had collaborated with Chris regularly, compiling reports about strange lights in the sky, visiting archives, checking data, comparing notes and developing research strategies. Since their meeting with Captain Crowley, Chris and Joy had found that they had more in common than merely investigating UFO's. Whilst it was true that their regular meetings about this subject had brought them closer together, their social lives had also slowly merged. Chris had learned to ride and the couple spent time at the weekends trekking over the moorland. A romance had gradually blossomed and the couple were rarely seen apart. They both had to be careful over what they wrote, what they said and who they spoke to. They had decided to restrict their enquiries to certain types of UFO report. They put on one side the abductee stories and those which involved people on their own. They tried to filter out doubtful reports that they suspected were hoaxes. Instead, Chris recorded all sightings where there were two or more people involved. Joy focussed on cases where there were radar traces. The plan was to look for stories that could be corroborated by more than one source or where hard evidence was available.

The summer was now coming to an end and shadows were lengthening as Joy stood with her hands on her hips pensively surveying the newly restored stable block. Today, with the sun reflecting off the newly tiled roof and the stables ready to house her animals, all the frustrations of the building work were forgotten. Work had continued on the renovation of the Manor House over the summer months with only minimal delays. The coach house had been the most straight forward task with just cosmetic changes plus painting and decorating throughout. Now that it was completed and awaiting its first customers the Penrose family were pleased with its appearance and facilities. Bob Mortimer had been true to his word and had done his best to ensure that the project was kept on schedule.

As Joy walked towards the rear of the stable block accompanied by her mother, she felt content, sharing her thoughts freely. "I am looking forward to moving into the apartment over the stables. It will be a good place to live and convenient if there are any problems with the ponies. As time has gone on I have become more and more convinced that we have made the right choices."

"I will have to commute from our house," Alice reflected. "I know it's only a short distance to go home, but it would help if I could stay overnight should we have to work late and the coach house is full to capacity."

"That shouldn't be a problem, but let's hope that our working hours are not too onerous." Joy was thinking that it would be so much more convenient for Chris to visit. He had been meeting Joy at Innyvale Farm and although he had got to know Bert quite well, he had yet to formally meet the Penrose family.

One of the hardest jobs that Joy had found doing was saying farewell to Bert Pennington. He had known of Joy's plans for a few months and supported her move. He was obviously sorry that Joy was leaving, but had told her how much he had appreciated her work on the farm. During their conversation on the subject Bert had spoken with regret.

"Things don't stay the same for ever. I'm sorry that you are leaving, but I understand that you need to move on while you are young." His words lingered in Joy's memory. She had assured Bert and his wife that they would be the first to get an invitation to the opening of the new venture. It still made her feel sad to be leaving her work at the farm. Every decision had its emotional as well as its financial cost.

Alice had recently turned her attention to marketing. Like any new facility it was a worry about generating customers when there were no previous reviews. Initially, they would have to try to make sure that nothing got in the way of building their reputation. The family had invited local dignitaries, neighbours, members of the business community, potential customers and the press to a 'Grand Opening Preview'. They had erected a small marquee at the rear of the coach house and had organised a buffet lunch. Today was the day when the 'Grand Opening Preview' was to take place. Alice knew this would be an important day and whilst she was thrilled that her venture had reached this point, she also felt a sense of trepidation. There were no guarantees that the day would go well. Joy was excited because this would be the first time that Chris would meet her parents. Secretly, she was hoping to encourage him to write a piece about the opening in 'The Cornish Gazette'. Chris did not need any encouragement. He wanted the venture to be a success and was willing to help where he could.

Henry Penrose had been willing to assist with the work on the centre when he had any free time. He had continued with his involvement in the 3D printing process and although his company were pleased with the results it had left him with limited scope to devote to setting up the new centre. The constant military presence in the muscular form of Dennis Torrance cast a regular shadow over the process. During his visits he required every minute detail of operations, checking and inspecting each part meticulously. His visits reminded Henry of the times at school when the Head Teacher had stood behind his desk when he was completing an exam paper. Still not convinced by the new process, Henry was persevering and was slowly adapting to using new production techniques. In his mind he knew that change was inevitable, but that did not mean it had to be embraced. Sometimes a product could be spoilt by progress and Henry wanted to be sure that his company did not throw the baby out with the bathwater in a rush to abandon the traditional casting process.

Today, at the 'Grand Opening Preview' he felt relaxed. He was relieved that the weather was fine. It would provide the best conditions to show off the site. As he looked across the parking area an old, red Honda Civic was just pulling into one of the spaces. The driver had a mop of brown hair which ruffled in the breeze as he opened the door. Something stirred in Henry's memory, but he was at a loss to know what it was. He felt sure that he had seen that car before somewhere. His thoughts were interrupted as his daughter walked briskly by attired in a striking yellow dress. He thought she looked so young and beautiful. It was such a contrast to her daily working clothes which were invariably a tatty pair of jeans and an old shirt. Working with horses was not the cleanest of jobs. She embraced the new arrival warmly and it was obvious that they were more than friends. Hand in hand they walked back towards the coach house where Henry stood. He now realised how little he had asked about his daughter's relationship with this young man. It was true that he had talked to Alice about his concerns regarding Joy's research affecting his job, but he had not wanted to make a big issue about it. After introductions had been made Joy left the two men talking as she went to help her mother greet the arrival of a member of the Parish Council.

"Joy tells me that she has been helping you research the UFO phenomenon," proclaimed Henry in an effort to start the conversation.

"We have been checking UFO reports," Chris replied. He knew from what Joy had told him that Henry was sceptical about this subject and did not want him to think that he was deliberately leading her astray. "She is a lovely person and I have grown very fond of her since we met. The investigations into UFO's are a common interest, but we enjoy being together and I value her help."

"Have you made any important discoveries as a result of your research?" Henry asked.

"Collecting and analysing all the data has taken us hours of painstaking work. It has involved recording all the selected sightings on a map in addition to collating the times and dates of each report. Patterns have emerged in reports of sightings which seemed to cluster along geometric aerial pathways. You could call them the ley lines of the sky. The behaviour of the craft also conformed to repeated patterns. Firstly, there is a rapid approach, often a beam of light, instantaneous acceleration, geometric movement followed by disappearance. Our analysis shows that sightings invariably occurred in the evening or at night. Furthermore, there has been a marked increase in reports proliferating from around springtime two years ago. These have persisted ever since."

As Chris outlined the research, Henry had become a little uneasy. Conversations with Dennis Torrance about conflicts of interest were resurfacing and he was beginning to feel a bit anxious about the direction of this conversation. "Have you come to any conclusions based on all your analysis?"

"We sat down one evening and evaluated our findings," said Chris. "There were notes spread all over the table which we tried to organise methodically. Eventually, we drew five conclusions." Chris pulled a notebook out of his jacket pocket and passed it to Henry to read.

- Sightings were not illusions in the mind of the individual person making the report, as radar traces had been reported independently.
- The area near Newquay airport appeared to be at the centre of the pathways of activity.
- Many sightings were reporting during the hours of darkness.
- The aircraft appeared to be under intelligent control, capable of extreme speed and manoeuvrability.
- It was hard to see that humans were piloting these craft as the force of acceleration was greater than the human body could survive.

Henry was impressed by these research efforts, but concerned about the implications regarding his own position. "I knew that Joy felt strongly that she had to report what she had seen. She was deeply shocked by that incident at the farm. Normally, I would not have given the matter a second thought except that I know my daughter quite well and she is not a person prone to flights of fancy. I must say that I am surprised about the lengths that she has gone to in furthering these investigations."

"It was that incident that brought us together," replied Chris cautiously. He did not know how much Joy had told her father about the incident. "I knew it was a genuine report as soon as I visited the farm. There was no doubt that something damaged the wind turbine and Joy showed me the metal panel that she found at the site of the crash."

"You found metal from the object that collided with the turbine? Joy missed telling me about that," said Henry with raised eyebrows. "I don't remember reading anything about that in your newspaper report."

"At the time I was not sure what the metal part was, but I had promised Joy that I would try to get to the bottom of the incident. I thought that if I got the part tested it would be incontrovertible evidence that her sighting was genuine. That is how we became a team," said Chris sheepishly, wondering how Henry would react.

"What was the result of the test?" asked Henry. "Joy hasn't told me anything, although I suppose I am guilty of not asking questions. We have all been so preoccupied with getting this centre ready for opening."

Chris felt defensive regarding the next sequence of events. He was conscious of the attentions of the authorities and the last thing he wanted to do was to make Henry think his daughter was being put into danger. He decided to be guarded as to how much of his story he disclosed.

"I took the part to The New Technologies Centre at Newquay airport. I thought that they would be best placed to check the part. I never saw it again and was told to refrain from further investigation by the national defence authorities," said Chris. "It was because they were so unhelpful that Joy and I started to research these sightings independently."

The mention of The New Technologies Centre acted as a springboard to Henry's memory. Now he knew why seeing the red Honda parking on his driveway had seemed familiar. It was the car that had held him up at the barrier on the day he went to meet Dennis Torrance. He remembered the aggravation with the security man.

Henry fixed his attention on Chris with furrowed brows. "I saw you that day. I was in the car behind you at the barrier. You were arguing with the security man."

"That clown made me feel like a terrorist even though I had an appointment," said Chris indignantly. "I expect that you got in without all that fuss. After all, you did not have part of an alien spacecraft in your car," laughed Chris trying his best to make light of the events.

There was a short pause as Henry thought back to that day. "My problems started after I got in," frowned Henry. "I work for an investment casting company and was there to attend a meeting about a new technique. I'm afraid I am quite a traditional person and I wasn't really looking forward to attending that meeting."

Chris saw a look of resignation cross Henry's face. "Joy knows that I don't really approve of her involvement with the investigations that you are both involved with. It could become an embarrassment to me as a person employed to work on processes at The New Technologies Centre. I respect her sincerity, but I need to distance myself from your activities both personally and professionally."

"I have to tell you that Joy and I suspect that there is a bigger story that links the UFO sightings to more earthly activities," Chris replied. "My enquiries have been met by mendacious statements and obfuscation by the authorities, which makes me more inquisitive."

"I would advise you to be careful. There are some powerful people who will not take kindly to your interference," said Henry forcefully.

As this conversation progressed a plan was forming in Chris's head. It was just a thought, not yet an inspiration. His idea was to spend a night near to the airport. This could be a worthwhile information gathering exercise as that was the epicentre of reported activity. He made a mental note of this idea. Just now there were more immediate matters to attend to, but a plan was forming in his head. It was a plan that he would eventually activate and live to regret.

Chris felt a tug on his arm. Joy apologised for interrupting, but wanted to take Chris to join with her mother. She knew that Alice had just finished ushering latecomers into the marquee and would shortly be addressing the gathering. The two men followed Joy in silence.

To Alice Penrose the day was a milestone. It marked the end of all the hassle involved with project managing the completion of the Centre, dealing with the legal and planning issues, insurance matters and checking equipment. One of the most time-consuming jobs had been marketing the facilities to potential customers. An agency had assisted with this aspect and although their commission was high it had procured several important customers, sufficient to kick start the business. The biggest success had been to secure a booking from Southfield College of Further Education in Birmingham. They had contracted to bring a group of young people who were on an apprenticeship scheme. This would fill the Centre to capacity from Friday to Friday during the second week in October and would require both herself and Joy to staff the timetable. A few customers had booked for single day programs; others were members of clubs who wanted weekend activities. There was a booking from a local company who wanted a two-day team building experience as part of their induction for new employees. Alice felt happy that at this early stage there was interest in the new venture. This day was an important stage in the publicity process aimed at raising their profile.

It was not the best timing for Joy to formally introduce Chris to her mother. There was barely time for Alice to greet Chris before she had to address the gathering. She did not want to lose the dynamic momentum of keeping the guests interested and informed before they indulged themselves at the buffet.

"It's lovely to meet you Chris," said Alice giving him a charming smile. "I hope you will be able to stay until after our little tours so that we can talk in a more relaxed atmosphere."

"Little tours?" Chris was unaware of any tours.

"Yes, it is just a brief look around our facilities," Alice replied.

Feeling slightly flushed with the stress of the occasion Alice thanked everyone for coming and summarised the company objectives from her elevated position standing on a pallet covered with a blanket. After raising a toast to the new venture, she introduced Joy as her business partner and explained that they would be pleased if their guests would accompany them on a short tour of the facilities. They would then return to the marquee to enjoy the hospitality. Alice headed one group in a tour of the coach house whilst Joy took her group to the stables and to see the Manor House. If their timing was right the groups would cross after about fifteen minutes.

Chris tagged along with Joy's group and they made their way to the stables. He found himself sandwiched between a woman who talked incessantly about horses and a man who remained largely silent. The extent of Chris's knowledge about horses would have fitted on the back of a postage stamp and so his contribution to the conversation was limited. The man was more of a mystery. Although he was quiet and courteous, Chris noticed that he was very attentive to his surroundings. As the group approached the stable block his dark eyes surveyed the building as if he were checking it for snipers. Eventually, he asked a question about the routes that Joy intended to take when trekking on the moor. There was something slightly odd about this man and it was not just the fact that he seemed rather too old to be interested in horse riding. Behind his casual charm and grey beard, Chris detected an innate furtiveness. He wondered if this visitor could have some ulterior motive for his visit. Could this man be spying on the venture for a competitor? Chris felt slightly uneasy about the man's demeanour, but he put this feeling to one side. He did not want anything to spoil the day. Later he found that this odd visitor was called Peter Vadim. Unknown to both men at the time, their paths would cross again soon

NINE

BIRTH OF A RESIDENTIAL

Two hundred and twenty miles away from Wadebridge, situated less than four miles from Birmingham city centre, the small town of Southfield nestles in the shadow of a factory producing chocolate. The smell of cocoa often drifted in the air during the confectionary process. For any person who liked chocolate this was a pleasing aroma! Sitting at his desk in the Business Studies staffroom of Southfield College of Further Education an accounting lecturer called Jim Pilkington was settling down to assess some student assignments. Jim had worked at the college for the last ten years after leaving a secure, well paid job, in the finance department of an energy company. It had not entered his head that while he had been on his summer vacation a contract had been made between the college managers and an Outdoor Pursuits Centre in Cornwall. Even more of a surprise would be the eventual disclosure that he was to be involved in accompanying a group of students on a residential visit to this Cornish Centre.

The college had a large intake of part time students drawn from commercial and industrial companies in the surrounding areas. Youth unemployment in the area had been higher than the national average for some time after the closure of a major motor manufacturing plant. Other local companies had been trimming their labour forces to cut costs and improve productivity. Over the years Jim had become slightly cynical about new educational initiatives. The advent of new courses was driven more by politics and economics than educational development. He had endured so many heralded schemes that often failed to live up to their objectives that he returned to the college each September resigned to hearing college management extolling the virtues of the latest package. He knew the management were usually well meaning, but wondered whether they would be so enthusiastic if they were the ones who had to deliver the courses. The latest manifestation to affect Jim's work at the college was a pilot scheme called the 'Jobseekers'. It was Southfield's contribution to addressing youth unemployment. It would generate income for the college and enhance the job opportunities of the clients. Who could argue with that?

There were only ten clients in this Jobseekers group, but they could be quite challenging. They were referred to as clients because it was thought to be more appropriate, bearing in mind their age and the nature of their contract with the college. Most of them had dropped out of the education system without any qualifications and had given up trying to gain employment. They were known as NEETS, meaning not in employment, education, or training schemes. Many of them had become despondent after endless job applications had resulted in rejection. They had drifted into a culture of dependency, becoming lazy and complacent. They felt victims of a system that did not seem to care about them, but were well informed when it came to claiming entitlements to benefits. In the space that unemployment created, some of the group had become involved with petty crime and drugs. There was a vicious circle of events. No job, too much spare time, antisocial behaviour, blemished record, no job.

Austerity measures introduced by the government meant that to remain eligible for benefits the claimant had to attend an approved training course. The aim was to improve their skills therefore enhancing their employment prospects. From Jim Pilkington's point of view many of this group of students would have little intrinsic motivation. Some would attend because they needed their benefits and they would perceive the training course as of little value. The course was a distraction from the sedentary lifestyle that they had allowed themselves to degenerate into. Jim Pilkington was under no illusion as to who would get the blame if students were to drop out. He knew that the college had less than altruistic reasons for accepting the contract from the government. They had enrolled the group of Jobseekers because special funding was available. It was funding that became more lucrative the more successful the training course was in helping the client into permanent employment. If students dropped out it was seen as the lecturers' fault for not inspiring sufficient interest in their clients.

Jim's usual area of work was mainly concerned with vocational training and most of his students were either on day release from their employers or attending evening classes in their own time. The courses the students attended were highly relevant to their occupation. Some of them had their fees paid by their employer and others self-funded their studies. They were intrinsically interested in their courses as the material related strongly to their work and they were extrinsically motivated by the career progression that opened to them after they became qualified. Given a competent, knowledgeable lecturer, these students were attentive and easy to teach. By contrast the clients in the Jobseekers group would be much more of a handful. They were not thirsting for knowledge, having been dragooned by the fear of losing their benefits, and without any innate affinity to improving their education. It would not be the degree of knowledge that their lecturer held, but whether he or she could motivate them sufficiently to realise their full potential. It would take time, patience and energy to show them that someone cared about their future.

Jim had been asked to teach the Jobseekers group on the dreaded Friday afternoon slot by his Head of Faculty. During the first week of this autumn term he had responded to a message posted to his computer inbox asking him to attend a meeting in the Head's office. Jim knew from experience that his boss could be quite manipulative, even ruthless in getting what he wanted. It was always best to try to accommodate his requests or risk some future retribution. He had tried to argue a case of why he was not best positioned to teach Literacy and Numeracy skills, but the problem was that the person who would normally have covered this part of the timetable was off on maternity leave. It had been nice to be complimented by the Head on his versatility, experience and empathy, but deep-down Jim knew that this was going to be a tough assignment. After this difficult period of verbal sparring there seemed little point in carrying on the discussion. He knew that his meeting with the Head was ending as, through the corner of his eye, he saw him subtly glance towards a large clock positioned high on the office wall. Resigned to his fate Jim returned to his desk in the staffroom.

The main timetable changes had been settled a few weeks ago. There had been a couple of weeks devoted to enrolment and administration. This was the first week in the classroom and all groups of students had to receive a formal induction to their studies. It was the week when teaching staff met their students face to face in a classroom.

On this last day of the induction week Jim Pilkington sat at his desk and switched on his computer. He was wearing the same

Harris Tweed jacket that he always wore at work. Having been accustomed to wearing a shirt and tie in his previous job he never considered changing to a less formal attire. The jacket had leather reinforcements on each elbow and was a sort of mini storeroom. The top pocket housed biros and a pencil. A range of whiteboard markers lived in the lower left-hand pocket and the lower right pocket held a couple of memory sticks and his mobile. One of his inside pockets held his calculator. Out of the other inside pocket Jim extracted his reading glasses and started to scroll through his e-mails. Most were routine matters to do with things like Health and Safety, parking arrangements, latest times for post collections, closure of the first-floor toilets etc. Jim scrolled down until an item with a special tag announced its importance. He was invited to attend a meeting in the boardroom at ten o'clock that morning. The agenda concerned some forthcoming social skills residential courses. Jim did not like the sound of it. The words social skills did not appeal to him. He saw himself as a trainer. His job was to lecture on vocational courses and meet the objectives set out by the professional accounting bodies. The area of social skills he considered to be like a cloud, ephemeral, lacking substance and difficult to assess. Worse still he had intended to use the morning for lesson preparation and marking. His first lecture session with the Jobseekers was at one fifteen that same afternoon.

It was with a slightly resentful attitude that he now found himself entering the boardroom of Southfield College of Further Education clutching his diary and an A4 tablet of paper. Jim Pilkington was familiar with this room after attending many previous meetings here. Modular furniture could be arranged to meet the requirements of whatever meeting was intended. Three of the walls were wood panelled, one of them housing a large interactive whiteboard. The outer wall was all glass giving a good view of the sports field. A group of students were playing football as the autumn breeze blew a flurry of brown leaves across the pitch. Vertical blinds hung from a rail above the windows and could be drawn for privacy or protection from the sun. Overhead hung a projector linked to a computer situated on a small desk.

On this Friday morning an island of tables had been created to accommodate a small gathering. Seated around the tables was the Head of the Social Work Faculty, Stella Goldman. She was an austere middle-aged woman dressed in what looked like a blue housecoat. A large scarf was draped decoratively around her shoulders. Stella had always felt a strong social conscience and she embraced her work with vocational zeal. The matter of social skill development was incorporated within her faculty and she was not looking forward to this meeting. Jim Pilkington would be there and he tended to make niggling, negative comments. He had a habit of insinuating double standards which made her feel insecure. Similarly, she considered his subject, 'Accounting', to be a cold numbers subject staffed by bureaucrat's intent on measuring and counting things. In her mind these were people who knew the price of everything, but the value of nothing.

Stella was accompanied by one of her staff, Laura Odubi who was now in her second year of teaching. Her parents were professional people who had fled to the UK from Uganda to avoid persecution. Laura had no memory of life in Africa having lived most of her life in Birmingham. After graduating she had been employed as a social worker by the Local Authority, but had become restless and decided to risk a career change. Now aged thirty-two, Laura lived with her long-term partner. She was an attractive, gregarious person, who had succumbed to the practice of body piercing. A silver stud adorned her lower lip which looked as innocuous as graffiti on an oil painting. Laura's first year of teaching had nearly been her last. She quickly realised that as a teacher, you were only as good as your last lesson. Working with the students was rewarding, but the pressures were unrelenting. Every minute in the classroom required attention and every lesson plan had to be created for the first time. After each lesson, an evaluation had to be completed and filed to meet inspection requirements. She just felt as mentally drained at the end of each day as she had been in her previous job. She would return to her apartment only to start the preparation of material for the next day, mark student assignments and complete outstanding administrative tasks. Then it was time for bed, sleep and the stressful cycle repeated itself. She wondered if there was something lacking in herself. The trouble was that she could not think of other ways of working that would not undermine quality. She was not prepared to do less than her best, but her social life was suffering. Stress was making her increasingly moody, irritable and a bit depressed.

One day she had slumped down in the staffroom next to Jim Pilkington looking pale and demoralised. Jim had bought her a coffee and although she had never spoken to him before, she could not help herself from expressing her negative feelings about the job. Jim was able to use his experience, suggesting coping mechanisms which proved to be helpful. Over the rest of that first year Jim had been a source of advice which she respected. Improbable as it would seem, coming from such different faculties, they had got on well.

The screen on the wall suddenly flashed into life as Stella Goldman activated the computer and the word 'Agenda' appeared for all to see. Stella clapped her hands together as if she were attracting the attention of noisy schoolchildren and immediately the murmur of conversation around the table evaporated.

"I can't wait any longer for Janet Cowley. She has not sent any apology and we all have other things to do." There was a hint of irritation in Stella's voice.

Janet Cowley was a member of staff within the Hairdressing and Beauty Salon. It was a facility to replicate a real salon where apprentices could be trained to industry standards.

Stella explained that the purpose of the meeting was to inform staff of the forthcoming residential component required for the apprenticeship courses. A click of the mouse revealed that there was only one item for consideration – 'Residential'. Further screens appeared showing the facilities at an outdoor centre called 'Grenah Manor'. A map illustrated the location of the outdoor centre on the edge of Bodmin Moor, North Cornwall. This was followed by a timetable of activities for the second week in October. The last screen contained a bullet pointed list of aims and objectives. It was obvious that a lot of time had been devoted to organising this residential. Stella eventually ended her commentary and turned away from her Powerpoint presentation to address the meeting.

"So, I expect you are wondering what this residential has got to do with you?" she said.

In answer to her own question Stella continued. "The faculty has invested a lot of time in organising this residential. I personally have had to check more paperwork than is contained in the Brexit withdrawal agreement. However, I do not really mind because our students deserve the best. There will be just two groups involved, the Jobseekers and the hairdressing apprentices. That will be sixteen students in total which fortunately includes equal numbers of males and females. All sixteen students have signed our residential trip agreement. There are a small number of students from each group who will not be attending because of personal or work commitments. However, for those who are going, this experience is going to widen their perceptions, develop their confidence and improve their self-esteem. Of course, this will only happen if we support them throughout the process and that is why you are here. We need you to be 'on board' to make this residential a success."

Although he suspected what the answer would be, Jim was about to enquire what this all had to do with him, when the door opened and in strode a woman with dyed red hair. She was dressed in a white laboratory coat and although probably in her late thirties was strangely attractive. She sat sideways on a vacant seat at the end of the table. Her white laboratory coat ended above her knees. Perching sideways on her chair, she casually displayed a shapely pair of tanned legs. If there needed to be an advert for beauty treatments, Janet was a mobile exhibit of what could be achieved. Her face never saw the light of day without the application of liners, creams and powders. She did not wear much lipstick, but the vivid colour of her hair made her distinctive.

"Sorry I'm late. Had to make sure that the apprentices didn't destroy my salon or themselves," Janet stated with a sardonic smile. If that was an apology it was minimal.

Jim looked at Janet and wondered what size of handbag she would need to house all her cosmetics. Then he turned to address Stella who, by the look on her face, was obviously unimpressed by the late arrival. Nevertheless, she passed a residential information pack across the table which Janet collected and began to read.

"Which staff will be involved in accompanying the students," Jim asked weakly. By now he knew the answer would confirm his presence at this gathering, but he wanted to hear it proclaimed officially.

"You and Janet," snapped Stella. "We have to maintain an appropriate gender balance as well as meeting the staff student ratios required by the insurance company, the Local Authority, and the Centre. I will be your first point of liaison at the college with Laura covering any times when I am otherwise engaged. She will have full access to all the essential details. I will give you our personal mobile numbers to back up communications."

Now he was convinced that all arrangements were in the category of 'non-negotiable' Jim felt compelled to protest. "I can't just drop all my other courses to go on a jolly," said Jim. "I have to think of the bigger picture."

"The bigger picture has already been taken care of," hissed Stella indignantly. "Cover has been organised and approved for all your students during that period."

"But, I am about to introduce the professional accounting students to their new module that week," Jim persisted.

"You are teaching on the Jobseekers course and I would have thought that you had a commitment to them," Stella retorted. This was just the sort of response that she had anticipated from Jim Pilkington. "It is not a jolly, as you describe it. It is a proven way to enhance personal development. Anyway, you and Janet are two of the authorised drivers for the two minibuses. When you get there, your role will be to support the specialist staff provided by Grenah Manor."

"The timetable you showed us involves activities that we are not trained for," said Jim in a last desperate attempt to find a technical reason which would exclude him.

"Your role will be to support the fully qualified Centre staff. They will lead each activity, elicit your advice on the composition of the groups and handle equipment. You will be required to assist by helping the students during the activities. You will be expected to deal with any disciplinary issues, hold feedback sessions on each activity and generally be on hand to reassure the young people who are away from their familiar surroundings. Think of your role as ambassadors for Southfield College and mentors to the students," said Stella grandly.

"I can assure you that the Centre has first class facilities. There is a seventeenth century manor house surrounded by thirty acres of farmland. All the accommodation in the manor house is privately reserved. Our groups will have accommodation in a separate building called the coach house. This has been newly refurbished with all bedrooms equipped with en suite facilities."

"What about the catering facilities?" asked Janet.

"There is a dining room at the rear of the manor house which adjoins the kitchens. We will have exclusive access to this room for eating and holding full group meetings," said Stella.

"How far away from the Manor House is the building where we will be sleeping?" Jim enquired

"The distance is walkable in minutes," Stella said firmly.

"Will the staff have their own rooms?" Janet enquired. "If I am to go on this residential, I don't want to be corralled with a group of students. I need some personal space." Janet was a straight talking, no nonsense type of person. Her manicured appearance disguised her down to earth approach which often surprised people.

"The old coach house has been converted to accommodate a maximum of eighteen people. Most of the rooms are furnished with two single beds, although there may be a bunk bed and a single in one or two. Only the teaching staff will have their own rooms. The students will share their accommodation." Stella carried on quickly, anticipating the next question. "I have asked the group tutors to provide a list of names. I will make sure that you all receive accurate rooming information well before departure to help with room allocation."

The only person to have remained silent was Laura. She did not need to ask a question. Working with Stella she was already well briefed about the residential. There was a silence around the table and so Stella quickly brought the meeting to an end with a final statement. "We will reconvene the day before you leave. Keep an eye on your inbox for the time and place."

Jim and Janet left the meeting together and headed for the canteen.

"I should never have agreed to work on this Jobseekers course," Jim grumbled. "What a stitch up! Not only do I have to teach them on a Friday afternoon, but I am expected to escort them around Cornwall in the middle of October."

Janet could not help seeing the positive side. "Stop looking so gloomy. Think of it as just another part of the job. It gets us out of the college for a week and I might even treat you to a free hair cut!" she said with a smile.

Jim sighed with resignation. "Well I suppose there are some perks to look forward to!"

He returned to his desk thinking that Janet did have a point, but he was worried about how easily things could go wrong on these residential courses. A colleague had once told him that the college had booked through a travel company for a group of students to attend an educational convention in Holland. After travelling overnight on the ferry, they arrived at their hotel only to be told that they were excluded from entry. The company they had used to book the trip had not paid the bill for their previous party. Only a personal guarantee to underwrite from the Principal had gained them entry. Meanwhile they had all been stranded on the pavement with their suitcases. Dismissing these thoughts Jim knew he had to be more positive and forced himself to think of the open Cornish moors, fresh air and beautiful seascapes.

TEN

ANATOMY OF A SPY

For a man in his sixties Peter Vadim still looked fit for his age. Surprisingly, his brown hair had kept its colour, although the same could not be said for his manicured beard, which had turned grey. He took care over his appearance, invariably wearing clothes with designer labels. Outwardly cultured and polite, it was hard to believe that this man, capable of such disarming charm, led a double life.

These days he had more time to sit on the veranda of his house near Plymouth and enjoy the view across the city. He was increasingly conscious of how reflective he had become of late, as he relaxed on his favourite recliner. Visible over the rooftops the busy waters of Plymouth Sound extended beyond the protective mole. A cargo ship with a red hull was anchored just beyond The Sound and after that the open sea stretched towards the horizon. Sometimes, especially on warm summer evenings, Peter revisited events in his life, reassessing decisions he had made, remembering people and pondering how he had ended up still being asked for information by the Russian Intelligence network. He knew inside that the harsh truth was that he was a traitor to the country he had been born and brought up in. It was not a path that he had chosen for ideological principles. The reality was that his naivety had allowed him to drift into espionage. When he had realised what he was doing, the blackmail threats of exposure had made it too late to withdraw. Peter remembered his Russian ancestry and consoled himself with the thought that at least he was helping the motherland of his ancestors.

Peter's father, Henrick, had lived in Leningrad in 1941 when the city was besieged by the Germans during Operation Barbarossa. This long siege had lasted from September 1941 until 1944 and during this time more than a million of the inhabitants starved to death. There had been so much hunger and suffering that many citizens had resorted to eating dogs to avoid starvation. Where people died in the street there had been a scramble to snatch their ration cards. Such was the desperation the normal standards of behaviour had been abandoned. Trapped in this nightmare situation Henrick had involved himself in a scheme to smuggle food and supplies into the city across a frozen lake called Lake Ladoga. One end of the lake was not occupied by the enemy, providing a tenuous supply lifeline.

During the winter months, when the temperature dropped to minus 12 degrees Centigrade it was possible to drive a lorry across the lake. Essential supplies could be loaded from the eastern shore of the lake which remained under Soviet control. This journey was dangerous, but provided an essential link to the city of Leningrad. It was whilst driving one of these supply trucks that Henrick had been spotted by an enemy dive bomber which immediately attacked. The truck was not hit directly, but the bombs broke the ice and caused the heavy vehicle to sink quickly. Although uninjured by the bombs, Henrick suffered severe exposure from immersion in the icy water. He was lucky to be rescued by Soviet troops who transferred him to a hospital in Murmansk. It was here that he met an allied Royal Naval officer who offered him work as a Russian interpreter. It was an important role helping to distribute vital supplies from the Arctic convoys. Spies and Soviet agents brought news from the besieged city of Leningrad. Information was sometimes incomplete and communication was spasmodic, but those with relatives trapped in the city pounced on any scrap of news that might shed light on the plight of their loved ones.

One day Henrick was summoned to meet an official attached to Soviet Intelligence. It was rare to receive a summons of this sort and Henrick felt concerned that something was wrong. Not really a premonition of doom, rather a feeling of foreboding crept over him. It was a cold bleak day and flurries of snow stuck to his clothing as he trudged through the freezing streets on his way to the Embassy. His fears were brutally confirmed with the terrible news that his family had not survived the siege. A combination of hunger and bitter cold had drained the life from them, as it had to many of the other inhabitants of the stricken city.

After the war Henrick came to Plymouth aboard a Royal Navy frigate and settled into a new life in Britain. He met Peter's mother whilst working at the dockyard in Plymouth and in 1947 they became the proud parents of a baby boy. They called him Peter after Peter the Great. Peter grew up in Plymouth and heard stories of his family's tragic history in Russia. He was a quiet boy who preferred keeping his own company to socialising with his peers. He was not particularly studious, but had inherited his father's penchant for language and was a fluent Russian speaker. His father died following an accident at work and not long afterwards his mother was diagnosed with an incurable cancer. This double tragedy caused Peter to retreat further into his shell. After inheriting his parent's house in Plymouth, Peter forged a career buying and selling paintings, making prints, and renting his spare rooms as a holiday let.

The stories that his father had told him about his Russian ancestry were deeply ingrained and Peter made several visits to Leningrad to trace exactly what had become of his historical family. Although renamed St Petersburg, records from the time of the siege remained in archives, in church records and in government offices. It was on one such visit to St Petersburg that Peter was befriended by an old priest in the church of St Catherine of Alexandria. Unknown to Peter was the fact that this priest was connected to Russian Intelligence. It was a proven strategy of the Russian Intelligence services to use people who were embedded in a foreign country. They were considered to be unobtrusive, fluent in the language and regarded as part of the landscape.

Initially, the priest helped Peter to research the church records and in return asked for photographs of Plymouth which Peter innocently provided. As each visit cemented their friendship Peter found himself being pressed for more information. He felt affection for the old priest who had survived the depravities of the war and recalled so many stories about the realities of life under siege. Slowly and almost casually the requests for information about Plymouth became more onerous. It was now a question of supplying photos of warships entering port and providing pictures of the dockyard. The demand for information escalated until Peter was asked to keep a diary of the movements of vessels in and out of port. Although the requests for information had at first seemed inconsequential and fairly innocuous the stage had now been reached where Peter realised that he was acting as a spy. He resolved to tell the priest that he was not able to supply any more detail. His statement fell on deaf ears.

On returning home Peter found a brown envelop placed in the middle of his kitchen table. It contained a large cash sum and a rendezvous location where he was to meet a member of the Russian Embassy staff. During this meeting he was told that unless he remained part of the information network his previous activities would be reported to the British authorities. Peter now started to lead a double life as a British citizen and as a Russian informant. He was only ever a low key operative, but over the years he had despatched a wealth of routine information about the shipping in and around Plymouth. He was not proud of what he had done. He had not consciously sort to betray his country for ideological reasons. He had been sucked slowly into the dark world of espionage and had not had the courage to reject it. Complacency had resulted in treachery.

Over the period of his long operational career Peter had provided his handlers with information about UK military operations, the movement of personnel, the location of bases, and photographs of the latest weapon systems on British warships. Now, following his years of service and feeling every one of his sixty-nine years of age, it had been his intension to retire from active operations after his last assignment. He felt weary after years of constant pressure. There were people he had admired, but had later been forced to deceive. There were people who he had counted as friends who had been exploited. He knew that he was only as useful as his last job and he felt he had pushed his luck far enough. The danger of exposure was an ever present threat and he wanted to retire peacefully in his home rather than fester in a jail.

He had arranged to meet his Russian contact in an old waterside pub in Plymouth. Peter intended to say that he had decided not to receive any future assignments. The agent's dispassionate eyes surveyed Peter critically, as if assessing his worthiness to be trusted with anything let alone a matter of state. It was as if the agent was reading his mind. Peter panicked as he remembered the threat that had been made to expose his activities to the authorities. There was a slightly unsettling delay before the agent discreetly delivered the mission objectives. His accented voice was barely audible above the background hum of conversation in the pub. Peter shifted uneasily in his chair. He leaned forward stroking his grey beard, listening carefully, whilst trying to remain impassive. It appeared that dissemination of reconnaissance data was showing that the British were deploying some new type of aircraft. Little was known for sure, but a prototype aircraft, capable of tremendous speed and difficult to detect on radar had been observed flying over the English South West peninsular. Peter's brief was to discover the existence, location and extent of any development program. He was expected to obtain as much information as possible about the capabilities of this apparently sophisticated aircraft. His plans to retire were yet again left unfulfilled.

After reading all the recent reports of unusual aerial activity in the South West area Peter had come to realise that much of it emanated from the area around the airport. This was confirmed by the Russian reconnaissance photographs taken from the air. One of his targets was known to the Russian Intelligence service as Dennis Torrance and he had been given a photograph of this person. He had wasted little time monitoring the activity around Newquay Airport. His preference was for careful planning with an alternative plan B should things go wrong. In his experience, sound preparation and attention to detail was essential. It had not been long before his observations had shown a connection between the image in the photograph named as Dennis Torrance who worked for the defence ministry and Henry Penrose. Peter had decided to follow various personnel who regularly used the base on the perimeter of Newquay airport. Experience told him that if you checked on the people first, they would lead you to the core of whatever business you were interested in. One day he had followed Dennis to a factory in Wadebridge. The name of the factory was written in large red letters over the entrance – Precision Castings (Wadebridge) Limited. After patiently waiting for over an hour,

Dennis Torrance had emerged from the factory in the company of another man who walked with him to his car. The shutter on Peter's camera clicked repeatedly as he photographed the two men. Shortly afterwards Dennis Torrance drove away. Peter did not follow. He decided to check the status of the other man who had now returned to the building. Entering reception on the pretext of making an enquiry about the range of products, Peter waited while the receptionist went to collect the company brochure. On the wall was a diagram of the line management structure with photographs of each manager. Their names were printed below the photos and Peter immediately recognised the person he had photographed as Henry Penrose. Peter suspected that Precision Castings (Wadebridge) Limited was probably manufacturing items for the military.

The name Penrose struck a chord, but for a while Peter could not figure out where he had heard that name before. That evening whilst reading his newspaper his memory was suddenly restored. It was a report in this same newspaper about a UFO. Peter went to the pile of old newspapers that he kept stored in a cupboard under the stairs. They came in useful for when he had to clear his cat's litter tray. It was not long before a systematic trawl through the grubby back copies revealed what he had been looking for. Written in a bold type was a heading about a UFO sighting near to Davidstow airfield on the edge of Bodmin Moor. Someone called Joy Penrose had reported an encounter with a strange craft. A picture of a damaged wind turbine had been included in the report. A visit to the library in Bodmin revealed that Henry, Alice and Joy Penrose were listed in the Electoral Register as living at the same address. It was probably a blind alley, but Peter pondered how he could find out more about the contracts held by Precision Castings (Wadebridge) Limited. He started searching through the entries for this firm on the Companies House website.

The opportunity to get closer to the family happened by chance through a circular advertising a new Outdoor Pursuits Centre. It had been sent to him as the owner of the holiday let in Plymouth. When he saw the name Penrose on the leaflet Peter decided to attend the opening day ceremony. It was a perfect excuse to make informal contact with Henry Penrose.

ELEVEN
TANGLED NETWORK

The mini tours of their new outdoor centre were brief, but they achieved their objective. The immediate visitor feedback sounded positive. Alice and Joy felt relieved and slightly elated as they exchanged thoughts on the way back to the marquee. The whole event had gone well with some genuine interest generated from several of the visitors. It was not the only reason for their optimism. Their new website page had generated numerous enquiries making the venture less dependent on the expensive Agency in procuring new business. They also had the definite booking from Southfield College of Further Education.

In the marquee Bert Pennington and his wife were enjoying the refreshments whilst chatting to Henry. In contrast to his daughter's involvement with the UFO issue, Henry was proud to hear how much Bert had valued Joy's work at the farm. When Alice returned to the marquee, she was able to resume her conversation with Chris in a more relaxed atmosphere. The glass of red wine she had selected gradually induced a mellowing effect, helping to lubricate the conversation. She soon found Chris a person well informed and knowledgeable about local matters. For his part Chris felt politely included by this enterprising family, comfortable enough to mention talk about his work and interest in UFO phenomena. Eventually, they were joined by Joy who had been distracted by another guest. She arrived to hear that Chris was enthusiastically describing the result of their latest research.

After embracing her fondly Chris continued, "Joy has been such a help in all this research! It needed a careful person to sift through the volumes of data that we collected. As a result of her efforts we have been able to reveal an intriguing pattern."

Joy smiled nervously in the direction of her mother. She understood her parents were sensitive to her involvement with this subject. "We have both spent hours checking timings and locations of recent UFO sightings in this area. It has become a bit like a hobby."

"It's really quite obvious when you stand back and look at the facts," Chris explained. "We know that most of the sightings from the public have taken place after dark. Plotting the locations of each UFO sighting over the last few months on a map of North Cornwall shows that certain tracks seem to repeat."

"It shocks and surprises me to think that my experience may not be isolated," said Joy pensively. The memory of her sighting in the Davidstow Woods still haunted her.

"There does actually appear to be a hive of activity near to a village called St Eval," Chris continued, following the theme of Joy's comment. "These sightings all seem to concern low altitude encounters with triangular shaped craft showing red and green lights."

"Isn't there an old disused airfield there?" asked Joy, looking towards her mother.

After having listened quietly, Alice realised how deeply Joy had become involved in this subject. She wanted to be supportive and decided to offer a positive contribution. "There was a second world war RAF coastal command station at St Eval. Some of the villagers were forced out of their homes because of a compulsory purchase order. Aircraft carried out photographic reconnaissance and anti-submarine patrols from there, but I heard that the station was closed in the late 1950's. I think parts of it are still used as a communication station."

"Well that is interesting. Perhaps we should have a drive around there to see whether there is a runway. Who knows it might be North Cornwall's Area 51," Chris remarked half seriously.

The comment evoked apprehension in Alice's perception of these matters. She remembered how concerned Henry had been about Joy's involvement with the UFO scenario. She could see how all this could compromise his work and did not want to make matters worse.

Chris cleared his throat rather overtly before continuing to communicate the findings from recent research.

"Anyway, more interesting than the low-level sightings is the fact that the flight paths seem to converge along an ancient ley line. They are clustered along the old Cornish ley line that stretches from Mont St Michel in France through St Michel's Mount in Cornwall. It continues through Glastonbury and Avebury all the way through to Great Yarmouth in the East of England."

A glance over to Alice showed raised eyebrows at the mention of ley lines. Chris explained. "Ley lines are reputed to be invisible lines of force. They are supposed to harness magnetic gravitational fields. I have read that they can be used to harness the Earth's magnetism to help navigation."

"So, you think that the unidentified craft are using these lines to navigate?" asked Alice.

"That's what the patterns of sightings seem to show," said Chris. "They do seem to be clustered along what appears to be a geometric aerial pathway when in flight at altitude. There is a predominance of low-level sightings around the village of St Eval. One person compared the aircraft to insects returning to a nest. When you read reports from local people about their sightings, they describe how they looked up and saw, delta winged craft pass silently overhead."

Alice had been listening carefully to the conversation about UFO's. Like Henry, she was sceptical about the subject and wanted to better understand Chris's attitude towards these matters, so she asked him whether he believed that Earth was being visited by extra-terrestrials. Chris himself was uncertain and had to admit that he was not wholly convinced.

"I believe that the sightings that we have analysed are from people who have genuinely seen things that they couldn't explain. There are too many reports just to reject them as figments of imagination. Then there is the fact of radar corroboration. There does seem to be something unusual happening in our skies, but I am not entirely sure whether it has anything to do with aliens. I have a deepening suspicion that the source of these sightings may be nearer to home."

Alice frowned. "Well, I would have dismissed it all as fantasy until I heard about Joy's close encounter. Now I am not sure what to make of it all. I hope that your research will clear up some of the misconceptions."

So preoccupied were Chris and Joy in conversation that they had failed to notice that standing just behind them was the mysterious man with the grey beard who had been part of Joy's group during their earlier tour of the facilities. He had been close enough to overhear their discussion. They did not think anything about it, as the man seemed preoccupied enjoying the refreshments which were on offer.

Sensing that he might have been noticed as invading the personal space of the group near to him, the man wisely moved to distance himself. His thoughts were focussed on the snippets of conversation that he had overheard and this lack of concentration resulted in him accidentally nudging Henry's arm. The sandwich that Henry had been eating slipped off his plate and onto the floor, narrowly missing Bert Pennington's boot.

Henry was about to apologise, but realised that there was no need. Unperturbed, Bert moved back a step and said with a smile, "Better than the usual mess that drops on my boots!"

The comment caused laughter in the group. Apologising for his carelessness, the man with the grey beard held out his hand and introduced himself as Peter Vadim, owner of a holiday let in Plymouth.

Bert and his wife moved away, suspecting that this guest wanted to talk to Henry one to one. "It has been nice to talk to you Henry. You must bring Alice round to the farm for a meal when things have settled down."

"We will look forward to that," Henry replied.

Peter Vadim now had the meeting with Henry that he had hoped for. "I have come to see if this new Centre could be of interest to my guests. I intend to let them know about your outdoor centre. I think that it may well be the sort of place that some of my younger visitors would be keen to avail themselves of," said Peter. "It must have taken a lot of your time to establish such a facility."

Peter's easy charm was received warmly by Henry who explained that the venture was really the brainchild of his wife and daughter.

"So, you do not work in the leisure industry?" enquired Peter in precise, polished English.

"No, I work for a company that makes investment castings in Wadebridge," replied Henry innocently. He had no idea that Peter already knew this and more.

"Is there a lot of demand for your firm's products?" asked Peter.

"We have made parts by the traditional lost wax process for years," said Henry. "It is good for manufacturing volumes of small parts in a variety of metal alloys."

"I expect that you supply the needs of industry in the South West." Peter was probing, fishing, for information.

"Well, obviously a lot of our customers are local, but we supply further afield too". Henry was conscious that he did not want to divulge too much information about his work to a stranger, so he started to steer the conversation more towards the visitor's life. "Tell me, are you enjoying high occupancy levels as more people take 'Staycations'? I know that the fall in the pound, international terrorism, and the uncertainty over our relations with the European Union are altering perceptions of where people want to holiday."

"I have been fully booked this summer," Peter replied. "It is mainly families during the school holidays and older couples at the off-peak dates. Of course, it helps if the weather stays warm and dry. I live alone and so it makes fuller use of my property to let part of it off. I aim to give my guests a clean and comfortable accommodation at competitive prices. When I read the feedback they give I think most are happy. Usually, I am pleased to have them stay. Living on my own it is good to have people around."

Henry concluded that Peter sounded like a lonely sort of person. He personally, would not have wanted to have lived on his own. Perhaps Peter's more solitary life was the reason why he seemed a bit odd. Although friendly on the surface, Henry sensed a faint insincerity about the man. It was just a feeling without any evidence. He decided to remain cautious in associating with this guest. Excusing himself Henry graciously moved to introduce Peter to one of the other guests involved in the holiday industry. It did seem a bit odd that a man as articulate and well dressed as Peter appeared to be reliant on a single holiday let for his income. He wondered what other streams of income Peter had coming in.

These thoughts swiftly disappeared as he joined Alice and Joy who were listening to Chris talk about some of the other assignments that he had worked on as a journalist. Henry was keen to get to know more about the man who was associating with his daughter. He also intended to give him a gentle reminder that he did not want his daughter to get any more deeply involved with these UFO investigations.

By late afternoon, the launch of the outdoor centre came to an end. The last of the visitors meandered on their way to their cars. The day had gone well and the Penrose family were all pleased with the responses that had been received. Chris returned to his car accompanied by Joy who was in high spirits. Approaching the car Chris saw that a small white envelope was trapped beneath one of the windscreen wipers. The letters CA were handwritten on the front in black biro.

"I hope it isn't a parking fine," grinned Chris. His grin was soon replaced with a frown when he opened the envelope. Inside was a scrap of paper that looked as if it had been ripped from the inside of a paperback book. It simply showed a hand drawn image of a flying saucer followed by one word written through the middle of a large red 'X'. Like those used on traffic signs. Shocked and surprised, Chris handed the paper over for Joy to see. It was the word 'ABDUCTION' that made her gasp.

"Who would bother to draw that meaningless twaddle?" Joy was annoyed that someone had trespassed on her land. She was alarmed that this intruder had been impertinent enough to interfere with Chris's car. Frowning with indignation she said. "It is pretty obvious that you must have been followed here by some nasty individual who wants to warn you."

Chris scratched his head. "Every time something bad happens it's usually connected to my reports on unidentified flying objects," said Chris. "There are people who are extremely sensitive to anything connected to this subject. I do not mean individual people. Ever since I took that metal part for analysis, I have had trouble. There was the visit from the defence people who pretended to be concerned for my health when warning me away from further investigation. My newspaper has been threatened by the Ministry of Defence. Now I think back I think that someone was following me on the way here. I remember it because the car I saw in my mirror had just one headlight on. At first, I thought it was a motorcycle, but after a while I realised it was a black car. When I turned in here it continued down the main road. It feels more and more like blatant intimidation."

A tide of anger was rising in Joy that overrode the warnings to be careful given by her family. "I didn't realise that you were being harassed to this extent. It is intolerable and I am going to make an official complaint to those defence people. It is unacceptable behaviour. They cannot persecute people just when they feel like it. That word 'abduction' implies involuntary removal."

Before Joy could say any more Chris held up his hand. "Hold on a minute. If we are right about it being the authorities, they are not going to take any notice of pleas from us. It just proves to me that there is something that they are hiding. The only way to deal with this is to find out what it is. I already have strong suspicions."

"You don't think that they are hiding an actual alien craft, do you? Perhaps they have the rest of the craft that hit the wind turbine. I have read reports about the crash in 1947 at Roswell in Mexico where alien bodies were said to have been recovered and subjected to an autopsy." Joy shuddered at the implications of her words.

"More likely they are using the reports of UFO activity to hide the fact that they are testing some new top-secret aircraft. Didn't Captain Cowley say that there was a project to develop some sort of drone?"

"I think he referred to it as 'The Transformer Project' if my memory serves me right," said Joy.

"That's it," said Chris excitedly. "I think a drone would look like an alien craft to the unsuspecting observer. How convenient to use stories of unidentified flying objects to divert attention. I need to spend time carrying out my own undercover observations at a location where I know that there have been sightings. It could be very revealing to spend a night observing aircraft movement at that airfield near to Newquay."

After a short silence where both looked enquiringly at the other Joy responded. "If you mean St Eval, I don't think it is a good idea to go there. It would be too risky. I went near there after I took a wrong turning a couple of years ago. There was a big fence with signs warning people to keep out."

Joy was less than impressed with this proposal. It was a headstrong idea that needed to be thought through more carefully.

"Apart from the fact that you could be arrested as a spy, you would waste endless time. If it is a top-secret aircraft, you have no idea when it will be operating and you can't be certain that it will be at St Eval."

Chris smiled. "I don't want to sound overconfident, but I know the pattern. There is a cluster of low-level sightings in that area. They are all on nights when the weather is clear and in the early hours when there are few commercial flights using Newquay airport. I have booked a couple of days holiday during the second week in October and can easily arrange to do a bit of night-time observation. If the weather is clear it would be a chance to test my theory."

Joy felt alarmed by this plan. "Look, you are letting your enthusiasm get in the way of common sense."

"I need to do this to follow through a new line of enquiry," said Chris firmly. "It's only one night and I won't trespass inside the fence."

"Well, I probably will not be able to come with you. You will be on your own. We have got that booking from a College of Further Education to organise. I will need to help mum plan and deliver a program of activities. It is important that we establish a good reputation considering that we are a new venture."

"No need to worry. It's better that I do this observation alone," said Chris. "The more people, the more obtrusive it would be. Obviously, it would be great to have your company, but this is one occasion that is better served by me working alone."

Privately he was glad that Joy would not be there. He did not want to be responsible for her safety if things went wrong. Neither did he want to cause any potential embarrassment to the Penrose family. He screwed up the message left on his windscreen and trod on it like a discarded cigarette. If the authorities were trying to frighten him, they were going to find that he would not be easily intimidated.

At around this time Peter Vadim was on his way home to Plymouth. As he drove along, he was thinking about the bits of conversation that he had overheard about UFO sightings, but he was not convinced that Cornwall was facing an alien invasion. Considering the information that he had been given by Russian Intelligence, he too thought it highly likely that the sightings had been of a terrestrial aircraft. It was during this journey home that Peter decided to make some observations of his own. He would take his camera and the camouflage tent that he used on his occasional bird watching trips. The problem was where to pitch his tent. He had heard St Eval mentioned during the afternoon. As soon as he reached home, he opened a map of the area and found the location of St Eval. He saw that it was near to Newquay airport and decided that would be as good a place as any to start his observation.

TWELVE

JOBSEEKERS

> I hear and I forget,
> I see and I remember;
> I do and I understand.
> *Old Chinese proverb*

It was Jim Pilkington's last session with the jobseeker group before their trip to Cornwall. He would need to remind any student under the age of eighteen to return the parental consent forms before the deadline which was the following Friday. Stella Goldman had already briefed the group regarding the timetable of activities for the week, and the list of essentials needed to survive this residential in reasonable comfort. Jim made his way down a long corridor with classrooms on either side. He always liked to enter a classroom well before the start time of a teaching session. It was reassuring to set out all the resources necessary on his desk and check that the connection between the laptop and the whiteboard was operating effectively. Some of the window blinds needed to be drawn so that the outside light did not obscure the images on the whiteboard surface. Finally, he made sure that each student had access to a calculator and that there were twelve pencils in a pot near the door. For this session four tape measures were required and Jim glanced in the desk drawer to ensure that they were available.

Jim had read the profiles of the ten students who had enrolled on the jobseekers course. They were in the age range of sixteen to twenty. There were eight males and two female students. One of the males would not be going on the residential as he had gained a work experience position and had to remain at his place of employment. None of them had been in permanent employment and a look at their application forms gave a clue as to why not. They had obviously read the sections on the form, but their writing was often untidy and sometimes illegible. There were lots of spelling mistakes, punctuation was conspicuous by its absence and there were multiple grammatical mistakes. One of the forms had been used as a coaster for a coffee cup and showed a circular brown stain. Some forms had smudges and it was common to find scrawled crossings of mistakes. Attached to each of the application forms were the results of a little numeracy test that all applicants had to complete at the time of their enrolment. This revealed further common problems. Addition and subtraction questions seemed to have been completed accurately. The main trouble had been in multiplication and division. It was evident that many of the students had not learned their multiplication tables. They did not know how to calculate percentages, which was a problem for business students when calculating value added tax.

It was what Jim had expected from a group of this type and having read through the school leaving reports he realised that truancy, bad behaviour, undesirable influences, drug abuse and brushes with the law were all too common. However, the reports also contained examples of hobbies where individuals had taken real interest. One young man was able to recite the current position of all the premier league football clubs from memory and could calculate the various permutations that would result from possible future results. Another knew every social security entitlement, every way of exploiting the system and how to effectively dodge getting employed. These young people were not particularly lacking intelligence and they could show initiative. The trick was to gain their respect by engaging with them. If they connected with the teacher, they tended to look on the session more favourably.

When he had first started teaching Jim knew that his students would all have individual differences. His ambition was to find a combination of factors that would be the blueprint for an optimum teaching method. He had soon discovered that this would not be possible. The differences between individuals were so diverse that the only strategy in designing a lesson was to include variety so that there was a chance that everyone received a bit of their preferred learning technique. So those who learned best from visual images got some pictures and those that preferred text got some written material. Those who liked a structured sequence would get some programmed learning, but the lesson would also have to appeal to the student who liked a more holistic approach.

It was not long before the tranquil atmosphere of the empty room was disturbed by a babble of voices just outside the door. Inquisitive faces peered in through the window and someone tried the door handle. Jim always locked the door before a class started. During his training he had been told that an effective technique in classroom management was to get the students in together quickly and then get on with the lesson immediately. At the end it was good practice to get them all out together efficiently. The other ingredient was to try to get on with them. Jim found that in recent years the default was that a lecturer started from a position of disrespect and any change to this had to be earned. He knew that it would make the residential visit to Cornwall much better if he had established some sort of basic rapport with the students beforehand.

Jim unlocked the door and acting like the traffic lights on the slip road to a congested motorway he ensured that there was a controlled trickle rather than a stampede into the room. He carefully observed the usual mixture of individuals filtering through the doorway. It was no surprise to see tattoos and assorted rings adorning the bodies of both sexes. Perhaps, they needed to decorate themselves to show their individuality. Some strutted in confidently others shyly hiding their faces behind a curtain of long hair or hoods. They did not appear to have any bags or coats and their pockets were devoid of pens or pencils. They had just turned up, still with their earphones dangling around their necks like stethoscopes. Mobile phones were their prize possessions. The most noticeable client was a large West Indian youth who wore a cowboy hat, shorts and green wellington boots. Jim remembered from reading the admission records that two of the men were of Pakistani origin. Although born in Birmingham, they entered the room muttering in Urdu. One young man stood away from the others closely grasping what looked like a laptop case to his side. Dressed in a patterned cardigan and blue jeans he seemed a little isolated. He stood erect, head bowed, looking at the floor. The only two females clung together as if they were a group within a group. They were chatting as if in another dimension, impervious to thoughts about education. They could have been waiting for a train. When all this assorted crew were seated, Jim sharply rapped the desk with the back of his board cleaner. He waited for a moment until he commanded a focus of attention.

"The purpose of this session is to give you practice making calculations. We are going to add and divide. We are going to measure and compare the proportion of one thing to another. At the end I hope that you will see that numbers can be magic."

A tall, willowy youth with blonde hair looked up from where he had been aimlessly fiddling with the buttons on his mobile phone and spoke. "So, I suppose you think you are a Paul Daniels!"

All the students could be identified by a lanyard which had to be draped around their necks for security reasons. It was helpful to glance at this at the start of a new course until the lecturer learned every name. This tall individual had his tag hidden beneath his jacket.

Ignoring the statement Jim addressed the youth directly. "Please can you remind me of your name?"

"Spartacus," replied the tall youth impertinently, but much to the amusement of the other clients.

Continuing to ignore the provocation, Jim clicked the mouse and said, "Well Spartacus, please make sure that phone is switched off. It could ruin the magic ingredients!"

A horizontal grid appeared on the whiteboard screen. Jim drew attention to a printed handout that he had distributed to each student. On the handout was an exact copy of the grid as displayed on the whiteboard.

"As I click the mouse the grid on the screen will slowly fill with a sequence of four numbers. I want you to examine the sequence and tell me what number you think should go in box five."

There was silence as the whole group copied the numbers and started to think about them.

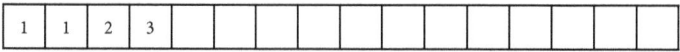

One of the females put her hand up. She was good looking with blonde hair which had been dyed with a blue streak. "Me and Becky think it should be five," she said confidently.

"Excellent, that is correct," Jim replied. "Can you tell us why?"

"Becky thinks you just have to add the numbers together in

the two spaces before the blank one," said the girl with blonde hair. Her friend obviously had the brains, but not the confidence to speak out. Becky smiled, pleased to have her correct answer acknowledged, but she remained silent.

"OK. Complete all the boxes using Becky's system. You can work together. Use the calculators if that helps." Jim liked to give clear instructions.

Five minutes later Jim flicked the completed grid onto the whiteboard to confirm the answers.

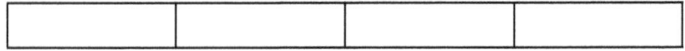

| 1 | 1 | 2 | 3 | 5 | 8 | 13 | 21 | 34 | 55 | 89 | 144 | 233 | 377 | 610 | 987 |

"That is called the Fibonacci sequence after the person who devised it in 1234 – Leonardo Fibonacci," Jim proclaimed before moving on quickly to display the next empty grid.

Again, it corresponded to blank grids printed on each student's handout.

Jim waited until he was sure everyone had his attention before communicating his next instruction.

"For this exercise you need to work in groups of two. Use the calculator. Select any number from the sequence, divide it by the number that comes before it and write your answer in the first of the four blank spaces printed on the handout. You can repeat this with any other numbers of your choice. Write the answers in the other three boxes."

Someone shouted indignantly, "You want us to do that calculation four times?"

"That's exactly what I want you to do," Jim replied. He thought about adding if that is not too much trouble, but decided against it.

When it became obvious that the groups had all made their calculations Jim asked one person from each group to write their answers on the main whiteboard. "What do you notice about the numbers?" asked Jim.

A youth in a leather jacket responded first. "The numbers are all close to 1.618, but I still can't see the magic."

"Perhaps the next exercise will convince you," smiled Jim as he changed the whiteboard image to show the outline of a person. "I need two volunteers for this demonstration."

To his dismay out came Spartacus and Struthers. They were both wearing a type of fashionable jeans which hung low on the waist and with a cut too big for their bottoms. It never ceased to amaze Jim how they walked in such clothes without their trousers falling to their ankles.

Jim extracted some tape measures from his drawer and passed one to Struthers.

"Measure the distance from the tip of Spartacus's head to the floor," he said to Struthers. "The rest of you make a note of the measurement."

"My name is Birch," said Spartacus.

"We call him Birchy because he's so tall," affirmed Struthers as he struggled to hold the tape to the top of Birch's head.

"Now measure the distance from his belly button to the floor," commanded Jim.

"I'm not going anywhere near his belly button!" exclaimed Struthers with a look of horror at the suggestion. Sniggers rippled around the classroom.

"Let Birch hold the tape to his own belly button and then you just extend it to the floor. Don't forget to record this measurement," Jim reminded the class. He updated the figure on the whiteboard to reinforce this action.

Addressing the class Jim asked them to divide the longer of

the two measurements by the shorter measurement. The clicking of calculator buttons echoed round the room.

"What is your answer?" Jim enquired.

A chorus of surprised voices responded. "Wow, 1.618"

So that proves Mr. Birch is human just like the rest of us," Jim remarked as Birch and Struthers slunk back to their table. By the time the jobseekers course ended Jim learned that Birch came from a household where nobody worked. His father had a severe drink problem and his mother seemed to be continually producing more children. They were all living in a house provided by the council on an estate plagued by gangs and drug dealers.

The next ten minutes involved another measuring exercise. This time it involved measuring the distance from the shoulder to the fingertips and then dividing it by the distance from the elbow to the fingertips. The results from each student were now collated and analysed to demonstrate the recurrence of 1.618.

"The nearer the proportions of a person to 1.618 the more they will conform to what we perceive as beautiful and that is why that number is used by artists like Leonardo Da Vinci in constructing their paintings," Jim explained with a flourish of his hands. "It is called the Golden Ratio. It is a concept that people have known about since the time of the Ancient Greeks."

He could tell that his group of jobseekers were impressed by these little experiments. Quickly, he displayed a few more pictures of buildings, plants and paintings where the 1.618 number featured, before referring his students to some web site addresses where they could find out more.

"I hope that you have learned that making calculations can be interesting as well as useful," said Jim as he issued each student with a handout containing the essential notes relevant to the lesson. "Your research project is to find evidence of the use of the Golden Ratio by architects, artists and where it occurs in nature.

Use the web addresses that I have given you to help you in this task. Computer time can be booked in the resource centre on the first floor. Have you any questions?"

The first response was frivolous "What time does the canteen open?" It was quickly followed by a request for information about the forthcoming residential. "Where will we meet next Friday for our trip?"

"I'm glad that you asked that question," replied Jim. "We will not meet again until the day of the residential. Please assemble in the college foyer next Friday at 8.30am. The buses will leave at 9.00am and I do not want to leave anyone behind. There are still a couple of parental consent forms to be returned and it is essential that these be handed to me on Monday morning. Have a good weekend and I will see you next week."

The jobseekers shuffled out and Jim felt a sense of relief flood through him now that the lesson had been completed successfully. The room that had been full of voices was now a silent, empty shell. Only the lingering smell of random human bodies remained as a reminder that the room had recently been populated. He collected in the tape measures, calculators, and pencils and returned them to the cupboard. Jim used this calm interlude to write up the lesson evaluation and mark the electronic register. Before he left, he glanced around to make sure that he was leaving the room tidy. The next session would have to be planned. Eventually he returned to the staffroom, filled his bag with a set of unmarked assignments and headed for the car park.

THIRTEEN
FURTIVE RECONNAISSANCE

A little learning is a dangerous thing;
Drink deep, or taste not the Pierian spring.
(Pope)

It was calm and surprisingly warm for late September. Peter was sitting in his favourite chair on the veranda of his house in Plymouth. Precariously spread across his knee, were the reconnaissance reports from the Russian spy planes which had recently flown near to the South West Coast. A photograph of Dennis Torrance was fixed to the top of one report with a red paperclip. Peter picked up an aerial photograph showing Newquay airport and the surrounding area. All the buildings, runways and aircraft appeared on the photograph and Peter knew that Dennis Torrance was based there. It was the area about a mile to one side of Newquay airport that attracted Peter's attention. The photograph showed the old airfield at St Eval which he had overheard being mentioned at the launch of The Outdoor Pursuits Centre the previous day. The strips of concrete were clearly indicative of runways. Peter was already wearing his reading glasses and he was reminded of how much his eyesight had deteriorated lately as he pored over the details of the photograph. Reaching into the inside pocket of his jacket he extracted a magnifying glass. It was always a handy tool to carry about when the need to inspect fine detail presented itself. There were dark marks on one section of the runway which, on inspection under the magnifying glass looked suspiciously like the signature left after repeated aircraft landings. Peter put the photograph down and poured himself a glass of beer. He started to evaluate the snippets of information at his disposal.

The pieces of a jigsaw do not mean much on their own and caution was required to avoid jumping to conclusions. Trying to link all the available data needed care. Firstly, Dennis Torrance was a military man and he worked at Newquay airport. He visited Henry Penrose who worked for an investment casting company in Wadebridge. Peter concluded that it was probable that parts were being made for delivery to the military and those parts could be fitted to aircraft. Secondly, there were persistent rumours of strange lights in the sky around the area, but Peter did not believe that all these sightings were of alien craft. It would be convenient for Dennis Torrance to use the UFO reports as a smokescreen to hide what was a secret aircraft project. Finally, if there was a secret aircraft, it would have to take off and land somewhere and Peter began to wonder if that somewhere was the old St Eval airfield. His handler at Soviet Intelligence was pressing for an information update and so Peter decided to allocate time the next day to have a look at St Eval airfield. He was feeling increasingly resentful of the intrusion that his spying activities were having on his life. He felt a distinct lack of enthusiasm for this job and his thoughts regularly turned to enjoying a more sedate lifestyle in retirement. It was so comfortable on the veranda that a combination of the beer and the warm fresh air made relaxation inevitable. Peter drifted off to sleep.

The journey from Plymouth to St Eval took over one hour. Approaching the little village Peter could see the wind turbines on 'Bear's Down' in his rear-view mirror. Large turbines grouped on the high ground like weird sentinels, reminiscent of a scene from 'The War of the Worlds'. Driving along the road that skirted the airfield Peter could see the square tower of a church to his right. On the left of the road sheep were grazing on grassy areas between the sections of concrete that had once been aircraft runways. Scattered around the airfield like giant Meccano structures were numerous tall radio masts. A first impression was that of neglect.

There was a right turn signposted 'Padstow 6 miles' and a few yards along was the parking area for visitors to the church. A memorial to members of the aircrew who had lost their lives flying from the airfield between 1939-1959 served as a reminder that this had been an operational RAF base. Peter leaned with his elbows on the roof of his car as he used a powerful pair of binoculars to scan the airfield. Towards one end of the main runway was a collection of low-level buildings painted white with several cars parked outside. There was a warning sign on the perimeter fence that stated in red letters 'Airfield Radio – Keep Out'. One of the white buildings had a curved corrugated roof and double doors. The hinges had been greased and there were scratches on the ground proving that they had been opened recently. Peter considered the possibility that this building could be a hangar for an aircraft. It had a low roof, but was wide enough to house a plane. Furthermore, the binoculars confirmed that the dark marks on the concrete runway were in fact tyre marks. The marks all seemed to be grouped along the same stretch of runway which suggested that they were made by landing aircraft rather than road vehicles on test. He put the zoom lens on his camera and took a sequence of photographs. Being preoccupied with his observations Peter had not noticed a rather rotund man carrying a rake over his shoulder, approaching from the church gateway.

"I don't think that you will see much to photograph over there." The man spoke with a gravelly voice and a distinct West Country accent.

Peter swung round and his face must have shown surprise. "Didn't mean to startle you," said the man with a wry smile. "Just come to do a bit of weeding around the church grounds. That's a fine camera that you have got there my friend."

This sort of situation required quick thinking. It was not the first time that Peter had found himself in danger of exposure. Experience told him to stay calm and allow his sense of self-preservation to take over.

"I have heard fascinating stories about this airfield and thought a few photos would add some interest to my book." It was a convincing lie and the man responded with helpful information.

"If it is information that you want, I can help. In the war, patrols came in and out of here all the time. They used the church tower as an aid to navigation. There were Spitfires, Hurricanes, Beauforts, to mention a few of the aircraft. I suppose that you know about the German bombing raids? They caused a tremendous amount of damage. Then came the Americans with their Liberators, but the field has been quiet since 1959. We get more noise from the Kart track just up the road."

"Did you live around here during the war," asked Peter.

"I've lived in these parts all my life. I cut grass, sometimes do a little landscaping, keep the cemetery clear of weeds and occasionally help to run the car park at Bedruthan Steps," said the man proudly. "Not as challenging as writing a book though is it?" he asked with good humour.

"It sounds challenging enough to me," Peter replied. "You must have noticed a huge difference after the airfield closed in 1959."

The man looked mystified. "What do you mean?"

"No aircraft rumbling in and out, fewer customers in the shops, empty pews in the church," suggested Peter.

There was a pause before the man spoke again. "It is certainly quieter now, although we get a lot of tourists here in the summer and the airfield is still not totally disused."

"I suppose there must be the occasional private plane connected to Airfield Radio," said Peter. "I saw the signs telling people to 'Keep Out' along the perimeter fence."

The gardener looked furtively from side to side to check that no one was listening and leaning forward towards Peter he muttered under his breath. "Folks say there's some sort of special plane using the airfield. We locals have all caught a glimpse, but whatever it is, it only seems to operate on clear nights after dark."

"That's interesting. Can you describe the aircraft?" asked Peter. "There isn't much room to operate with these tall masts in the way."

"Personally, all I saw was a dark delta wing shape. It had green and red lights. Whatever craft it was it moved at great speed and was gone before I had chance to see it in detail."

"That is intriguing," said Peter. "Perhaps, I can mention it in my book."

"Well don't mention that I told you anything. I don't want a visit from the defence people." The man had a genuine look of concern on his face. "Folk around here keep themselves to themselves."

There was a shout from the church gate. "Looks like the Vicar wants you," said Peter. "It was nice to talk to you."

"Send a copy of your book to the church when it's published," called the man as he headed towards the gate. "I will let the Vicar know what to expect." Then he was gone, hidden from view by the hedges that surrounded the church.

Peter packed away his camera and returned to his car. His suspicions about a secret aircraft reinforced. He felt under some pressure to report back to his intelligence handler something of substance. So far, he had only obtained bits of hearsay, some circumstantial evidence and a few photographs of an abandoned airfield. Unfortunately, to be certain of the facts, it was going to be necessary to penetrate the airfield and look inside the white hangar. To do this would require some careful planning and Peter decided to spend the rest of the morning surveying the airfield.

After driving around the perimeter of the airfield it soon became apparent that there were a couple of entrances usable by vehicles. The whole airfield was surrounded by a six-foot chain mesh barrier with warnings to 'Keep Out – Private Property – Airfield Radio' posted at regular intervals. Peter parked discretely amongst some roadside hedges adjacent to an entrance located nearest to the buildings. Tyre tracks betrayed its regular use as a vehicle access point. It was in a place where one of the old runways had cut across what was now the public highway. Large rocks had been dumped on each side of the entrance to prevent parking and so there was a narrow avenue of concrete that ended at a galvanised metal gate. Next to the gate was an intercom fixed to a post with a camera attached higher up. Just inside the fence was a grey concrete circular turret that looked as if it had been used for airfield defence during the war years. Through his binoculars Peter could see the old sections of runway stretching towards the group of buildings. Clumps of grass were growing between the old crumbling sections of concrete and sheep were grazing on the flat scrubland prairies that had once been populated by planes and aircrew. A second inner chain link fence surrounded a cluster of white single storey buildings. A double security perimeter was a concern. There were high posts at each corner of this fence with mounted cameras and only a single pedestrian access gate controlled by an intercom with keypad. It seemed that a lot of security was being used to protect 'Airfield Radio'! No vehicles were parked inside the perimeter of this internal security fence. Observation of the gateway over the next few hours revealed visits by several private cars, small vans and a skip lorry. The driver of each vehicle pressed a button on the intercom and after a few moments the gate swung open. Once the vehicle was safely through, the gate closed again automatically with a resounding clang.

It was time to leave. Hunger was beginning to gnaw at Peter's stomach as he considered his options. It would be impractical to cut through the fence and walk across to the buildings. Any disturbance to the fence immediately alerted the attention of the nearest camera. Peter had tested this by throwing a log against the fence and watching from behind a gorse bush as the camera swivelled around to view the point of impact. Similarly, climbing over the gate would be immediately detected by the camera. Once inside the fence there was absolutely no cover and with acres of open ground to pass over, an intruder would easily be detected by the cameras. Then there was the problem of the internal fence with its own security. Peter quickly concluded that the only way to get access would be by deception. As he drove home, he started to develop a plan. He had noticed that a dark blue van bearing the letters 'Reed Contracts' had made two visits to the airfield during the day. A search on his mobile through the Companies House 'Webcheck' service soon revealed that this was a firm called 'Reed Contracts Ltd.' with a registered office in Newquay. The business was listed as providing maintenance, heating service, and general repairs to offices, shops and business premises. The basic germ of an idea started to develop in Peter's head and by the time he arrived home he had formed an action plan. Tomorrow he would visit the offices of 'Reed Contracts Ltd.' in Newquay under the pretence of enquiring about a repair contract for his holiday let.

FOURTEEN

VISIT TO ST EVAL

Peter decided that his incursion of the airfield would take place on a Friday. It was late in the afternoon on the second Friday in October, a mild bright day for the time of year. The clocks were not due to be turned back for another couple of weeks and there would be enough time to complete outdoor work before dark. His initial visit to the offices of 'Reed Contracts Ltd.' had helped enormously. It had provided an opportunity to rummage through the bins at the rear of the premises on the pretext that he was looking for a spare part for his central heating boiler. This had been an unsavoury job, but the reward had been a treasure trove of discarded company documentation. Additionally, Peter had thoroughly photographed the company vans ensuring that his hired van matched them in every detail including the stencilled lettering on each side. Even more useful had been the visit he had received from a member of the company maintenance team. This was in response to a request he had made for a quotation to cover the maintenance needs of his holiday let business. During this home visit Peter had managed to discretely photograph the engineer's identity badge which contained a bar code. A request to his Russian handler resulted in the forgery of an identical duplicate plastic badge, courtesy of the Russian Embassy in London. Peter would now assume the name of this authentic employee although it was his own image that had been inserted on the badge photograph. Still there were weaknesses in Peter's plans. He anticipated that it would be unlikely that he would be able to withstand maximum scrutiny. Luck would be needed to help him bluff his way in. He thought that on a Friday afternoon there would be a slight relaxation in the thoroughness of the security checks. Using his experience, he calculated that not only were there likely to be fewer staff around, but those that remained would not want the week to end with extra hassle. It was a gamble based on human psychology. He decided that Friday must be the preferred day.

Peter was driving a blazer blue Ford Courier van, procured by his Russian handler using a false identity. The logo on the van was an exact match to the vans which Peter had so carefully photographed. The van had been parked in a nearby multi storey car park ready for his collection. It had been hard work carrying his bag of tools and equipment from his home and Peter was glad when he reached the van. The drive to St Eval seemed to take longer than usual and the anticipation of the forthcoming operation raised Peter's stress levels.

The gate on the perimeter of the St Eval airfield loomed ahead. Catching a glimpse of himself in the rear-view mirror was not an edifying image. The baseball cap and dark blue boiler suit that all company employees wore was not an image he would have chosen for himself. It made him look like an aging prison warder. On his exit, following his visit to the premises of 'Reed Contracts Ltd.', Peter had noticed this soiled, crumpled boiler suit embroidered with the company logo, discarded in a skip. He had discretely commandeered the garment. It was torn, faded and smelly.

Although cleaned and repaired, the boiler suit still betrayed its frequent use with stains and patches in various places.

If his appearance depressed him so did his mission. Peter had never wanted to continue with these assignments and now his dreams of retirement had been postponed again. He was weary with the subterfuge, furtiveness and pressure that the work brought with it. He was always careful, but the worry of detection was constantly there in the back of his mind. He had taken risks year after year and even though he had achieved the required objectives he had never gained any feeling of satisfaction for his efforts. On the contrary, he often felt ashamed to be involved in what amounted to be a betrayal of the country in which he was born. These feelings had grown more profoundly as he had aged and as he approached the gate in the perimeter fence, he vowed to himself that this would be his last job. He imagined a new life in St Petersburg where he could live his remaining years in the place where his ancestors had lived and died.

The security camera adjusted as the van pulled up at the gate. Peter pressed the intercom button. There was an electronic static hiss followed by a voice which sounded as if it was in an empty room miles away. "Base Security", was the distant response.

Peter's heart rate increased dramatically and he felt suddenly hot. "Mike Brown from 'Reed Contracts Ltd.' I am responding to a breakdown call," he said boldly.

There was a pause, followed by a click as the intercom switched off, and then the gate slowly swung open. Ahead was the empty acreage of the airfield. Peter was in. The van thumped over each joint of the concrete sections of the runway making the tools in the back vibrate. A green plastic case marked 'Bosch Sander' did not hold the sander. It contained a small handgun together with a clip of ammunition and a silencer which could be attached to the barrel. It was an item that Peter had owned for many years and fortunately had never had to use. On many jobs he had never bothered to take the weapon with him, but this assignment carried much higher risks. His philosophy was to plan carefully so that the need to use force was minimised. The gun would only be used as a last resort if things went horribly wrong. It might need to be used if Peter had to fall back on plan B.

Parking near the pedestrian gate which gave access through the inner security fence to the white painted buildings clearly visible from the road, Peter opened the rear doors of his van and collected a large tool bag. He took his time because he needed to be sure that the air ventilator in the wall of the hangar building which he had viewed through binoculars was what it seemed. Relieved to confirm that it was indeed an air vent Peter walked casually up to the gate and pressed the intercom. It crackled into life and this time the Controller wanted more information.

"Nobody told me to expect a maintenance visit this afternoon," barked the security Controller suspiciously.

"I received a late request on my radio," Peter replied. "Just on my way home too. Fortunately, I was in your vicinity when the message came through."

The sound of clicking on a computer keyboard came through the intercom. Muffled voices could be heard in the background. "There is no record of a RFM here on the database. Better come back on Monday."

This is what Peter anticipated would be the first weak point in his plan and where the paperwork retrieved from the dustbin at the back of the 'Reed Contracts Ltd.' offices would be useful. He realised that the maintenance team had to have a 'RFM' (Request for Maintenance) before deploying to a job. Using the layout of an old 'RFM' form retrieved from the bin, Peter had produced a mock version with a fictitious job number. He had sent an email from his desktop computer to his mobile phone purporting to be from 'Reed Contracts Ltd.', with an attachment showing the RFM. It was a request to check the filters on a pump that sent oil to the heating systems.

"One of your people just emailed confirmation to my mobile. It concerns a problem with the filters on your oil pump. I might as well have a look at the filters now that I'm here," stressed Peter as insistently as he thought appropriate under the circumstances. "It is probably an intermittent fault, but if it acts up over the weekend your heating system will go down."

Reluctantly, without grace, the Controller agreed to meet Peter at the security gate. "I need to see that RFM and check your ID before you access the site," he grumbled.

A couple of minutes later the lumbering frame of the security Controller emerged from the doorway of a building that had a large sign saying, 'Airfield Radio'. He gave Peter's ID badge a cursory glance and then stared at Peter. "Mike Brown," he sighed as if making a mental note of the name of the person stupid enough to turn up late on a Friday afternoon without the usual clearances.

Peter held his mobile to the fence trying to keep his fingers carelessly positioned over the job number at the top of the form. "There must have been a mistake recording the request somewhere along the line," suggested Peter. "I will probably be able to rectify the problem in less time than it takes to stand here talking about paperwork."

There was a slight delay as the controller weighed the consequences of opening the gate without his database fully updated. Alternatively, he did not fancy the prospect of a cold weekend if the heating malfunctioned. His brain worked so slowly that Peter could almost see the cogs turning in the man's beefy head. Then without another word, he moved to unlock the gate and Peter entered the inner sanctuary of the compound.

"You need to make it snappy mate," said the charmless controller. "My shift ends at 1830 hours and I do not want you here when I leave. It's Friday and I want to end the week without any outstanding problems." That was a sentiment that Peter shared.

The Controller escorted Peter to the oil storage tank which was perched on a platform between the old hangar and the other buildings. This is where careful planning was paying off. Peter was fully aware of where the tank was and he knew that the air vent in the hangar wall was just a few feet from the platform and at about the same level. Careful observation through the powerful binoculars had been time well spent. The factors that Peter was less sure about concerned the real function of these buildings. There were certainly lots of huge radio masts straddling the airfield, but it was unlikely that they were being used to transmit Pirate FM! Another unknown factor concerned the number of personnel in the buildings. There never seemed to be many people around although there were always half a dozen cars parked outside the compound. Could it be that they were all working within the hangar building?

"Rather you than me climbing up there with that bag," chuckled the Controller unsympathetically. He reminded Peter of Vlad, the infamous 'Impaler' who had appeared in a film that he had been watching. "I'll be back shortly after I've completed my rounds."

Vlad moved out of sight around a corner of the hangar building. "No need to hurry," Peter muttered under his breath as he climbed the vertical steel ladder which led up to the platform. It was a climb of about thirty feet from ground level although it seemed more. The tool bag he was carrying across his shoulders was very heavy and Peter felt every one of his sixty-nine years as he hauled it up to the platform. Sweat was turning the collar of his overalls a darker colour. He started to unscrew the cover of the oil pump. This gave him time to see where the security cameras were pointing and to check whether the vent was within reach. He had brought a camera probe attached to the end of a cable which fitted into the rear of a small TV monitor. It was the same sort of devise used by plumbers when probing for blockages in narrow drains. The nearest security camera was fixed to a bracket on the side of the hangar building and it slowly turned in an arc to survey the area around the oil tank. Peter watched the camera through the corner of his eye. When it was pointing away from his position he leaned across and jammed the camera hinge with a pair of long handled grippers. The camera gave a little shudder and emitted a distressed electronic buzz. Peter hoped that the fault would not be noticed immediately, giving him just enough time to film the interior of the hangar. He carefully directed the cable with the probe at the end through the air vent. Fortunately, it went through smoothly, with no discernible resistance. A glance at the little TV monitor revealed the shape of a small black delta winged aircraft. Peter pressed the record button and panned the probe to both the left and the right. Finally, he pressed the zoom control before switching off. Leaning from the platform to haul back the cable from within the vent Peter caught sight of Vlad returning from his little excursion. He urgently pulled the cable back, but it became caught on a rusty bolt just inside the vent. There was insufficient time to retrieve the probe, pack it away and release the grippers from the security camera before Vlad reappeared. In desperation, Peter grabbed a pair of heavy-duty pliers from his overall trouser pocket, cut the cable as near to the vent as he could reach, and wound the remaining section around his arm. After dumping the remaining length of the cable in his bag he swiftly removed the grippers from the hinge of the security camera. Initially, the camera jumped erratically as if indignant that its graceful movement had been impaired, before settling back to resume its orbit. Vlad rounded the corner to approach the oil tank just as Peter was bending down to fasten his tool bag.

"I've just finished," shouted Peter hoping to distract Vlad from looking up towards the vent which now had a short length of cable protruding from its interior. "Take a look at this." Peter let go of an old oil filter which fluttered down towards the security man and as quickly as he could he descended the ladder. Once at ground level he joined Vlad who was vacantly gawping at the filter. Now he would have less need to look upwards.

"That was your problem, a blocked filter. It was the easiest job I've had all day."

"In that case let us get you off the site then I can lock up before the end of my shift. I have an appointment with a pint of bitter in my local tonight." Vlad was not a man who would win a prize for gratitude or civility.

When he felt anxious Peter had to exert a lot of self-control. He found it hard to resist the temptation to rush when walking from the gate to where he had parked the van. The sensation of being watched was strong and it was difficult to maintain a calm, natural posture. Once in the vehicle the same problem emerged. The sections of tarmac were flashing past and Peter had to force himself to slow down. His collar felt uncomfortably damp as sweat trickled down the back of his neck. His heartbeat was stampeding as a rush of adrenalin swept through his body. The exit gate loomed ahead in the failing light. If that gate did not open Peter knew he would be forced to ram it. There was only a short distant to go and Peter was willing the gate to open. He had slowed the vehicle to a crawl. As the wheels of the van passed over a pressure pad embedded in the concrete surface, the gate swung open. Relief flooded through his body as he exited the airfield and started to turn right with the intension of driving in the direction of the car park at Bedruthan Steps.

The previous day Peter had parked his own car in the National Trust car park at Bedruthan Steps. He knew that there would be no attendant on duty as the café and tourist shop was closed after the end of September. All that was open was the gate that led to the coast path. He had walked from the NT car park to Mawgan Porth where he had taken a local bus to Newquay Airport. There were lots of taxis available. It was a good fare to cover the journey from the airport to Plymouth. Peter would submit a claim on his expense account to recover the money. His Russian contact would collect the blue van from the car park once Peter gave the code to indicate that the mission had been completed successfully.

Just as Peter was making his right turn onto the narrow road that led around the airfield perimeter a red car appeared travelling at speed from the direction of St Eval. The front of his van was now halfway across the road and Peter hesitated, not sure whether to accelerate or make an emergency stop. Instinctively, he stamped hard on the brake pedal. The oncoming car swerved violently to avoid a collision, the driver trying to get through the gap between the front of the van and the grassy bank at the side of the roadway. The car clipped the nearside front wing of the van. The impact diverted the wheels of the car into a drainage ditch which ran parallel to the road. There was a shower of grass and earth followed by a metallic screech as the underside of the car came into contact with the ridge between the ditch and the road. The vehicle came to a grounding halt leaving debris across the tarmac. Peter now completed his turn with the van wheel making a discordant scraping sound. The last thing he wanted to do was to stop, but he knew that he would not get far with the damaged wheel. The noise from the tyre increased with every yard. It sounded as though the metal from the front wing was in contact with the front offside tyre. Peter pulled up just beyond where the red car had stopped to check the damage. He got out and sure enough the dented wing had been pushed back towards the tyre. Peter bent down and tugged at the twisted metal wing vigorously until the tyre was free from contact. He was angry at the stupidity of the other driver, but this was not the time to get involved in an argument. Before he was able to get back into his van a grey Land Rover passed the two stricken vehicles. Immediately, it reversed so close that it blocked the way forward. A tall, muscular man with a shaven head emerged from the Land Rover and jogged aggressively along the roadway. He was dressed in military fatigues which blended well with the roadside foliage in the fading light. Attached to his belt were two sets of handcuffs. It was Dennis Torrance.

FIFTEEN
FUGITIVES

After returning home from the opening of the Outdoor Pursuits Centre Chris started to reflect on the events of the day. He felt frustrated that all the investigations that he had carried out over a long period were getting nowhere. Enquiries to Government departments had met with evasive, sometimes obstructive responses. Politicians were afraid of being ridiculed or afraid to venture into uncharted territory. Even Chris's own newspaper was unable to report freely. He was irritated beyond compare at the thought of all the smug officials secretly pleased to be stifling investigation. They must be very content to know that their controlling strategy was blocking any inconvenient research. The time had come to take some direct action.

Chris had intended to pay a visit to the airfield at St Eval during a weekday, but had changed his mind. He wanted to help Joy at the Outdoor Pursuits Centre. Another pair of hands would be welcome in supporting the activities for the college students. If they gave positive feedback at the end of their stay the college might use the facilities again in the future. In the end he decided that if he was going to make observations at St Eval he might as well start straight after work on the Friday evening. The weather on that second Friday in October was forecast to be clear, but chilly. He knew the students from the college would be arriving that day, but he thought that it would be more convenient if he arrived to help on the Saturday. This would give the party time to unpack and familiarise themselves with the facilities at the centre after their long journey.

Leaving his workplace earlier than normal on the Friday evening, Chris arrived at the airfield whilst it was still light. He parked next to the perimeter fence on a grassy bank surrounded by trees. Thinking that this would be a discrete place to park he started to eat a supply of packed sandwiches. He had prepared the ham sandwiches before leaving for work that morning and they tasted good. He could see the white buildings and the hangar clearly through his binoculars. Now that the engine was no longer running it was becoming chilly and Chris got out of his car to fetch his overcoat from the boot. Immediately, he noticed that another vehicle had parked at the point where he had exited the road. It looked like a grey Land Rover. Worse still, a large shaven headed man, was approaching through the trees. The man gave every appearance of being a member of the military. Chris quickly got back into his car and started the engine. As he glanced in his rear-view mirror, he was horrified to see the man now running at speed towards him. The old red Honda was not the ideal vehicle to be driven off road, but Chris had no intension of entering any dialogue with the panting, shaven headed creature, which now filled his mirror. The Honda lurched forward swaying heavily on its aging suspension as Chris steered through the trees, desperately trying to find a suitable place to regain the road. Just ahead was an open section of grass which bordered the road. The grass banked upwards at the point where it met the roadway and Chris wondered whether the car could clear it without grounding. There was no choice but to go for it. The car surged over the bank with an ominous thump, scattering the remains of the ham sandwiches into the foot well. Adrenaline pounding through his veins Chris sped down the open road like a getaway driver after a robbery. After a quick glance in his mirror Chris realised to his dismay that the Land Rover was following. He now started to think how naive he had been not to guess that his car had been bugged. It all became suddenly and brutally clear. This was the reason for the message on his windscreen and all the other inconveniences that he had suffered recently. As Chris turned to view the road ahead, he was confronted by the sight of a dark blue van turning across the carriageway from a gateway on the opposite side of the road. He braked hard and swerved to avoid a collision. His car clipped the front wing of the van and his nearside wheels dropped into a drainage ditch at the side of the road. The Honda grounded heavily on the edge of the tarmac grinding to a shuddering stop. Fortunately, the air bag had not been activated and Chris could see the blue van parking just ahead. The driver got out and went to inspect the damage to his vehicle. In a weird sort of way Chris was glad that he would not be left alone at the mercy of the military man who now overtook the stricken vehicles and reversed to park closely in front of the van. As Chris sat motionless, still shocked by the accident, the man in military fatigues wrenched his door open and dragged him out. The shaven head was attached to a face that looked like thunder.

"Hands on the roof," barked the angry man who roughly grabbed his arms.

Chris looked up the road and his gaze was met by the van driver. Both men held their stare in surprise as they struggled to remember where they had seen each other before. There was recognition and then realisation. This van driver was the visitor at the opening of the Outdoor Pursuits Centre. He was the furtive character that had aroused Chris's suspicions from the moment they had met. Chris realised that he was in this predicament because he had been electronically tracked. What puzzled him was why the owner of a holiday let should be driving a maintenance van out of a secure airfield at this time on a Friday night.

Seamlessly, Dennis applied a set of handcuffs and Chris found himself hauled up the road and forced into the passenger seat of the Land Rover. Feeling indignant and a bit frightened Chris sat and reflected for a moment. He wondered about his options. Would it be wise to stay where he was or attempt to escape? As these questions circled in his head Chris became aware that a confrontation was taking place between the other two men. Their raised voices sounded muffled, but their body language and the presence of a gun betrayed their hostility to each other. He watched with growing trepidation, feeling safer in the car than outside, as events unfolded violently.

Peter's head was racing because he knew the man was the one he had photographed leaving the Precision Castings factory in Wadebridge. Soviet Intelligence had given him a photograph identifying him as Dennis Torrance and it was known that he worked for the Ministry of Defence. Peter wondered how he could have been intercepted so soon after his visit. How cruel fate had been to him. The open road had beckoned only to be blocked by some stupid speeding motorist. These thoughts temporarily rendered him inert and he stood like a statue as anger surged through him like a fever.

The man in fatigues rushed past, ignoring Peter completely. He wrenched the door of the red car open and roughly dragged the driver out as if he was a worthless crash test dummy. The driver appeared to be in shock. His hair ruffled, falling across his startled face. He looked at Peter as his arms were dumped on the roof of the red car and there was recognition. Peter recognised him too. It was the journalist he had met at the opening of the Outdoor Pursuits Centre. This was the person he remembered who had filed reports for a newspaper about Unidentified Flying Objects under the name of Chris Arbor. He was also fully aware that it was Chris Arbor who had introduced himself to the group tour at the new Centre only a few days before. Peter felt shocked as he realised that his undercover role working for Russian Intelligence was in grave danger of exposure. Chris was bound to ask questions about his activities. He would wonder why a holiday let landlord was driving a maintenance van out of a secure airfield. It felt gutting to think that after so much time and effort had gone into gaining access to the interior of the hangar, the mission could be compromised by this unfortunate incident. Instead of one person causing problems by the roadside there were now two. Peter knew that he had no room to dither. He needed to take complete control of the situation without delay. He had never killed anyone and he had no intension of changing that today. However, he was so close to finishing this job and the prospect of retirement weighed sweetly on his mind. The only reason that he had brought the gun was to provide insurance that he would be able to sustain his freedom, but deep down he knew that he probably would never use deadly force. It was not his style. He was not a killer by nature.

The attitude of Dennis Torrance was unmistakable. He showed every sign of someone whose patience had been severely tested and was in no mood for tolerance. Aggressive and determined to assert his authority he extracted a pair of handcuffs from his waist band and unceremoniously started to apply the cuffs to Chris Arbor's wrists. Aware that he was in imminent danger of becoming embroiled in this farce, Peter opened the rear doors of his van and found the box marked Bosch Sander. He knew that of the two men Dennis Torrance was the biggest threat to his freedom. He quickly attached the silencer to the barrel of the handgun and inserted a clip of ammunition whilst Dennis was preoccupied manhandling Chris. He collected the tool bag which contained the recording equipment, closed the rear doors and waited.

Chris was protesting that his rights to freedom were being infringed. Dennis was triumphantly explaining that all rights to freedom had been forfeited because they had been abused. So involved with the argument, Dennis had paid no attention to the driver standing at the rear of the blue van. Peter watched as Dennis frogmarched the protesting journalist back up the road and bundled him into the passenger seat of the parked Land Rover. After locking the doors, he walked back around the front of the vehicle whilst extracting his mobile from a pocket in his jacket. It was at this point that he found that he had made a serious tactical error as he looked up to be confronted by Peter, still dressed in his overalls, standing a few yards away. A gun was aimed at the centre of Dennis's shaven head. Dennis quickly accessed whether he could disarm his assailant. The odds were not in his favour and he knew that he was now the one who would have to obey.

"Put your phone and the ignition keys on the bonnet," instructed Peter gravely.

"Who are you?" enquired Dennis angrily. He was annoyed with himself for not checking earlier. He pointed towards Chris who was seated in the Land Rover observing events with growing horror. "This man is a threat to national security and needs to be interrogated. You are threatening a member of Her Majesty's government and impeding my authority to protect the defence of the realm."

Peter ignored the question and the pompous statement. It was only a matter of time before another vehicle passed by and raised the alarm. It was also possible that the airfield cameras were picking up the action. He did not want to approach Dennis as he knew that he was probably trained to disarm an assailant given half a chance, so he continued to stand well back. The veins on Dennis's neck stuck out like red string as he assessed his predicament. It was embarrassing to be thwarted by some interfering maintenance engineer. His eyes flicked furtively around as he searched for an escape route. He moved towards Peter menacingly, his body taught like an animal about to spring. Peter had no choice but to fire a warning shot into the road just in front of his assailant. Bits of tarmac seared through Dennis's trouser leg and he dropped to his knees in pain. Perhaps now he believed that Peter's threats had substance.

"Move and I will shoot you," Peter growled. "Do not make me kill you." He was angry and the violence of the situation was inciting him towards even greater force.

Blood was staining Dennis's clothing and as he looked up towards Peter, he could see the malevolence in his face. He now felt convinced that Peter was fully prepared to use deadly force.

"This is the last time that I shall tell you to put your phone and keys on the bonnet," instructed Peter gravelly. "Do it now, meathead."

Dennis knew that he had little choice so crawled to the front of the vehicle and deposited the items as directed before slumping back down on the road in a heap. As he bent towards the bonnet Peter noticed the second set of handcuffs attached to the webbing on his belt.

"Now put your handcuffs around one wrist and crawl to that post." Pointing at an old rusty signpost that had long since lost its sign, Peter commanded that Dennis attach the cuffs to the post."

Dennis remained inert. He did not take kindly to being told what to do, he was normally the one who did the dictating. However, he knew that he was going to have to suffer this indignity. He had no other choice. Better to be embarrassed than dead and so he reluctantly complied. "I don't know who you are, but you won't get far," he snarled. "This place is festooned by security cameras. In fact, I wouldn't be surprised if the alert hasn't been sounded already."

"Throw the keys to both sets of handcuffs onto the road scumbag," said Peter sternly.

Dennis decided to use delaying tactics in the hope that he would be able to attract the attention of a passing motorist. He started to make a pathetic, fumbled attempt to reach into his pocket. "I can't reach my pockets whilst handcuffed to this post," Dennis protested defiantly. He hoped to entice Peter nearer to him in the hope that he could make a grab for the gun with his free arm.

There was no time to argue. Peter did not want to shoot his prisoner, but he had to restrain himself from pistol whipping the arrogant slob. It was with the utmost of self-control that he stayed back. He knew Dennis was desperate enough to gamble his life on any opportunity to escape. He took a last look at Dennis slumped against the post and jumped into the Land Rover. After dead locking the doors, he turned the ignition key. The Land Rover's engine burst into life with a powerful roar. In less than a minute the vehicle was just a shape disappearing into the distance. Meanwhile, Chris sat uncomfortably in the passenger seat with his wrists handcuffed behind his back. His brain racing wildly as he wondered whether he had escaped from the frying pan only to land in the fire.

This was now the time for calculations. Peter was concerned as to whether he would have sufficient time to reach the car park at Bedruthan Steps before the alarm went out. He knew that Dennis would free himself from the handcuffs almost immediately, but without the car radio or his mobile there would be a delay before he could raise the alarm. The probability was that sooner or later a helicopter would be scrambled to track the Land Rover's route. There were few roads in the area and it would be impossible to escape the helicopter's camera even if he went off road. The distance to the car park at Bedruthan Steps was only a few miles, but the roads from St Eval were narrow and winding. They were only suitable for the width of one vehicle and as they were travelling along at a most inconsiderate speed, oncoming vehicles had to dart into laybys to avoid a collision. If they were lucky, they would reach the car park and leave the area before the authorities could set up roadblocks.

On the other hand, it was going dark and there was a hint of sea mist drifting in from the Atlantic. The seawater, still warm from the summer, when meeting with the cold evening air often caused mists in October. Peter hoped that the mist would thicken and cause the helicopter to be grounded. If this happened, he estimated that he would be able to abandon the Land Rover and switch to his own car. Once he reached the main A39 he would merge with traffic and put distance between himself and the airfield at St Eval. The dice had been thrown and the odds of escape were evenly balanced.

SIXTEEN

JOURNEY TO CORNWALL

The foyer of Southfield College of Further Education was a hive of activity on this Friday morning. Some of the jobseekers were sitting on their cases whilst others huddled together exchanging thoughts about the coming adventure. Birch and Struthers were outside enjoying an early morning smoke whilst furtively surveying the girls from hairdressing through the glass entrance doors. Members of the hairdressing group had a sort of conformity in their appearance. Fashion was important in their chosen vocation and they paid homage by virtue of their stylish clothes. The jobseekers by contrast appeared more bohemian. Many excited voices hummed through the air punctuated by short outbursts of nervous laughter. It was interesting to see how in the space of a few weeks the different groups of students had forged their own identities. Although it was easy to see who belonged to each group, they had in common their vocational training aimed at securing a job. After a week down in Cornwall it would be interesting to compare the dynamics on the journey home!

Much to the relief of the staff in reception, whose peaceful existence was being temporarily disrupted, two college minibuses pulled up outside. Jim helped by a member of the college support staff loaded the suitcases onto the roof rack, covered them with a waterproof membrane and secured them. Meanwhile, Janet checked the names of each student as they boarded the respective minibuses. The names of students with dietary requirements, allergies or medical conditions were highlighted with a code letter.

As expected, there were a couple of students missing. Janet's mobile started to send out a muffled ring from deep inside her rucksack. She urgently fumbled through her belongings to retrieve the phone. By the time she found it the caller had gone, leaving a voicemail message. It was one of Janet's students who wanted to explain that she was too ill to attend. One of Jim's students worked for a few hours each week in his uncle's restaurant. There had been rumours circulating that he had decided to spend the week working full time in the restaurant rather than attend the residential. It was no surprise that he had sent a last-minute message to say that he was indisposed. His absence was in the category of 'unexpected unavailability' which meant that there would be no blemish on his attendance record. By the time the checks had been completed it was past 9 o'clock.

Laura Odubi had called down from the Social Work Facility to see the groups off. She was carrying a ring binder under her arm. She sat in the vacant passenger seat next to where Jim was perched in the driver's seat and opened the file.

"I'm glad someone wants to sit next to me," said Jim with a wry smile.

"To be honest I wish I was coming with you." Laura turned to the students. "It would be a relief to get out of this place for a week even if it meant being stuck with you lot."

"You could share a bunk with me," shouted Struthers from the back.

"In your dreams," replied Laura as she pulled out some papers from the file. "It seems that one of your clients will not be coming Jim. I hear that his uncle needs his help in the family restaurant!"

Jim shrugged his shoulders. He privately wondered if the lad would improve his skills just as much by working with his family. The fewer the numbers involved the less the complications with accommodation and personal requirements. Almost reading his thoughts Laura handed the contact details for the Centre staff in Cornwall, their address, postcode and visit confirmation sheet.

Laura squeezed Jim's shoulder as she turned and smiled at the sea of faces behind. "Have a good trip everyone," she said before walking over to see Janet in the other bus.

After setting the postcode of Grenah Manor into the satnav the two buses headed south down the M5 motorway. The passengers soon began to settle down. The hardest part was leaving familiar surroundings to venture into unknown territory. Once on the way a sort of peaceful resignation settled into the brain. Some students were chatting, some had their headphones on. As usual, many were fiddling with their mobiles. Early on Jim had found it necessary to advise Birch to adjust his behaviour. He had seen him holding his folded newspaper against the rear window of the minibus. From the responses of each lorry driver that they passed, Jim suspected that the page must be displaying some salacious picture. Realising that he would have to sit in the front seat next to Jim for the entire journey Birch agreed to act more sensibly. Fortunately, the atmosphere on Janet's bus was calmer. She wondered if most of her group had been out late the night before. They did have a reputation for partying.

As they travelled down the motorway Jim thought about the visit. In recent years there had been a drive to ensure compliance to the practices demanded by Her Majesty's Inspectorate. There had to be a trail of evidence that could be audited when required.

Conformity to the system was mandatory. Jim sometimes thought that if the people who designed the paperwork were the same ones who had to fill it in, the forms would be much shorter. In reality, every simplification that was announced resulted in extra pages. Then there was the issue of Health and Safety, and the costs of the insurance. He could not stop himself from wondering whether the benefits of these residential trips could be justified against the costs, plus the time and trouble of organising them.

The journey took over four hours which included a toilet stop at a motorway service area, where the groups purchased fast food or sandwiches. The eating habits of the youngsters never ceased to surprise him as he watched them swill down their half-eaten meals with cans of coke. They always seemed in such a rush to get on to the next thing, with little regard to their diet or digestion. Why there was such a fuss about vegetarian meals at the Outdoor Pursuits Centre Jim found hard to understand.

There had been moments of amusement en route. Passing the sign on the A30 that announced 'Kernow – Welcome to Cornwall' a cheer had gone up on Janet's bus after someone shouted 'Poldark Country'. One of the lads on Jim's bus had caused a stir as they crossed the edge of Bodmin Moor, insisting he had caught a glimpse of a strange beast with red eyes.

"It's probably a drunken tourist," Birch snarled. On closer inspection it turned out to be a large black sheep.

Finally, there was a buzz of excitement as they turned through the granite gateposts and parked outside the refurbished Coach House in the grounds of Grenah Manor.

Understandably, the students were rather weary after their confinement on such a long journey and there was the usual stampede to get off the buses. Many of their lives lacked structure and discipline. An objective of this residential process was to address this problem. They needed guidance as to how to act in civilised ways. Jim went round to the door of the bus and asked everyone to sit down until he had announced their arrival to the Centre's Reception. Mercifully, they all waited patiently for instructions as Janet remained to supervise until Jim returned.

Alice and Joy Penrose had been awaiting the arrival of their guests and immediately came out to greet them. The weather was fine and it was agreed that the students could get off the bus whilst the cases were unloaded from the roof racks. Everyone lent a hand retrieving their cases as they were passed down and Alice and Joy shepherded the students into their prearranged groups.

"We expect you to stay in these groups for the duration of your visit," said Alice reinforcing the arrangements agreed with the College. "I will be responsible for the activities for group A and Joy here will be responsible for Group B. After we have shown you to your accommodation, we all need to meet again outside the front entrance of this building at 4pm dressed in track suits and trainers. There will be a short tour which will include reference to Health and Safety concerns on site. Then we go on a little ramble. When we return you will have time to get changed ready for a meal in the Manor House at 7pm. Are there any questions?"

"What time does the bar open?" asked Birch with a facetious smile.

Alice addressed Birch directly. "You are going to be too exhausted to worry about the bar tonight." Turning to the full assembly she continued, "That reminds me. Later this evening you will be given the full timetable of activities for the week. You will all need to keep a clear head because you will need both stamina and tenacity."

"Doesn't sound like much fun," Birch muttered half under his breath.

"I will make sure that you are the first person to offer feedback at the end of the week. Please save your thoughts until then." Alice knew that she could not show any sign of irritation or she would end up being goaded all week.

The last thing that Janet and Jim felt like was to go jogging, but they knew that it was important to keep the students busy. It was also a fact that they all needed to exercise after their travels. Perhaps, the students would sleep better later on if they were physically exhausted. So, at 4pm they all met outside the Coach House as agreed. Alice directed the students into their designated groups so that they could be accompanied by either herself or Joy as guides. She checked off the names of her own group which consisted of people from both courses. Jobseekers and hairdressers had been merged in roughly equal numbers. Two people were missing. Birch and Struthers had not arrived. Jim moved towards the building intent on rounding up the two stray students. Alice held up her hand to stop him.

"I am afraid we will have to wait until the two missing gentlemen decide to join us," she announced. "There is no way we can leave without them."

There was a murmur of complaint that ran through the assembled groups. This was late in the afternoon in October. And there was a chill in the air. It was not ideal to be standing around inactive in a tracksuit. They waited for a further twenty minutes before the two miscreants appeared laughing distractedly, absorbed in their own little world. Jim stalked over to meet them and immediately detected the smell of lager on their breath. They must have smuggled a couple of cans in their clothing.

Someone shouted at Birch, "Come on mate we're freezing out here. What are you playing at?"

Birch made a rude gesture in the direction of the voice, but his lack of contrition was causing a ripple of anger from the rest of the students and both he and Struthers decided it would be wise to keep quiet. Jim sent Birch to one group and Struthers to the other. Divide and rule.

Alice led one group down the lane outside the Centre which joined the start of the Camel cycle trail about a mile away. Joy led her group in the opposite direction down a steep lane that brought them to an ancient bridge over the River Camel. It was a shorter route, but much more hilly.

Both parties returned to the Coach House without incident. There had been one or two moans about wanting to be back in Birmingham, but generally they all felt refreshed by their exertions. Their lives were in the city and the sights and sounds of the countryside were unfamiliar. This new environment would be a challenge, but also an education. There was an hour before the evening meal in the restaurant and then the students would be briefed about the activities for the next day, Saturday. It was interesting that neither Birch nor Struthers were late for either the meal or the briefing. Evidently, peer group pressure had exerted itself in a positive way.

It was made clear to all the students that for the next day they would remain in the groups that they had already been in earlier. One group would accompany Alice and Jim on a walk over Bodmin Moor where they would climb to the top of Roughtor. There would be an opportunity to try an introduction to abseiling as part of this day long activity. A packed lunch would be prepared for later when their energy levels were depleted after trekking over open moorland. The other group would be with Joy and Janet for a cycle ride along the Camel Trail on the section from Wenford Bridge to Dunmere. Refreshments could be taken at a pub called 'The Borough Arms' at Dunmere. Both groups would meet by the minibuses straight after breakfast at 9am prompt. Alice's group would take the minibus to the furthest edge of Davidstow airfield where they would park before heading onto the moor from a track near Trevillian's gate. Janet would drive the other bus and park at Wenford Bridge where Joy would arrange the bike hire. On their return all students would gather after the evening meal for debriefing.

Predictably there were no questions. After the travel and the ramble, the students just wanted to go to their rooms and rest. As the students dispersed Alice and Joy hoped that the weather would be kind. The forecast was for fair weather, but they had an alternative plan on hand should it be needed. Joy wondered if Chris would be able to meet them to lend a hand. Unfortunately, she was going to be disappointed.

SEVENTEEN
FALSE IMPRISONMENT

All thoughts of making an escape had left Chris's head. His journalistic instincts had returned as he felt less intimidated and wanted answers. There was a story here which could provide a scoop. A tsunami of inquisitiveness was engulfing him and he could see possible closure to the mystery of the sightings. After all, these had been the focus of his investigations for a long time. He did not know what to make of the man in the blue overalls who now sat straining at the wheel of the Land Rover as they bounded dangerously along the narrow country roads. Strangely, he was not afraid of his chauffer. Here was someone who could have used deadly force, but had chosen to preserve a life probably at his own expense.

"My name is Chris Arbor and if you remember we met at the opening of the Outdoor Pursuits Centre," said Chris by way of starting a conversation. "I can't recall your name I'm afraid."

Unable to take his eyes off the road and stressed by the precarious situation he found himself in Peter was reluctant to enter into any sort of conversation.

"My name is not important, but I remember you from that occasion at the Outdoor Pursuits Centre. I know that you are a journalist. Just remain calm and no harm will come to you," said Peter in truncated sentences.

Chris leaned back in his seat. He did not know this man and he certainly did not trust him. He knew that he had become a player in a game that he had not been invited to, but he believed Peter when he said that he would not be harmed.

The Land Rover crossed the coast road and entered the lane leading to the National Trust car park at Bedruthan Steps. It was twilight with a darkening sky and patchy mist rolling into every hollow. Looking towards the sea there was only a void of greyness. The car park was deserted and the nearby buildings, so crowded in the summer months, were unoccupied. The two fugitives abandoned the Land Rover leaving it parked hidden under the branches of a tree next to a hedge. They raced over to where Peter had parked his car and quickly regained the coast road. Peter had decided to take a risk by following a route through Trenance, Mawgan Porth and Trevarrien which would direct him past Newquay airport before joining the main A39 at St Column Major. He had left his blue overalls behind in the Land Rover and was now wearing a navy-blue fleece and jeans. The only item that he had brought with him was the small TV with the recording equipment from the hangar. Chris was still clamped uncomfortably in the cuffs that Dennis had roughly applied. Fortunately, he had put his overcoat on when he was at the airfield, so he was reasonably warm, but the cuffs were chaffing his wrists. He had allowed Peter to dictate his movements not just because he was the one with a gun, but because he wanted to know more.

The mist had temporarily grounded flights at the airport and the threat of roadblocks did not materialise. Once on the A39 heading swiftly towards Wadebridge Peter began to relax a little.

The thought that Dennis had not been able to extricate himself from the post very quickly pleased him greatly. Perhaps, he had lost the key that he had said was so hard to reach! Chris sensed that the atmosphere in the car had become less tense and decided to strike up a conversation.

"Why were you at the old St Eval airfield today?" He asked casually.

Peter smiled. "The same reason as you. I don't believe those stories about Unidentified Flying Objects."

"You were exiting the airfield in a van. I have no idea how you got in, but did you find see anything in the hangar?"

"Sometimes you have to go where you are not invited," said Peter. "Otherwise you will never know what is going on. I had to find out."

There was a period of silence whilst Chris pondered Peter's replies. He was concerned about the gun and the fact that Peter had been prepared to break the law. What sort of person would go to all the trouble to plan what amounted to a military operation just to check a rumour? No ordinary person would have been capable of thwarting Dennis Torrance. Could it be that Peter was a spy?

"Are you working for yourself?" Chris asked. He did not expect a straight answer, but Peter's evasive reply told him what he needed to know.

"It is better that you don't know who I work for," Peter replied abruptly. "The less you know the safer you will be."

"I can tell you that I got involved in these UFO investigations after I found a damaged section of an alien craft up on Bodmin Moor. Stupidly, I handed the part over to the defence people thinking that they would confirm where it had come from. Instead they warned me off, which only made me more determined to find out the truth. Do you know any more now that you have visited the hangar?"

"Perhaps," said Peter cautiously. "When we get to base, I intend to check. I have signalled my controller who will be meeting us at the base. It is a place we sometimes use when we need to meet urgently."

They drove on in silence. Chris was content to stay with Peter for the time being. He wanted to know what Peter had found before planning his escape. The car drove along the A39 through Camelford before making a right turn down a narrow road that Chris knew led to the disused RAF airfield on the edge of Bodmin Moor. The car rumbled over a cattle grid its headlights picking out the dark shapes of trees that formed the edge of Davidstow woods. During World War 11 this had been the highest airfield in the country. Aircraft had been able to divert here from the coastal airfields which were often closed due to sea mist. Tonight, the mist affecting many low lying areas of the countryside was absent. The moon was silhouetting the derelict airfield buildings. These decaying, ghostly reminders of a bygone era marked the edge of crumbling concrete runways. They were heading to the far end of the airfield near a place called Trevillian's gate, a place where visitors parked before walking onto the moor. Chris estimated that they were less than three miles from Cornwall's highest Tors. He could see the dark, desolate shapes of Brown Willy and Rough Tor against the lighter backdrop of the night sky.

The car came to a sudden stop outside what at first looked like a large grassy mound. It was one of a number of bunkers originally used to store bombs. These bunkers had been located far enough away from any parked aircraft to avoid damage to them following an accidental explosion. Peter got out of the car and gestured with his gun for Chris to head towards the bunker. Just visible through the undergrowth was a short flight of steps that led to an open entrance beyond which was a concrete wall. Chris had to turn 90 degrees to his right before stopping at an old wooden door. He noticed the rotting door still had flecks of dull green paint and wondered about the lives of the people who had passed through here nearly 80 years ago. Peter tapped the door twice with the muzzle of his gun. A man wearing a balaclava and navy-blue coat opened the door and Chris was invited to sit on an upturned ammunition crate as Peter returned to the car to fetch his bag. The only light was from a storm lantern the man had hung from a rusty hook in the ceiling. It was such a dim, yellow light that it made everything appear monochrome. The man did not speak until Peter returned with his bag containing the TV equipment. The two men set the little monitor up on another crate and Peter switched on the battery power for the monitor and pressed play. The faces of the two men appeared pallid in the light from the monitor, their shadows cast huge against the far wall. Chris stood up, moving towards a position where he could also view the recording. He was roughly pushed back by the man in the balaclava and fell heavily onto the wet floor. The man raised his foot to stamp on Chris's head, but was restrained by Peter who tried to calm the violent thug.

"He's only a journalist who knows little. Once we are away it will make no difference. Who will believe someone who thinks he's seen a UFO. It will probably divert attention from reality."

The thug in the balaclava backed away with an angry grunt and Chris defiantly returned to a position where he could view the monitor.

The recording showed a triangular shaped craft resembling the shape of an inverted ice cream cone. It had a smooth polished black surface area. Along the central section, about midway to the top were a regular series of dark panels like the blackened windows of a drug dealer's car. No door was visible from the angle of the filming. There was no discernible cockpit, just the narrowing fuselage where significant damage was visible. A violent impact must have occurred, as two of the black panels were missing and a deep scrape scoured the adjoining section. The whole craft was resting on trestles. It did not appear to have any wheels. For a short time, Chris forgot about his predicament as he was overcome with a strange feeling of surprised elation. At last, after all his searching, here was physical evidence of what must be an alien craft. It was just as Joy and Bert had described during the night of their encounter in Davidstow Woods.

The recording continued, with the camera panning from side to side, and revealing a second slightly smaller aircraft. This craft had a more conventional shape with wheels supporting two stubby wings and a long nose wheel at the front of an elongated fuselage. There was no conventional cockpit, which led Chris to think that he was seeing a drone. It appeared that the aircraft was being modified. A large section of the engine housing had been removed and a technician was working inside the engine bay. It looked as if the drone was being cloned with parts from the cone shaped craft. Various parts from the alien craft were spread methodically on the floor of the hangar. The recording ended abruptly and the three men stood back, momentarily speechless, before Peter bent to disengage the battery.

"Looks like they have recovered some sort of unmanned probe and are using the parts to improve their new drone," said the man in the balaclava as he forced Chris back to the upturned crate.

Peter nodded. "It's taken them long enough. There have been months of test flights which people have reported as UFOs. The truth is the people were not always mistaken. We have now seen a secret aircraft still under development next to what I am convinced is a recovered alien craft."

It appeared that the man in the balaclava was Peter's senior. His speech had a heavy foreign accent which Chris thought was Eastern European. He packed the TV equipment into the bag and walked towards the door. Pointing at Chris he barked, "Are you going to dispose of him, or shall I?"

The words were so cold, so matter of fact. Chris was appalled that someone could so casually contemplate an execution. His thought turned to Joy and his promise to help her with the newly arrived guests. He felt deeply sad that he may not ever see her again. This potentially fatal situation had sharpened his focus and he pledged to himself that if he survived, he would open his heart to her.

Reality harshly returned as Peter shouted to his accomplice who was now exiting the bunker, "You go ahead to the car and I'll follow when I have cleaned up here." He had heard so many stories of brutality from his father about the days of siege in St Petersburgh that he had grown up repulsed by unnecessary violence. There was plenty of time to escape without the need to kill the hostage.

After the euphoria of the recording in the hangar Chris now feared the worst. In hindsight, he wished he had tried to escape earlier. The irony was that he had found out what he wanted to know, but would never be able to tell the story. He feared for his life. Peter pulled the gun from his pocket and bent down behind where Chris was perched. Chris heard a metallic scraping sound. He thought about torture before realising that Peter was using a pick to spring the lock on his hand cuffs. Then suddenly the cuffs released and he could free his arms. It felt wonderful to be free, but unfortunately it would not be for very long. Peter reattached one side of the cuffs to Chris's left wrist and pulled him to where a rusty chain dangled limply from its fixing in the wall. He threaded the other cuff through the last link and locked it. Then he carried the crate over so that Chris could at least sit down. There was only enough slack in the chain to allow movement from a sitting to a standing position.

"Sorry, but we need time to make our escape," said Peter with one finger over his lips to remind Chris to remain silent. "Now you know where the panel you handed to the authorities came from you will not be surprised at their lack of response to your questions."

Peter thrust a bottle of water into Chris's free hand and fired two shots into the floor. The shots echoed loudly around the old bunker as Peter collected the storm lantern and disappeared through the door. Chris was left sitting in the dark, damp, dungeon, attached to the wall like a medieval prisoner. Still, he was alive, and he knew that in the morning it should be possible to attract attention. If he made enough noise someone passing nearby may hear. Silence was now restored and Chris felt disorientated in the inky blackness. A sense of fear invaded his attempts to remain calm. What he had seen on the TV monitor haunted his mind. It was going to be a long night and Chris had no way of keeping time. Although he was wearing a watch, it was so dark in the bunker that he was unable to read it.

After what seemed like eternity, a sliver of light appeared around the edge of the door frame. His eyes fully accustomed to the dark, this tiny sliver of light was just enough for Chris to see the dark shape of an old metal bracket just on front of him. He stretched his leg forward and dragged it to where he could reach to pick it up with his free hand. The bracket made a dull clunk when struck against the wall which was very disappointing, but better than nothing. There was absolutely no sound coming from outside and after a while the effort of shouting and banging on the wall drained Chris's strength. He had not eaten properly for over 24 hours and his spirits were dropping. Desperation was seeping into his brain and he slumped down on the crate with his head bowed in submission. The hand cuff was biting into his wrist and he had just finished the last drops from the water bottle. It was hard to resist the urge to panic. He began to think about scratching a message onto the wall, but his thoughts were interrupted by a distant sound from outside. At first it was just a muted hum, but it got louder and Chris knew it was a motor vehicle. Then there was silence again. Chris was wondering if it was his imagination when he caught what sounded like a car door slamming shut. Then he heard it again, a second door closing. He started to bang and shout frantically in the hope that someone would hear him.

EIGHTEEN
THE BUNKER

———

Alice had checked the Saturday weather forecast before they had left Grenah Manor and although there was the threat of mist and fog later, the sun was melting the dew across the grass around Davidstow airfield. The bus juddered and rattled as it crossed a cattle grid. Alice joined the students at the rear of the minibus and checked that they had all got copies of the Ordinance Survey sheet covering the area of Bodmin Moor relevant to their expedition. Each student had a compass and the maps were inside acetate folders fixed flat to a board. Jim parked the bus near grass covered bunkers that bordered the edge of the airfield. After dispersing the packed lunches and climbing equipment around the group Alice beckoned them to follow as she headed for the gate that led to the moorland path. One person remained behind sitting on the ground next to the minibus. Jim could see that it was Birch. He was fiddling with the laces on his boots.

Sensing Jim's irritation Alice volunteered her help. "You go on ahead and wait for us at the Lanlavery Rocks." She indicated the point on Jim's map. "I'll follow with our friend as soon as we get his laces repaired. Make sure you keep your mobile handy."

Jim rolled his eyes and looked skyward as if expecting some divine intervention "Thanks, good luck with that. I'll, see you both later unless you strangle him with his own bootlaces." He marched off with the rest of the group glad to be free from responsibility for sorting out Birch's boot laces.

Alice bent down in front of Birch and managed to tie the two broken ends of his lace so that he could refasten his boot.

"Right, no more excuses, let's go and join the others," she said standing up. She hoped that Birch would follow her example without the need to issue an ultimatum.

Birch appeared to be transfixed by something behind her near the entrance to one of the grass covered bunkers. Neither of them spoke, but Alice turned to look in the same direction. The morning sun was quite low in the sky sending a golden glow over the top of the bunkers. A sparkling hue shone from the wet grass and in this iridescent light she could see the outline of a figure. It was a woman in a long dress wearing a bonnet. Although she was unable to see the woman's features in detail it was clear that she was pointing directly towards the door of the bunker. As Alice turned back towards Birch, she heard his phone camera click. They looked at each other, their faces etched in surprise, but when they looked back the figure had disappeared. Without warning, Birch marched off in the direction of the bunker. The spectral figure could no longer be seen.

"Where's that chick gone?" Alice heard him shout.

"I don't think it is wise to go near there," Alice shouted. She knew that the bunkers were sometimes used by drug addicts.

It was too late. Alice had to run to catch up. However, Birch was now approaching the steps to the bunker entrance. To their alarm they could now both hear banging and a muffled voice shouting from inside. Alice tried to impress restraint on Birch, but he was intent on rashly forging ahead. He was no stranger to violence. There had been some of that at home. He had seen his own father kick the front door in whilst under the influence of alcohol. Fuelled by a mindless, primeval resolve Birch charged into the bunker and turned to see the door. Adrenaline pumping through his veins he did not anticipate that this door would be weak and rotten. Launching himself at the old door with his full body weight he crashed through and landed in a heap on the damp floor of the bunker. He raised his head and saw the silhouette of a man before him. Instinctively, Birch fumbled in his pocket to get his mobile phone and immediately switched it on. There was no signal. Chris, dishevelled, and cuffed to the wall would have hugged him if he had been able to move.

Birch was shocked by what he saw in the dim glow of his phone. All he could manage to say was, "Are you alright mate?"

"Do I look alright," Chris responded weakly. "Just get some help so I can get out of here."

Birch half staggered half climbed out of the bunker. The sudden sunlight was blinding him. He felt someone take hold of his arm. It was Alice.

"There's some guy in there chained to the wall," he gasped as he wrenched himself free.

"Chained to the wall?" Repeated Alice like an echo.

"He's in a bad way and needs help. Go and see for yourself."

In the trouser pocket of her fatigues Alice took out a small torch. As they entered the bunker, she switched it on and shone the beam towards the far wall. Immediately she recognised the forlorn figure hooked uncomfortably to the wall, arm raised is if in salutation.

"Chris Arbor," she gasped. "How did you get in this predicament? Joy told me that you were taking a holiday."

"Well I hadn't planned on this part of it," Chris replied with a weak smile. "I'll explain later because it is a long story. It is so good to see you though. I was beginning to think I would never get out of here alive."

There was a pause before Alice remembered that she had a half dunk bottle of water in her jacket pocket.

"Help him to drink this," she commanded, passing the bottle to Birch. "I'll go outside and call the emergency services. They will have to cut through that rusty chain. Try to keep him talking."

Once outside, Alice notified the emergency services as to their exact location. She also used her mobile to contact Jim who had arrived at the Lanlavery Rock and was starting to worry where she was. It was decided that Jim would lead the party to the top of Rough Tor before returning to the minibus retracing the same route. The abseiling would have to be cancelled on this occasion as both would be needed to safely supervise the activity. In any case Jim was not a qualified instructor. The trek would take an hour each way plus time at the top for lunch and photographs. It was now 10.30am so it would probably be mid-afternoon before the party arrived back. As she put her phone away Alice could see the blue flashing lights of a police car approaching from the far side of the airfield.

Meanwhile, Birch had adjusted the crate to make it more comfortable for the shackled prisoner. He had been trying to chip away the mortar from the anchorage of the metal ring to which the cuffs were attached. Alice was impressed by his behaviour. This was a person who could be very obtuse, but in this difficult situation he had shown courage, initiative and consideration. She made a mental note to make sure that Birch's actions were included on his residential report.

Emerging from the police car were two officers. One of them introduced himself to Alice as Sergeant Stone. He was a burly, authoritative figure, who towered above Alice.

"There's a man trapped in there," explained Alice as she pointed towards the bunker.

"Fetch a torch from the car," barked the burly officer to his colleague. He turned to look at Alice. She felt his piercing eyes assessing her. "Can you tell me what has happened here?"

Alice explained how it had been by pure chance that they had heard Chris's cries for help. "We were delayed from leaving the minibus after the other students had left and heard sounds. When we got inside the bunker, we saw a man chained to the wall. Then I realised that I recognised the victim." She omitted to mention the ghostly apparition who had directed them to the exact location.

"So, you know him?" said the Sergeant abruptly as they made their way to the bunker. "What is his name?"

Alice was worried about what trouble Chris had got himself into, but she felt that she had to be honest with the policeman. "He's a journalist called Chris Arbor who works for the local newspaper," was all she could think of in response.

Sergeant Stone instructed the other officer to wait outside while he entered the bunker closely followed by Alice. The powerful beam of the Sergeant's torch revealed the pathetic sight of Chris slumped on the crate with his wrist still attached to the bracket. Birch was still trying to release the cuffs.

"This is Mr. Birch," Alice said in anticipation of the Sergeant's next question. "He is with me and our group of students. We are on an orienteering exercise across the moor."

"You've got yourself into a right pickle here my friend," said the Sergeant as he moved close in front of Chris to inspect the cuffs in more detail. These little gems are different to the ones we normally use. They look like the ones used by the military."

They were interrupted as a shout echoed around the bunker from just outside. "The Fire Brigade has arrived Sergeant."

"We'll come out now to give you more room," shouted the

Sergeant gesturing to Alice and Birch towards the exit. "The Fire Brigade lads will free you in a few minutes," he said to reassure Chris that his ordeal was ending.

The Sergeant gave a quick appraisal of the situation to the firemen, who then entered the bunker with a set of heavy-duty bolt cutters. A couple of minutes later they emerged supporting the weak and exhausted journalist. Strong arms helped him into the back of an ambulance which had now arrived on the scene.

There was a crackle from the radio as a message came through in response to an enquiry regarding a person called Chris Arbor. Sergeant Stone's face turned a severe shade of red as he listened to the call. Apparently, an alert had been issued within the last twelve hours for a person of this name to be apprehended. He was classed as a fugitive, possibly armed and wanted in connection with a spying incident. This information changed the complexion of his enquiries dramatically.

Striding directly to the parked ambulance Sergeant Stone subjected Chris to a thorough body search. All his personal possessions were removed from his clothing and placed in a polythene bag. Satisfied that he was not carrying weapons or other incriminating items he then instructed his colleague to accompany Chris to the hospital which he had been told was in Bodmin. "Don't let him out of your sight until your relief arrives," he said sternly. "I will request this area to be sealed off as a crime scene. The forensics staff should be here soon."

His relief at rescue had been short lived. Not only had he been subjected to the indignity of a body search he was now being treated like a dangerous criminal. Chris felt his euphoria melt away as he contemplated the implications of his new status. Surely, the authorities could not be thinking that he had been in collusion with Peter? The more he thought about the events of last night the more worried he became. Yes, he had been reporting on UFOs and he had visited St Eval, but he had not trespassed on the airfield. He had been falsely imprisoned by people that he had no connection with whatsoever. He had met Peter once before at the opening of the Outdoor Pursuits Centre, but it was an absolute coincidence that he should collide with his van. He was really a victim of false imprisonment, but would the authorities see it this way? As the ambulance doors closed Chris saw Alice standing nearby. He leaned forward to speak to her, but was pushed back by his police minder and the doors slammed shut. As the ambulance moved away Alice asked the Sergeant where Chris was being taken.

"He's going to Bodmin Hospital for a check over, but that will be the least of his worries. I have been informed that an alert was issued last night for his apprehension. He is in serious trouble. All I can say is that there is a National Security issue here. I think that you and Mr. Birch had better come for a sit down in my car so that I can make a note of your names and addresses. You will have to come to the station later to give detailed statements."

By the time Jim arrived back with the rest of the group, men in white suits were swarming around the bunker. Streamers of blue and white tape fluttered around the perimeter of what was now a restricted area. Once everyone was accounted for and seated in the minibus Alice gave a summary of events.

"Sounds like Birch did well today," said Jim. "Who'd have thought that a broken lace would have led to saving a man's life!"

"Looks like you may be in the newspapers tomorrow Birch," called someone from the rear of the bus.

"Won't be the first time," smiled Birch. "He was secretly enjoying his new status as a hero. "I used more energy trying to get that guy's handcuffs off than I would have spent on your entire walk!"

NINETEEN

INTERROGATION

The minibus with the orienteering group arrived back at Grenah Manor first after having had their activities curtailed because of the events at Davidstow airfield. Both Jim and Alice knew that when the other students returned there would be an excited exchange of information about their experiences during the day. Alice wanted to make sure that both the college staff received the facts concerning her daughter's connection to the rescued journalist. She knew how quickly false stories and rumours could spread. The last thing she wanted was for this incident to undermine relationships to the detriment of their program. It was going to be a shock when Joy heard what had happened and Alice wanted to be the first person to tell her. It was agreed that Jim and Janet would supervise the students whilst Alice took Joy aside to break the discomforting news.

The bike ride had been a great success and Joy knew that her group had enjoyed the activity. They were all feeling a bit weary and Joy was looking forward to a shower before the evening meal. From the moment her mother took her arm and directed her away from the others she could tell that something was wrong. The anxious look on Alice's face was something that Joy recognised immediately. At first, she thought it was something to do with the Centre, but as her mother told her about Chris's plight, she felt slightly ambivalent. Of course, she was saddened by his ordeal, but could not suppress annoyance that he had gone ahead with his trip to St Eval without telling her. This was a week when he knew she would be busy with the college visit and she had advised him against going to the airfield alone. Her first reaction was to go to see Chris, but Alice explained that she would not be allowed to speak to him as he was under arrest. Anyway, nobody knew where he would be taken after his check-up at the hospital.

Alice was distracted from the conversation when her mobile rang. She could see that it was an incoming call from Henry. He had decided to go to work that morning to deal with an urgent production problem. Henry wanted the family to know that he had been taken to Bodmin Police Station earlier in the day. It was for questioning in connection with a breach of security concerning the contract between his firm and the Ministry of Defence. Suspicion had fallen on him because of his connection to Chris Arbor. The uncomfortable fact that he had inadvertently conversed with a spy at the Grand Opening of the Outdoor Pursuits Centre had also conspired to compromise his integrity. He had rigorously resisted suggestions doubting his loyalty to the project and had now satisfactorily answered all the questions. He had been told that he would be released pending further enquiries as all the evidence against him was circumstantial. As he read through and signed his statement, he felt indignant and embarrassed that his integrity had been questioned. It was a situation that Henry had fearfully anticipated ever since his daughter's involvement with the UFO story. He assured Alice that although he was going to be home later than expected there was no need to worry.

After a night in the hospital Chris was transferred to Bodmin Police Station and taken to an interview room. Fortunately, his injuries were superficial. Scratches, bruises, dehydration and shock had been treated successfully. Feeling a bit the worst for wear, he was invited to sit behind a large teak desk which had a recording machine perched on one side. A uniformed police officer stood stiffly by the door like a toy soldier. Nobody spoke and it seemed like an age before the door suddenly opened and in came Sergeant Stone accompanied by Dennis Torrance. The pair sat down at the opposite side of the table to Chris and the officer who had been guarding the door left the room. Dennis placed a manila folder on the table and smoothed his hand over the cover as though he was removing dust. Chris could feel the tension as Dennis looked at him with his cold blue, piercing eyes. There was no greeting, just a dispassionate silence. Then Sergeant Stone switched on the recorder and read out the time and date of the interview. Chris had lost track of time. It was reassuring to hear that it was Sunday 16th October at 11am.

"You are being detained under the Ministry of Defence Police Act 1987 on suspicion that on the evening of Friday 14th October you conspired with others to undermine National Security protocols," said Dennis before reading out Chris's rights.

"That's ridiculous," replied Chris angrily. "I am a newspaper reporter and I have been investigating UFO reports. What I have been doing is working to keep the public informed about a matter they have a right to know about."

"You were found spying next to an installation in a restricted area and when approached you drove off at speed. You then joined an accomplice and disappeared."

"I drove off because I realised that I was being followed by someone who I had every reason to distrust. In any case, I was not within any restricted area. For all you know I might have been enjoying a picnic on my way home from work," said Chris indignantly.

"Except, we both know that you were not having a picnic, you were spying on the activities at the airfield," snarled Dennis.

"I was observing the activities at the airfield as part of my duty to report on a matter of public interest. Matters that people like you want to hide away. I resent the use of the word 'spying' because it implies that I am some sort of traitor. I was in fact carrying out research."

Dennis did not intend to be drawn into a long discussion. He opened the manila folder and withdrew a photograph of Peter Vadim which he passed over to Chris.

"How long have you known this man?"

"The only thing I know about this person is that I collided with his van while you were chasing me on the road outside the airfield. Obviously, I now acknowledge that he is a spy because of what happened after he imprisoned me during his escape," said Chris with a tone of exasperation.

"So, you didn't know this man before the collision?" Dennis betrayed a triumphal smirk as if he thought he had just played a winning card.

Chris hesitated before replying. He remembered the day that he went to Joy's opening event at Grenah Manor, the note on his windscreen and the suspicion that he had been followed. Dennis or some member of his team must have been watching his every move. He had to tell the truth, but the truth would make it look as if he was involved in a conspiracy. There was no way that he was going to give Dennis the satisfaction of proving him a liar.

"I'm not prepared to say another word until I speak to my legal representative," Chris asserted.

It was with a shrug of resignation that Dennis retrieved the photograph and replaced it in the folder. Sergeant Stone turned off the recorder and the pair retired from the room. One hour later the interview continued with a solicitor provided by the police force sitting next to Chris.

"My client wishes to make one phone call before we continue," the solicitor asserted.

"He can make his call if I think it safe for him to do so when we have concluded this interview. National Security cannot be compromised by attention to trivialities. Returning his attention to Chris he said, "You were about to tell us whether you had met this man before the incident outside the airfield." Dennis held out the photograph for everyone to view.

Feeling a sense of impending doom Chris admitted that he had met the man before.

"I recognised the man after we were involved in the collision," Chris explained. "He had attended the opening of an Outdoor Pursuits Centre which was a venture that my girlfriend was involved with. I never actually spoke to him personally as I just presumed he was a customer interested in using the facilities."

"Well I am glad that you have told us that," said Dennis, because we have just searched the spy's house and found a flyer of that event with his papers. What I would like to know is why a man known to us as a Soviet informer would take the trouble to go to some open day event at an Outdoor Pursuits Centre."

"I can't actually remember conversing with this man that day. He was just there in the background. I think he owned a holiday let. He asked a few questions when Joy and I took a group of the visitors on a tour of the facilities. Later he just blended in as we all ate refreshments." Chris felt his face flush as a vague memory emerged of Peter Vadim chatting with Henry Penrose. It was a memory that came with a sharp warning surge of anxiety. There was no way he was going to report that conversation because he knew Henry did some work for the MOD and would be seriously embarrassed by any association with a spy.

As if reading his mind Dennis continued. "Did Peter Vadim talk to any member of the Penrose family?"

"I didn't take any notice of Peter Vadim and was more interested in talking to my girlfriend, Joy Penrose. I told you I had no knowledge of this man, not even his name. There were lots of people talking in groups. You can't expect me to make notes of every conversation." Chris knew that he sounded defensive.

A shadow of disbelief clouded Dennis's face. "It seems odd to me that you as a journalist known for your reports about UFOs and mysterious objects never spoke with Peter Vadim who we know had a common interest in these subjects. In fact, I wouldn't be surprised if you were one of the reasons that he attended that day."

"That's absolute rubbish," said Chris angrily. "It was a complete coincidence that we collided at the airfield. It took me a few minutes to remember where I had seen the other driver before. If I had been in collusion with him, I wouldn't have been stupid enough to crash into his van."

"Be careful not to jump to conclusions prematurely," warned the solicitor.

There was a pause before Dennis spoke again. This time his voice took on a more sinister tone. "That is as it may be. Perhaps, he was more interested in someone else that day at the Centre. Do you know what Henry Penrose does for a living?"

This was what Chris had been dreading so he decided that the best form of defence was to go on the attack. "I know where Henry works, but we have never talked in any detail about his job. It is his daughter that I am interested in. The Penrose family are honest, hardworking people. Anyway, do you really think that if we were plotting to betray state secrets that we would be so naive to meet a spy at a family gathering within earshot of the public? It was a pure coincidence that Peter Vadim happened to be at the airfield at the same time as me. If I had known he was going to be there I would not have collided with him. If I were colluding with him why would I be left to die in that bunker? If he had got the information he was after from me, he would have had no need to trespass on the airfield. I am just an inquisitive journalist and everything that has happened since I handed in that fragment of metal at The New Technologies Centre has convinced me that there is a hidden agenda."

"Let me respond to that by saying that I think it is you with a secret agenda. I suspect that you have more than that metal fragment hidden away somewhere. Don't you think we know that there is a missing panel?"

"I have absolutely no idea what you are talking about," Chris could not disguise the disdain he felt regarding this accusation.

The Police solicitor looked at his watch. "I think that you are going to have to decide whether to charge or release this person fairly soon. Have you interviewed Henry Penrose separately about his involvement in this matter?"

Dennis gave Chris a severe look. "I will be comparing the statement that Henry Penrose has already made very carefully with yours my friend. However, there is one more issue I need to clear with Mr. Arbor." He put his elbows on the table and leaned forward.

"When Peter Vadim trespassed on the airfield, we know that he used a small camera capable of filming the interior of the hangar. Part of it was left dangling from an air vent. Can you tell me whether he succeeded in making a recording?"

Chris had anticipated this question. He knew that it would be unwise to let Dennis know that he was fully aware of what was in the hangar. Heaven knows what draconian measures Dennis would impose on him. There were cases where people who held too much dangerous knowledge suddenly disappeared or were declared mentally unstable. Chris decided that he would recount all the facts except for the part where he saw the recording. His account would be incomplete, but he hoped that it would remain credible.

"When we got to the bunker there was another man waiting there," said Chris. "It was dark and shadowy with just the torches giving a little light. I was still in the cuffs that you put on my wrists at the airfield and I was forced to sit on an old crate while they checked the recording. They were bent over a tiny TV monitor and appeared quite animated. When I tried to look, I was forcibly pushed backwards and fell to the ground banging my head. The other man went to the car and that was the last I saw of him or the recording. Peter was instructed to kill me, but he fired into the ground. He may have been a traitor, but he was not a natural killer."

There was a knock on the door and a police officer entered the room. He whispered something in Dennis's ear. Whatever was said activated Dennis as sharply as if he had received an electric shock.

"Interview terminated at 1300 hours," announced Dennis with an air of finality. He nodded at the solicitor indicating that his services would not be needed for the time being. "Sergeant Stone will call you if we decide to press any charges."

Next, he spoke quietly to Sergeant Stone before turning to fix Chris with a cold stare. "There's been an important development. You had better come with us. The body of a man has been found at the farm where you reported the original UFO activity. There may be a connection with the events of last night."

"You mean a body has been found at 'Innyvale Farm?" Chris asked in alarm as they exited the police station. "I sincerely hope that the farmer and his family are safe."

"That is the farm I am referring to. You may be able to help because the reports we are getting about this incident sound very curious."

"Do I take it that any charges against me have been dropped?" asked Chris.

"I will make that decision after we have been to the farm," replied Dennis. "In the meantime, you remain in my custody."

"Guilty until proved innocent," said Chris under his breath.

Dennis heard and ignored the comment. "Just get into the car."

The three men travelled together in silence. Sergeant Stone was driving the police car with Chris and Dennis in the rear seat. None of them spoke. Chris was familiar with the route they were taking along the Bodmin to Camelford road and he wondered about what Joy was doing as the car passed near to Grenah Manor. She had warned him about going to the airfield. He knew that Alice would have told her about his plight, but he was unsure about how sympathetic she would be. Maybe he had been inconsiderate, acting impulsively at a time when Joy was occupied with the new business. Contemplation in hindsight was not going to help now, so Chris sunk deeper into his seat and tried to clear his head.

The car climbed the long hill out of Camelford on the main Atlantic Highway towards Bude before suddenly turning right on the road that Chris knew led along the perimeter of the old Davidstow airfield. As they turned, he caught a glimpse of the brown and white sign that directed visitors to the 'Military Museums'. He knew that the museums were dedicated to the role of the airfield during the Second World War. The memories of his first visit to Innyvale Farm flooded back. This was where he had driven in response to the report of a UFO. It was where he had first met Joy. It was also near here that he had been imprisoned and could have died. Just as he was wondering whether he was being taken to the site of the wind turbines they passed a sign that Chris remembered with amusement from his first visit. It was fixed in the hedge of a neighbouring farm on the perimeter of a sharp bend in the road. It read 'FOR FOX SAKE SLOW DOWN'. He knew that the sign was just before Innyvale Farm and when the car turned right through the two stone pillars into the farmyard, he experienced a mixture of apprehension and relief to be back at the place where this whole saga had started.

Bert Pennington emerged from behind the barn and strode directly to meet them. The place assumed a different atmosphere today. It was like a business that had closed on a bank holiday with the normal bustle of activity temporarily suspended. Bert's serious expression did not give the impression that this was to be a social visit. A phrase from a book he had read by T.S. Eliot jumped into Chris's head. 'The traveller returns to the place from whence he started, but knows it for the first time'. Bert nodded an unsmiling acknowledgement towards Chris and beckoned the visitors to follow him. Chris was glad to suck in the fresh morning air after his confinement.

"Have you come back to enquire about the UFO story Chris? As you can see, I've got other problems here." He shouted over his shoulder. He privately wondered why the police had brought Chris along with them to what seemed to him an unrelated incident. Chris did not respond. He knew that Bert would find out the reason for his presence soon enough.

They walked to the rear of the barn where a small grassy field was used to park the tractor and store feedstuffs for the animals. In the centre of the field the grass had been flattened to form a pattern. It was triangular. The grass at the top of each of the points of the triangle was flattened for about a metre in length. The triangle was just about big enough to park a double deck bus inside. It was as if something flat and heavy had been dropped on the grass leaving a symmetrical imprint. Lying in the centre of the triangle of flattened grass were the fully clothed bodies of two men. The bodies were not twisted or contorted in any way. There was no blood or visible sign of injury. They were carefully laid out in a star shape formation with the top of their heads touching and arms outstretched backwards as if they were about to skydive. Their fingertips were just touching and their legs splayed wide open like gymnasts on a vaulting horse. Dennis indicated that they should approach the circumference of the triangle to get as close a look at the bodies as possible without disturbing the crime scene. Forensics had been called and would need to have access to an untouched scenario.

Chris could see immediately that it was Peter Vadim and his violent accomplice. There they lay flat on their backs with eyes wide open, vacantly staring at the sky. Peter was wearing the same clothes as when Chris had last seen him. The four men walked slowly around the circumference of the triangle, surveying the scene from every angle. There was not a speck of dust or grass on either of the men's clothing. It looked as if they had been placed carefully down in the geometric centre of the triangle. It was a grotesque display. Their positions were reminiscent of two people who had fallen asleep in the middle of some bazaar ritual. The only injury that was visible was a red mark around Peter's neck. It looked like the burn from a rope. A green, jelly type substance had been rubbed on the wound probably to sooth it. Chris attempted to speak, but his mouth was dry and all he could utter was confirmation that this was indeed Peter Vadim and the other man who had met them at the bunker. Now he knew why Dennis had been willing to bring him on this journey. He was the only person able to provide a positive identification of both men.

"Best end to them," snarled Dennis. In his mind they had condemned themselves by spying. "A couple of traitors who got what they deserved. The autopsy is going to be remarkably interesting. In the meantime, we will need to take photographs, and try to get a time frame on this event. I want anything found in their pockets reported to me immediately."

"Don't you want to know how they got there?" asked Chris cautiously. He was fully aware of how deeply implicated he was in this affair.

"That is something that I am expecting you to contribute to," replied Dennis. His muttered voice sounded ominous as it carried over to Chris in the breeze.

"Who is Peter Vadim?" asked Bert.

Sergeant Stone turned to address Bert ignoring his question. "Why have you only just reported this matter?" He asked accusingly.

Pointing to the prostrate body in the centre of the triangle Bert spoke sharply. He did not like the Sergeant's tone. "As soon as I saw the victims, I called the police. It's not my fault you took so long to get here."

"That was just over an hour ago. Didn't you notice this pantomime on your land earlier?"

"I don't spend all day looking behind the barn when there's work to be done elsewhere," said Bert.

"There must have been some noise, the sound of an engine, strangers crossing your land," the Sergeant persisted. "To make that shape and place the body so carefully must have taken time. I would have thought that it would have been obvious to you that something odd was happening."

Bert desperately searched through his memory of what he had been doing that morning. "It's Sunday, but the sheep don't know that! They needed my full attention."

Ignoring the sarcasm Sergeant Stone continued his line of questioning. "So, you were out in the fields and you did not hear or see anything unusual?"

"There was nothing specific. I did go down to the cellar below the farmhouse to retrieve some heavy-duty gloves so it may have happened then. When I walked back towards the fields some of the animals did seem agitated and that's when I saw the body." Bert explained.

"I see," said Sergeant Stone although he plainly did not understand how Bert could have been so unobservant. "Was your wife around?"

"She was at Church all morning so she wouldn't have seen anything," snapped Bert. He was getting rather annoyed by this rude police Sergeant. "You lot waste my time and I say nothing by way of complaint. Months ago, I reported an encounter with a UFO." Bert pointed towards Chris. "My friend the journalist here came around to report about it. I even handed over a metal panel from the site of the collision with the wind turbine. All I received was obfuscation and threats. Well enough is enough. You are going to need to treat me with a lot more respect if you want to gain my cooperation."

Sensing the negative escalation of the conversation, Dennis held up his hands in a gesture reminiscent of a traffic policeman stopping traffic. He took Sergeant Stone to one side and the two of them appeared hunched together in animated discussion, their heads regularly turning in the direction of the recalcitrant farmer with expressions that did not indicate admiration.

Meanwhile, Bert took the opportunity to ask Chris about what his part was in this unsolicited drama. Chris hurriedly explained the sequence of events that had led to his detention.

Their huddle ended, Sergeant Stone walked over to meet the newly arrived forensic team while Dennis beckoned Bert and Chris towards the parked police car. He held the rear door open and invited Chris to enter.

"Just sit in the car whilst I get a statement from Mr. Pennington," was all he said.

"There is nothing that I am unable to say about this matter that the journalist cannot hear," said Bert. A strong suspicion had seeped into his head that there was a link between this death and the previous UFO incident. Why else would Chris Arbor have been brought to the farm? Chris had been involved in the original UFO investigation and from what he had just told Bert he had got too near the truth. Memories of the patterns left on the ground during his previous encounter with the UFO flooded back.

"He is helping us with our enquiries regarding a matter connected to the dead man."

"Mr. Arbor is a journalist. He has been a party to everything that has happened here about the UFO incident near this farm. I entrusted him with the panel that came off the craft and I have every confidence in him." Handing the panel to Chris had not really helped to clarify anything. It had just resulted in threats and misinformation, but Bert could be a stubborn man when thwarted.

"He may be implicated in espionage," Dennis spat out the accusation, confident that this would disenfranchise Chris from any further inclusion.

"Espionage my arse," shouted Bert angrily. His bald head had turned red and there was rage in his eyes. "This man is just doing his job as a journalist. The fact that he reports on things you don't want to be heard does not make him a spy."

"You do not know the full story," Dennis replied defensively.

"Well, I could say that you don't know the full story either," Bert responded triumphantly.

"What part of the story do I not know?" asked Dennis in a voice that did not hide his scepticism.

Bert was beginning to enjoy this conversation. He could see that he was putting Dennis on to his back foot.

"Let's say that the metal panel that I asked Mr. Arbor to investigate is not the only one."

Surprise registered in Dennis's eyes, but he retained his official composure. "Withholding evidence is a serious matter."

"I was never asked to submit any evidence," said Bert. "I volunteered the damaged panel for public scrutiny, but it disappeared and all I received back was threats. I decided to keep the other panel hidden just in case I encountered a rainy day. I think that day has now arrived."

This revelation had focussed Dennis's mind. He was intrigued to know that a second panel had been found. It had been a mystery as to where it was after the recovery of the main wreckage. It was like a jigsaw with a piece missing. His team had been examining the original panel for some time. They had noted the markings engraved on the surface, but could not decipher them. They had tried to analyse the metal compounds that the part was manufactured from. The experts had not anticipated the complexity of the metal and were perplexed as to its constituent parts. All that was clear was that the metal retained properties that were unique from all other manufactured metals produced on Earth. It was an extremely malleable, but resilient material. The possibility of a second panel could make all the difference in tracing the origin especially if it continued the sequence of markings. He had to persuade Bert to hand over the panel. He could threaten to take the farm apart although this would raise the profile of the location and the part may not actually be hidden there. Dennis decided to try coercion rather than force.

"What can I do to encourage you to consider handing over the second panel?"

"I want the immediate release of this journalist. Those stupid spying charges wiped from his record and the truth about the UFO phenomena."

Dennis looked down at his feet and let out a long sigh. Life had been straight forward when he had been a soldier on active service. He was getting weary with all this verbal sparring. The subterfuge, the lies and evasions attached to his current role were unrewarding. Yet he was dedicated to the success of 'The Transformer Project'.

"Come with me to the car," he said directing Bert to follow.

Inside the police car Dennis wound up the windows and looked round to face Chris in the rear seat. He saw a pale and despondent creature with his head tilted back using the headrest for support. Bert had been invited to sit in the front passenger seat. Privately, Dennis had formed the opinion that the journalist had been in the wrong place at the wrong time. He was a meddlesome nuisance, but the circumstantial evidence alone was not enough to convict him of spying.

"Your friend the farmer has convinced me to withdraw the charges against you. I am still not convinced as to whether you are a naïve journalist or an incompetent spy. Stay local in case we need to have further talks. In the meantime, you are free to go home. However, I will have to make it conditional on the matters concerning events at this farm remaining between ourselves. No newspaper articles or press releases other than the ones I authorise."

"That sounds like censorship," protested Chris.

"There is some information that is sensitive and which would be detrimental to the welfare of both the country and individuals within it. If you want to be privy to confidential information you also must accept the responsibility that comes with it," Dennis replied. "This is not about blabbing in a newspaper to further your career by boosting the circulation. These are sensitive issues that will not be enhanced by public disclosure. You need to grow up and shut up. It may be censorship, but that is preferable to anarchy."

There was menace in Dennis's eyes. His fixed stare bored into Chris's head. He knew that what Dennis said made sense, but somewhere deep inside he resented being told what he could and could not say. Ultimately, there was no choice, but to agree to the conditions of confidentiality. The need to be free from custody and the thirst for knowledge overcame the indignity of being treated like a pawn in a game where there was no say in setting the rules.

"I have spent much time on this subject and I feel an overwhelming need to know the truth. I just hope that whatever you say deserves the secret status you have bestowed upon it," Chris said wearily.

Dennis turned to Bert and frowned. He was not a person who took kindly to loss of control. "I have had a bad feeling about this case. I do not understand how those wretched bodies could have been placed there so neatly. There is something very sinister, almost unworldly about it. Almost as if they were laid out in a pattern akin to a crop circle. Then there is the fear that our National Security may have been breached, which has serious implications."

It was not clear to Chris or Bert what Dennis meant about 'something unworldly'. Chris decided not to press the matter. His more urgent personal thoughts were taking priority. His thoughts kept returning to Joy. Would all these unpleasant events have a negative impact on their relationship? He felt an overwhelming desire to get away from Dennis and resume his life.

Dennis looked around furtively and rechecked the car windows were closed. In a hushed voice he said. "You asked me to answer your questions about UFOs. That is classified information, so I am prohibited from any disclosure. You have already witnessed certain events with your own eyes. I cannot deny the reality of what you have seen. You can take the absence of my denial as confirmation if you like. In this context, I can say that the authorities of each superpower in the world have accepted for a long time that there are certain cases where there is no rational explanation for penetration of their defences by unidentified craft. There has been collaboration to share information as a precaution to ensure that there is no mistake between them about breaches of sovereignty. This is to minimise the risk of confrontations. The full details in each country are classified and treated as so sensitive that only a handful of officials are in possession of the files. It is a subject treated as 'Above Top Secret'. As you now know there have been mishaps where craft of unknown origin have crashed. In these cases, it is our responsibility to clear up the mess as quickly as we can and make reassuring public statements while we carry out investigations."

"You mean providing disinformation," Chris sneered.

"Call it what you like, but the object is to prevent unrest and maintain the status quo," retorted Dennis. "There is no one on Earth who knows where these craft come from, why they come or how they work so it would be impossible to provide plausible explanations. No information is better than incomplete explanations over such profound matters."

"It is very convenient for you to keep everyone in the dark whilst at the same time hiding away wreckage and trying to incorporate the technology into your own projects," said Chris.

"It is true that we try to reverse engineer wreckage to see what we can learn from it. If it helps us in the technological race, then this can only be good for the UK".

Bert had been listening intently and decided to make his own contribution to the conversation. "When I approached the craft in Davidstow Woods it was relatively small and windowless, I got the feeling that it wasn't a manned craft. More like a remote-controlled object or a drone. Observing the way it moved I am in no doubt that it was being intelligently operated."

"In the near space, just outside the Earth's gravitational pull, our satellites have registered large unidentified objects. It is unclear whether these are alien mother ships or space debris. It is plausible that some of the objects we see are unmanned shuttles. Some may be manned and some remotely controlled," Dennis replied. "Their mission is unknown and that is why we try to keep track of them."

"Why haven't you tracked where they have come from?" asked Bert. "Have you no idea of their source or location?"

"The answer to that is a definite no, but it makes your disclosure that you have another panel from the crashed craft even more important. If we can supplement markings from the first panel by any on the second, it may help us to form a view on the source."

"You have a second panel?" asked Chris with unconcealed surprise. "Why didn't you tell me before?"

"If he had told you earlier you would still be under detention," Dennis interrupted abruptly in response. Pointing to Bert he continued, "This farmer friend of yours has used his little secret to barter for your release. If I were you, I would say that you owe him a favour."

Although he felt sceptical about the highly moral stance that Dennis was describing to justify the secrecy and obfuscation Chris could not resist asking a final question. "Have you managed to incorporate the technology from the craft that you have salvaged?"

"Why are you asking me questions that you already know the answer to? I am not at liberty to discuss classified information," Dennis snapped. "All I can confirm is that we are working hard to make sure that we retain an edge over our enemies in the race to develop new systems."

It was obvious that nothing further was going to be said on this matter.

Dennis got out of the car indicating that their talk was over. He had picked up a clipboard with some papers attached from the dashboard. The paper pages fluttered up in the breeze as Dennis walked forward. The two other men followed and Dennis asked a colleague to drive Chris home. As Chris was about to walk away Dennis blocked his path and placed his hand over the surface of the papers on the clipboard.

"You need to sign this," Dennis commanded holding out a pen.

"What is it?" asked Chris.

"It's a non-disclosure agreement," Dennis hissed. From the look on his face there was no prospect of discussion.

Chris was weary and wanted to leave. He thought about protesting, but knew that resistance was futile. He signed.

Dennis whispered in his ear and Chris cringed as polluting

TWENTY
CLASSIFIED INFORMATION

Freedom is one of those things that can be taken for granted. It is only when it is removed that its value is fully appreciated. When he had been told that he was being released Chris had felt huge relief. He was weary after enduring captivity, interrogation and hostile suspicion. Now he had to consider the future consequences for his relationship with Joy. Her father had been implicated in the affair and he wondered if the family would blame him for dragging them into the whole sorry saga. His release had brought with it a sense of euphoria, of excitement about the future, of hope after adversity. On the other hand, the fear of what the authorities might do next deeply concerned him.

His first impulse had been to visit Joy and explain his side of the story. Newspapers had been reporting the attempts of the authorities to break up a ring of spies. Dennis had been working his magic in diverting attention away from St Eval and eulogising the efforts of the MOD in keeping the country safe. Nevertheless, rumours of strange lights in the sky continued to circulate in the locality. Chris fully intended to confide the full story of what had hot damp breath breached his personal space. "If a word of our conversation gets printed in your newspaper, I will deny everything and you will lose your freedom".

By this time Bert was making his way towards the barn. Dennis hurried to catch up still clutching his clipboard. He intended to get Bert's signature on the agreement, but he thought it prudent to wait until Bert had revealed the hidden panel. Bert looked back and waved towards Chris. He put one finger on his ear as he shouted, "I'll give you a call."

When they reached the huge stinking pile of manure under which the panel was hidden Bert pointed to a shovel. "If you want the panel you will need this."

"You've hidden it under there?" gasped Dennis in disgust. "We'd better find it quickly or you are going to literally find yourself in the shit."

happened with Joy. This was despite the warning that Dennis had issued. He wanted Joy to know that their suspicions had been well founded after all their long months of research. He was desperate to tell her that he had seen the craft that had collided with the turbine and that it was in a hangar being dismantled by the MOD. Few things could be more sensational than the sight of a crashed UFO. It was confirmation that humans are not alone in the Universe. Yet the warnings that Dennis had given forbidding disclosure worried him. It was one thing to risk retribution personally, but what about the risk to Joy if she also knew the full story. One problem was that Joy had been fully occupied with meeting the needs of her customers. This was the first test of the new business when hosting a full complement of guests. It was regrettable that they were working with the shadow of the spying allegations hanging over them. The business needed to get a good review and the whole family were doing their best to make sure that the outdoor experience for the college students was a good one. It was not good for his ego, but realistically Chris knew that Joy was too busy to see him. On the positive side, it gave him more time to consider what to say when they next met. He decided to send her a text message asking for a convenient time to meet.

Chris turned his attention to recovering his car from the police compound in Bodmin. He had received the paperwork to facilitate collection of the car and a breakdown truck had been sent to deliver the damaged vehicle to a garage approved by his insurance company. The insurance policy enabled Chris to use a car supplied by the garage until his own was made roadworthy.

Joy could understand why her father had been implicated. She felt annoyed that he had suffered the indignity of having his integrity questioned. After his return from questioning he had confirmed to his family that he had been working on a special defence project. He had no idea that he had been the subject of

Russian surveillance and had convinced the authorities that he was a victim of espionage not a participant. Joy was embarrassed that he had become involved because of her relationship with Chris. The two of them had delved in matters that were extremely sensitive to the authorities and they had not thought through the consequences. She knew that she shared some of the blame for what had happened. It was her who had encouraged Chris to continue digging for information. Personally, she had helped with the research over the last few months. In hindsight, they were way out of their depth in the murky world of official disinformation. She still felt annoyed that Chris had chosen that moment to carry out what was always going to be a risky observation. To embark on such a foolhardy venture at a time when she could not help or support him was reckless. She thought that they were in a partnership. Although her feelings were confused, Joy wanted to meet to talk things over. She had grown fond of Chris and needed to see him, but the realities of work restricted the opportunity.

The text message from Chris spurred her into action. The last day of the program for the college students would be Thursday. In the evening, the students were scheduled to make group presentations as part of a final social event. Joy checked with the other staff as to whether it would be possible to invite Chris. There were no objections and so she sent back a text message inviting Chris to attend. They would have a chance to talk things over later the same evening. Thursday evening was something that Chris was now very much looking forward to so that he could set the record straight.

As the end of the outdoor pursuits week approached, Jim reflected on what had been achieved. Fortunately, the October weather had been benevolent and the students had been able to partake in the full range of activities. The programme of activities had worked well. Each day the students had been split into their two groups with each group involved in a different activity. The group who had been cycling on the Camel trail on Saturday switched to the orienteering activity on Sunday. The Saturday orienteering group switched to cycling on Sunday. This made the best use of the available staff and equipment. The program of activities had also included, canoeing, abseiling, pony trekking, visits to Camelford Leisure Centre and Tintagel Castle.

The plan had been to keep the students busy so that the risks of homesickness and boredom would be reduced. Encouraging them to embrace the tasks had not always been easy, although the majority reacted positively. They knew that they had an opportunity to gain new skills. Jim had found the physical activity demanding and although he had shared the night duty rota with Janet, he had never felt fully relaxed. He had suspected that Janet would be a less than enthusiastic member of staff, fussing about her hair or worrying about breaking a nail. This had been an error of judgement on his part. She had thrown herself into the activities and joined the spirit of the venture. The students had respect for her and she had total control over them. This had not been a holiday and the responsibility for the safety of the students was ever present. The pleasing thing was that overall, the objectives of the residential had been achieved. Of course, there had been the usual hassles concerning clashes of personality, fraught romantic associations and occasional outbreaks of unacceptable behaviour.

Some surprising things had happened. Birch had responded to his new status as a courageous hero following the incident at the bunker. He was using his strong personality to demonstrate positive leadership to the others. He had participated and contributed to all the demands that had been made of him. Many of the students had formed new friendships and gained confidence. One of the most belligerent students had been humbled, his respect undermined, after his refusal to abseil off the summit of Rough Tor. He remained a muted foghorn for the rest of the week, much to everyone's relief. Some of the quieter students had visibly gained in confidence. A program of outdoor activities was never going to be Jim's first love in the education world, but he was pleased to observe the positive changes to each student's skill set. The residential had not been the waste of time that he had expected. It had demonstrated the contribution these courses made to personal development. Changes in the affective domain were not so easily measured. It was just that he felt more comfortable with his training manuals, measurable objectives and occupationally committed students. He was looking forward to leaving what he humorously referred to as 'The Wild West' and returning to the West Midlands conurbation.

Preparation for the Thursday night presentations was underway. Students would make group presentations about what their favourite moments had been, what they thought had worked well, what they had learned and what changes they would recommend for future visitors. There would be a ballot as to man and woman of the trip. Everyone would be eligible to cast a vote for the person who they thought had demonstrated the most in terms of personal development. Certificates of participation would be issued to all. Last, but not least, the highlight of the evening would be 'music night' in the Manor House.

Chris arrived at Grenah Manor just before the student presentations were due to start. His journey had not been without incident. He had driven along the Atlantic Highway, the road which connected Wadebridge with Camelford. Halfway between the two towns was a sign which pointed to a village called St Tudy. This right turn off the main road would cut sixteen miles off the journey to Grenah Manor as he knew that St Tudy was only a mile away from the Manor house. It was a cross country lane of variable width with intermittent passing places for vehicles in the narrowest sections. The lane wound its way through farmland and undulated dramatically making navigation treacherous. It was dark, but Chris decided that the detour would be worth taking as he expected little traffic at that time of day. He had been half aware that a single bright headlight had been following behind for some time. He had given it little regard. After making the turn Chris noticed that the single bright headlight had followed. The light dazzled in his rear-view mirror. If it was a motorcycle it was following dangerously close behind. Up ahead was the entrance to a farm with enough space to pull off the lane. Chris decided that he would allow the biker to pass. As expected, the motorcycle sailed past and disappeared up the road. Feeling glad that he would be able to continue without the constant dazzle Chris drove on carefully without incident until he approached a crossroad. Suddenly, without warning the motorcycle roared out from the left and skidded to a stop in the centre of the crossing. Chris braked hard and stopped a few yards short of the bike. It was hard to see any detail, but the rider stood astride of his machine dressed in black leathers and with the visor on his helmet pulled down. It would be easy to mistake him for Darth Vader. As Chris considered what to do the leather clad figure leaned forward, pressed his body onto the fuel tank and edged slowly past the stationary car with just inches to spare. As he passed, he gave the car roof a heavy thump with his fist before speeding away. Shock soon turned to fury as Chris felt a wave of anger surge through his veins.

"What an idiot!" Chris muttered to himself. "Does the arrogant fool think he's clever?"

His impulse was to turn and chase the biker. Perhaps, he could nudge him off the road to teach him a lesson. After a few seconds Chris realised that he was suffering from road rage and slowly more rational thoughts returned. Anyway, there was no chance of turning in time to follow the motorcycle and so he continued his journey, the anger slowly subsiding. Slowly, it dawned on him that although he was driving a different car, someone may still be tracking his movements. His arrival at Grenah Manor was comforting and after Joy had greeted him convivially, Chris began to relax.

Although less than a week had elapsed since they last met it seemed longer. There was the gulf of interrupted communication. It was like the ice had to be broken again. Time had mellowed Joy's irritation at what she thought to be Chris's impulsive behaviour. Chris had been freed and her father exonerated from accusations of involvement in the spying scandal. She realised that it was only because of her feelings towards these two important people in her life that the whole affair had stressed her so much. It had been hard to maintain professional focus with this drama going on in the background. A deep concern remained in her mind about how Chris had become mixed up with a spy and she was eager to ask Chris for his story about what had happened.

All the staff who had participated in the program needed to be fully occupied supervising the presentations and so Joy showed Chris to a seat next to her father. Henry had insisted that he wanted to be present to give respect and support to his wife and daughter at this important stage in their business. For the Penrose family a successful end to this program would greatly help the promotion of the next one. It was the first time that Chris had met Henry Penrose since the open day. He felt guilty that his actions had dragged Henry into the mess.

"I've heard that you have been questioned about the security issues at St Eval," said Chris apologetically. "I am so sorry that my actions have impacted on you."

Henry shrugged his shoulders. "It has been a horrible experience. Perhaps you should have thought more deeply about the consequences of your actions on others. My livelihood was put at risk and my honesty questioned. Thankfully, I have been exonerated. I presume that you have now been cleared of charges, or you wouldn't be here."

"That doesn't mean that I can just forget what I have observed or what I discovered," Chris replied. "I was released because I was innocent of the spying charges. I never went inside the perimeter of the airfield at St Eval, but the military started to chase me. I then had a road accident. Unfortunately, the other vehicle was driven by someone who had been spying on that old airbase."

"I was questioned about that man who came to the Open Day. You know that odd character who said that he had a holiday let in Plymouth. Was he the person who you collided with at St Eval?" asked Henry inquisitively.

"I have been censored by the authorities from discussing certain matters," Chris replied with a tone of disgust." I can say that we are thinking of the same person though."

The conversation was curtailed as the presentations began. Birch saw Chris sitting at the back of the room and gave a cheeky wink in recognition. Later he was given the 'Man of the Trip Award' partly in recognition of his role in the bunker rescue. It may have just been a paper certificate, but Birch was doubly pleased because it had been awarded by his peers and it was the only award he had ever received. Jim applauded warmly. It was good to think that Birch now had the chance to build on this positive experience.

The formality of the presentations eventually ended. There was a buzz of excitement as the meeting broke up and the students readied themselves for the entertainment. They had survived the week. They were going home tomorrow. There was going to be music and dancing. It would be nice to dress in something other than waterproofs.

Henry was not a lover of modern music and made his excuses to leave the gathering. Chris made his way over to where Alice and Joy were talking to the college staff. Janet always attracted attention with her coloured hair and she laughed as one of the students stopped to share a joke with her. On his way Chris stopped to congratulate Birch on his award and thank him for his help with the rescue.

"No problem," said Birch. "You were lucky though. If I had not had to hang back to fix my laces, you might still have been in there now. It was strange too, seeing that weird chick pointing towards your place of imprisonment."

Chris was mystified by this comment. "Who was pointing, I thought it was just you and Alice."

"There was someone pointing. We couldn't see very well, but it was the figure of a woman." Birch pulled out his mobile. "You've just reminded me. I took a photo on my phone."

Birch scrolled through his photo album and stopped at the photo of the bunker. "There she is. It's a bit hazy because of the light."

There was no mistake. There was a figure pointing towards the bunker. It was definitely a female shape wearing what appeared to be old fashioned clothing and wearing a bonnet. Her features were obscured by the poor light.

"Without her attracting our attention we might never have gone close enough to hear your calls."

Before Chris was able to say anything more, they were joined by Alice who smiled at Birch. "You have done well and deserve to enjoy yourself tonight."

"Will you be buying me a drink?" asked Birch in his usual cheeky manner.

He did not wait for a reply and quickly moved the conversation on. "Just showing that picture I took of the woman at the bunker. Don't you remember her pointing? Odd looking babe, isn't she?"

Alice had been meaning to ask about the photo, but she had been so busy it had slipped her mind. Now she saw the picture the image stirred a memory. She would need to investigate further to be sure. "Would you object if I copied your photo onto the pictures folder in my laptop? It will not take a minute and then you can join your friends. I would like to check a few details."

The two of them went in search of the laptop and Chris found a chair next to where Joy was sitting, chatting to the two college staff. Jim was talking about life in Southfield College of Further Education. Joy introduced Chris to the two college staff and he asked Jim whether he thought the visit had been successful.

Jim thought carefully before answering. "To be honest I haven't got a lot of experience of this type of outdoor residential. I did once visit the Lake District with some foundation level apprentices who were employed in a factory. I was lucky to get back in one piece!"

"What happened?" asked Chris.

"The Centre where we stayed organised a search and rescue mission. I was taken to a remote crag and told that as I had a broken leg, I would have to await rescue. The apprentices were given a briefing including map references and they had to find me and bring me to safety. I was not allowed to call out."

"It sounds like you must have had a long and boring wait," said Chris.

Jim grimaced as the memory returned. "I could hear the apprentices crunching through the forest and making a lot of noise, like a herd of elephants. Eventually, one of them found me and called the others by blowing a whistle. When I told them of my fake injury, they told me to keep quiet or they would break my other leg. They bound me tightly to a stretcher and started to drag me at speed down the steep hillside. The idea was for two people to carry the stretcher down the track, but one of the lads decided to take a short cut through the trees. He dragged me on the stretcher as though he was being chased by demons. Any sapling in the way he tore out of the ground, we bounced over rocky areas as if they didn't exist."

Joy was appalled by this reckless behaviour. "Was there no other supervisor there to check on them?" she asked.

"No, it was supposed to be a teamwork exercise where the apprentices were expected to use their initiative."

"Were the apprentices disciplined afterwards?" asked Joy.

"I never said anything. I was just relieved it was over. In fact, I could see the funny side, although it could have been a disaster. Later the team was given an award for the fastest rescue in the whole year! I must admit that I had been sceptical about the value of the trip, but by the end of the residential I recognised a real change in their confidence and attitude. You asked me about the success of this visit and I would answer that by pointing out the change in young Birch for example."

"I can understand that your job requires a lot of patience," said Chris.

"Well yes, I think that's true," said Janet. "You need patience, perseverance and sometimes a sense of humour as Jim has just explained. People think that teaching is an easy job. Short hours, long holidays, trips to Cornwall. I can tell you that it is not what it seems. The hours are long and both staff and students need the breaks to recharge their batteries. As a lecturer you must constantly prepare and refine each lesson. It is a bit like acting except that the audience are not all thirsting to experience the performance. You must develop and deliver your material, manage the group, assess and feedback. At the end of the day you can get a lot of satisfaction though when you see someone has made progress."

Both the college staff had some interesting stories to tell about life in the College. It was quite different work to that which Chris was used to, but interesting to listen to a different perspective. "I have never thought that teaching was easy, but I can see that it can be rewarding," Chris reflected.

Although they were good company, Chris was glad when the college staff went to check on their students. He was impatient to talk to Joy alone He had been thinking about this coming conversation with Joy for days. She was the person who had endured the close encounter that had started the whole episode. The thought of all that they had gone through together over the summer months. The fact that they had spent so much time and energy investigating this matter only for the truth to be discovered but not disclosed was wrong. Joy deserved to know the truth. She was entitled to know what he knew. The problem was that if he shared his knowledge, she would also share the burden and the danger that accompanied it. Chris wondered if Dennis already suspected that he had been economical with the full story. He had been summoned to a meeting with Dennis tomorrow morning. Apparently, Dennis wanted to review his story and give an update about the results of Peter's autopsy. It was not a meeting that Chris was looking forward to.

As Chris recounted to Joy all the events that had led to his ultimate detention the memories flooded back. The car chase, the accident, Peter's gun, imprisonment in the bunker, rescue, and the spying suspicion poured out from his memory. Chris found himself physically flushed with the stress. He held back from mentioning seeing Peter's recording of the hangar contents and that Peter's body was found on Innyvale Farm.

Joy had listened earnestly to the story. "I can see why the defence people would suspect you of spying. They would not think it was just bad luck that you chose the same Friday night as Peter to do your snooping, especially when they knew that you had met Peter before at this address. Peter also spoke to my dad on the same day and I understand that's why he got involved."

"They made a wrong evaluation of the circumstantial evidence," Chris sighed. "He was spying for a foreign power. I was just observing the airfield to check on the substance of the UFO sightings. The thing that saved me was the tracking that the Defence people subjected me to. They knew that I had been honest in handing in that metal part and they had tracked my movements for months. My editor gave me his backing although he had to say that he had not authorised observation of the airfield. Peter was already known to security as a low-level spy and I suppose they were tracking him too. As for your dad I had no idea that he was working on a project for the MOD. No wonder he wasn't overly impressed with our research into UFO's."

"He would never betray the trust put in him and I feel awful that I have been the cause of his integrity being questioned," said Joy sorrowfully.

"It was absolutely unintentional," Chris replied. "I need to talk to your dad more fully at some point."

Joy was not consoled by this comment. "We both need to think more carefully about the consequences of our actions. Also, you haven't explained about how you eventually got released."

This was the moment that Chris had to decide whether to divulge his knowledge of the contents of the hangar. He was thinking about the consequences of telling Joy. What would the defence authorities do if they knew that their secrecy had been compromised? From his work as a journalist Chris knew how ruthless the state could be. There were cases where people had been undermined by misinformation, even declared to be mentally unstable. Some had been treated with drugs, subjected to hypnosis or been imprisoned for years. Occasionally, people disappeared and were never heard of again. Others had been poisoned. He was reluctant to expose Joy or any other member of her family to these risks. Yet, Joy had already become involved by her encounter on the moor. There she sat next to him in all innocence. How could he pretend to care about her whilst continuing this awful deception? It would be cruel to keep her in the dark after all they had been through.

Chris chose his words carefully. "I agree I need to be more cautious. Our future safety is more important than research. Anyway, my editor has forbidden any more reports on this matter.

Let us look to the future without dark shadows hanging over us." Dennis Torrance's voice was ringing in his ear about the need to ensure secrecy.

Joy frowned. "You still haven't explained what convinced the authorities to release you. I suspect that you haven't told me the full story."

"They remain suspicious of me, but only have circumstantial evidence which is insufficient for a conviction. I am in the position of being released without being completely believed."

"There is another thing that worries me." Joy was too intelligent to be fobbed off by anyone. "Peter was a traitor, but he spared your life in that bunker. If the Russians know that you are still alive, you are going to be in danger?"

Chris thought about the fate that had befallen Peter. His death was unexplained. If it was not the Russians who had killed him, who on earth could have left him so ceremonially positioned in that field? The chilling thought that there may be more danger from extra-terrestrial sources than earthly ones haunted Chris's mind.

Hiding his concerns behind bravado Chris spoke optimistically.

"Peter is dead. Bert found his body together with a second Russian spy on Innyvale Farm. I have no idea what the Russian controllers have discovered." Immediately he realised that he had made a mistake.

"Bert found the bodies on his farm?" Joy exclaimed. "Why would two spies be found on dead on Bert's farm?"

It was time to confide the whole story. There was no point in prevaricating. Joy would have to be told the full story of Peter's recording of the contents inside the hangar and the role of the second spy.

As Chris told the story of his captivity in the bunker Joy found herself becoming increasingly frightened. "Did you see what he recorded?" she gasped.

"Yes, but I didn't tell the authorities because I was worried about what they would do."

"Well you need to tell me, as I am the person who had the close encounter," said Joy sternly.

"They have a damaged craft in the hangar next to a drone aircraft. It is almost certainly the craft that hit the turbine near the farm. It looks just as you described. I think it must be the same craft because the damage is consistent with a violent collision. I only saw a bit of the recording, but it looked as though the military were trying to reverse engineer the technology so that it could be used to improve the prototype of their drone."

"So, this was incontrovertible evidence that an alien craft had collided with the turbine that night." It felt as though a burden had been lifted off Joy's shoulders.

What happened that night was not the product of her imagination or a case of mistaken identification. She never thought that she would hear confirmation of what all her instincts had told her. This news was scary, but exciting. The implication must be that there was intelligent life elsewhere and they had the technology for interplanetary travel.

Chris touched Joy's arm. "We must keep this to ourselves. Do not tell anyone, not even your family. When it concerns a project which is above top secret, knowledge can be a dangerous thing. We must never underestimate the power of the authorities. We could become another case of people who have disappeared without a trace."

"That sounds a bit melodramatic," said Joy reproachfully.

"It won't be melodramatic if we both end up dead like Peter and his associate. Not to mention the effect on your family. Remember your dad is doing work for the defence people. Besides that is not the end of the story." Chris was concerned that Joy's naivety could be their downfall.

"You mean there is something else that you haven't told me about?" said Joy indignantly.

"Bert never told anyone that he had a second section of the crashed craft. When Dennis drove me to the farm to help identify the two bodies, Bert heard him threaten to keep me locked up. Bert bartered my release in return for showing Dennis a second panel that he had hidden since the time of the crash."

This revelation was both a shock and a surprise to Joy who could not hide her feelings. "I think we need to pay Bert a visit. We need to talk through the whole saga. The thought of knowing what most other people do not know makes me fearful, but I cannot leave our investigation incomplete after what you have told me. There are some loose ends that we need to tidy up."

There was a determination about Joy that Chris had never seen before. She brushed her hand through her hair and smiled. "Let's try to relax and enjoy the rest of the evening." Joy accepted that she had finally heard the full story. She was unaware of the consequences that her knowledge of it could bring.

She took Chris's hand and together they walked towards the pulsating sounds of the 'music event' where the students were celebrating the last day of their course.

TWENTY-ONE
DEPARTURE

The final checks had been made under beds, inside drawers and bathroom shelves. Each student trundled out of the building with their heavy suitcases. Some felt that the week had been an ordeal. Most had gained something from the outdoor experience even if it was only personal pride in surviving the week. New friendships had been made and a newly formed spirit of teamwork was in evidence as the students helped the staff to load the cases onto the buses. When this essential task was complete Jim sat down on a bench next to Alice so that the final paperwork checks could be completed. Joy and Janet were busily checking names as the students boarded each bus. Alice beckoned for Birch to join her on the bench. She explained to Jim that she had received some news about Birch's photograph of the spectral woman at the bunker.

Struthers nudged Birch to alert him. "Your friend is calling for you," he said sarcastically.

"Get lost you loser," Birch sneered as he sauntered over to join Jim and Alice. "Any jobs going here, or do I have to go back with the rest?" he asked cheerily.

Alice smiled. "We'll keep you in mind for the future, but I wanted to tell you about your photo before you leave."

"Did you find anything interesting?" asked Birch.

"I have to tell you that more than 170 years ago, there was a murder committed not far from where we were that day on the edge of Davidstow airfield. I had a vague memory of viewing a television documentary about this murder. I think it was featured on BBC Spotlight. Anyway, something about your photo struck a chord. It was partly the location and partly the clothes that the woman was wearing. Not really expecting much I ran a Google search and the details of the murder case emerged. It seems the murder took place in 1844 and the name of the victim was Charlotte Dymond. Eyewitnesses described her appearance as wearing a green and white striped dress, a red shawl and white bonnet. She also carried an umbrella".

Alice fumbled in her bag and compared the printed image taken from Birch's phone to an artist's impression of Charlotte Dymond embedded in the internet article. Although not totally identical it was obvious that the two photos were of the same person.

Jim and Birch looked at the images in awe. "That is weird. The similarity is unmistakable." gasped Jim.

A low whistle emerged from Birch's mouth. "Cool, but how can that be?"

Alice's frowned. "At first I wondered whether your camera had an earlier image of someone etched into the memory card and this had become partially overwritten by the new image. On close inspection this does not seem to be the case. I can only say that the camera has captured an image of this person who lived and died near to the airfield bunker. She was alone, on the edge of the bleak moor with nobody to help when her assailant cut her throat."

"Was the murderer caught?" asked Birch.

"The story is that Charlotte was murdered by a jealous boyfriend. He was arrested, tried and found guilty. Later he was hung for the crime in Bodmin jail. It was a crime of passion. Apparently, there have been occasional sightings of Charlotte at various locations on the moorland. So, if it was her that we saw, we were not the first".

"So, a ghost showed us where the victim was. Wait 'till I tell the lads back home about this," smiled Birch proudly as he stood up, about to reunite with the other students by the minibus. "I still don't understand why she would appear to us. We had no connection with her past".

Alice handed the copy of the photo to Birch. "I can't explain it. It is an anomaly. If you want to read the details of the case, you can look it up on the internet when you get home. Charlotte Dymond had a traumatic ordeal which ended with her murder. Chris Arbor was enduring a traumatic ordeal imprisoned in the dark bunker. Maybe the energy generated from the desperation of Chris Arbor's predicament fused with the surrounding environment. After all, it was a location soaked with vibrations from the past. I have heard that physical objects can store patterns of energy from the past, a bit like rings which record the life of a tree. It is possible that his mental anguish activated that left behind by Charlotte Dymond and the result was the spectre captured on the photo. Whatever it was, her intervention saved his life."

Birch laughed. "I heard that you Cornish people had pagan beliefs. Now I am beginning to believe it's true." He started to walk away and then stopped abruptly as a new thought entered his head. "Is the victim buried near here?"

"She is buried in a church graveyard next to the A395. In fact, there is a stone memorial in her honour near to where her body was found at Roughtor Ford" Alice replied. "Read the full story when you get home."

Birch nodded and walked towards his bus, deep in thought. The story had captured his imagination.

"I think I will read the story too," Jim smiled as he searched in his pocket for the minibus keys. "It is a bizarre mystery which is going to raise eyebrows when I report this back to my colleagues in the staffroom."

Before they left the two members of the college staff offered their thanks. "On behalf of us all we would like to thank you for your hospitality and the hard work you have done this week. It is certainly a residential that we won't forget in a hurry." It was a heartfelt sentiment.

Packed, loaded and refuelled, with all students accounted for, the minibuses left on the long haul back to Birmingham. Birch cheerily blew a kiss through the window. There were many other faces pressed to the windows and lots of waving hands. Alice and Joy looked at each other and laughed, before breathing a sigh of relief. It had been tough work, but they were pleased that their business venture was proving to be a success. The Centre seemed deserted after all the activity. No voices, no activity, just the strong memories of the people who had been there moments before. It felt like standing on the platform of a condemned railway station after the last train had departed.

Not too far away on that same Friday morning Chris Arbor was sitting in the interview room inside Bodmin Police Station. It was uncomfortable returning to the place where he had so recently been interrogated. Chris could feel his body temperature rising as the stressful memories returned. This time it was different though because he had volunteered to meet with Dennis. Also, the door was not being guarded and he could leave if he wanted to. He was curious to hear the results of the autopsy on the body of Peter Vadim. Ever since viewing the bodies on Innyvale Farm Chris suspected that there was something symbolic in the way the bodies had been arranged. This was not some random murder with bodies dumped or hidden. It was a ritualistic display. Some form of unspoken communication.

Dennis was late. He liked to keep people waiting in this featureless room. It gave them time to reflect. It raised anxiety levels, making people more nervous, more prone to revealing their true feelings. Eventually, the door opened and Dennis took his seat at the opposite side of the table. He placed a folder on the table and impassively started to flick through the papers inside. The silence was making Chris feel uncomfortable, so he decided to speak.

"Have you found the cause of Peter Vadim's death?"

Dennis looked up from the folder and checked his watch. He stared across at Chris with a deadpan expression. There was an uncomfortable pause before he replied.

"It would appear that he suffered a catastrophic heart attack."

"Well that's not surprising. He had been having a stressful time. What about the wound on his neck?" Chris enquired.

"The report says that it looks like a restraint wound, probably a burn from a rope. It had been treated with a substance that the laboratory has been unable to identify."

It was beginning to annoy Chris that Dennis never volunteered information without having to be questioned first. Worse still, Dennis had a habit of turning the questions you asked around, making you feel uneasy. Choosing his words carefully Chris asked, "So we are no further forward?"

Dennis leaned back in his chair and folded his arms across his chest. His body language suggested that he anticipated an argument.

"When we made a thorough search of the victim's clothes, we found that the lining of his jacket pocket was ripped. A small scrap of paper torn from a notebook had become trapped between the lining and the fabric of the jacket. Our friend, Peter, had scribbled a note which he may have used to convey a message to his handlers."

"He wrote a message?" Chris repeated. "What did it say?"

"It was a coded message which had to be analysed by our experts," Dennis stated triumphantly.

He returned to the file and extracted a plastic bag containing a grubby fragment of paper. He held it up for Chris to see, like a magician revealing the final playing card at the end of a trick. Just legible were six groups of letters: **wkuhh fdpe wkuhh ydz wkuhh nqrz**

"It seems that your friend was fond of the writings of Julius Caesar! He used a cipher known by our experts as a Caesar Shift. If you write out the twenty-six letters of the alphabet on one line and then underneath repeat the alphabet shifting the places to the left from anywhere between one to twenty-five places you have a cipher. By testing the six groups of letters in Peter's message we started shifting one letter, then two and so on. Eventually, by shifting just three letters to the left we got a meaningful result. I will leave it for you to decode from our grid." Dennis provided the key to the code and pushed a pencil and paper across to Chris.

Plain	A	B	C	D	E	F	G	H	I	J	K	L	M
Cipher	d	e	f	g	h	i	j	k	l	m	n	o	p
Plain	N	O	P	Q	R	S	T	U	V	W	X	Y	Z
Cipher	q	r	s	t	u	v	w	x	y	z	a	b	c

Chris reluctantly set about the task, although he felt that he was being manipulated in some sort of mind game. It did not take very long until Chris had the decoded message which read

'three came, three saw, three know'.

Chris felt Dennis's piercing eyes survey him. It felt as though these sharp blue eyes were trying to penetrate his head as he read back what must have been some of the last jottings that Peter had ever made.

There was a silence before the ominous sound of Dennis Torrance's voice vibrated through the room. "Our analysis concludes that there were three observers to the DVD we know that was viewed in the bunker. Peter and his contact make two people. Who do you think the third observer could be?"

Chris gave a hollow laugh. "That phrase could mean a number of things. You can only speculate. There is nothing in the message that would prove anything. You do not know when it was written. Even if it did refer to three people in the bunker it remains vague and ambiguous."

"We know it was written at the time you were in the bunker with the spies," said Dennis. "If you look carefully there is a date written on the top right of the note. It is faint, smudged and hard to see, but you can just about read it."

Chris knew as soon as he had spoken that his attempts to undermine Dennis's suspicions were doomed to failure. He just hoped that his terse reply would not betray his growing sense of panic. He knew that he had potentially been incriminated. Why Peter had been stupid enough to write things in his diary under such circumstances was difficult to understand. Maybe he could not get a signal whilst in the bunker and decided to note down a message for later transmission.

"He can't have been a very professional spy if he wrote that down and failed to destroy it."

Dennis shrugged his broad shoulders. "Well I have given the statement you made the other day a lot of thought and I have concluded that on the balance of probability you did observe the DVD. I think it highly likely that in the dark with a glowing screen near to you, given your past interest in the subject of UFOs, that you were not able to resist a look. Maybe you only had a glimpse, but coupled with that message I strongly suspect that your statement is not a complete account of the events in that bunker."

Chris quickly considered his options. He could try to continue the story he had told when last interviewed. Alternatively, he could hold his hands up and admit that he had seen the recording. In the end he decided to say nothing. An awkward pause followed before Dennis reacted. His response was surprisingly casual. His tone was sharp as though he had lost all patience and had made the decision to move on regardless.

"Alright, you are exercising your right to remain silent. I trust that you will remain silent about the whole affair as we discussed the other day. We will be watching every move you make, checking every word you say. You know that bad things will happen if you don't remain discrete."

Dennis closed his folder, swivelled round as if on parade and left the room. The door shut behind him with a heavy thud. He had what he wanted. His own experts were busy examining both the panels from the crashed craft. Nothing much was to be gained from detaining the troublesome journalist. He would make sure that an eye was kept on Chris Arbor in the immediate future. Another name would be added to the list of people whose loyalty to the Crown was doubtful.

Leaving the threatening atmosphere of the police station felt liberating. Chris drew a deep breath of clean Cornish air before making his way home. He knew that he would have to be careful with the knowledge of what he had seen on the recording, but it was the fate of the Russian spies that concerned him most. Their deaths remained mysterious and the circumstances unresolved.

TWENTY-TWO

SYMBOLS

—

After the recent events Chris was finding it difficult to settle back into the routine of his job as a journalist. It was the same desk in the same open office, but it felt different. Maybe it was just his imagination, but people seemed a bit more furtive when they spoke to him. He thought he noticed eyes being averted when he walked through the office. Of more worry though were his own thoughts, which kept returning to things that Dennis Torrance had told him about alien craft. The confinement in the bunker and the shock of seeing the dead spies on the farm haunted him. If they could be so easily disposed of the same thing could happen to himself, Joy or Bert. He was about to leave his desk to check a story that had come in about a robbery in Wadebridge when his phone rang. It was Joy. It was good to hear her soft voice again.

"Bert has been in contact with me," said Joy. She sounded quite excited. "He wants to know if we can call at his farm this evening. He has something to show us and wants to disclose it urgently. Will you be free to travel over there tonight?"

After flicking through his diary Chris was able to respond immediately. "Yes, I can pick you up at the Outdoor Pursuits Centre about 7 o'clock if that suits you. Did Bert give any clue as to what he wants to disclose?"

"He didn't say specifically. I got the impression he has one or two photos of the farm that he wants us to view. He was quite insistent that we visit in person."

The couple arrived at Innyvale Farm with their expectations raised, wondering just what it was that Bert thought so important that it necessitated a visit to his farm. They had decided to use Joy's car and were in good spirits, busy in conversation, unaware that unseen eyes were watching from a distance through powerful binoculars.

Scattered over Bert's living room table were a couple of enlarged photographs that had been produced on a colour printer. They were from exposures on his camera taken on the night of the close encounter. They had since been deleted from the camera. He had been keeping the photographs under lock and key, worried about them being confiscated by the security forces. The quality of the photos was not brilliant, but it was immediately clear that they showed each of the damaged panels from the unidentified craft that had collided with the wind turbine. There was a blurring because of the camera not being kept steady and they were very dark. However, there was enough definition to show that the panels had suffered a violent impact. The impact area looked to be where there had been openings on the surface of the craft. It was not possible to tell if each of the panels was a door or an inspection hatch of some sort. The stricken craft had offered its most vulnerable area to the point of contact with the turbine blades. They were scuffed, distorted and spattered with mud. The impact had torn them violently from their connections to the main body of the craft. Fortunately, there were markings faintly visible. They were engraved or moulded into the surface rather than being painted. Lacking colour definition and hard to see, as they were the same colour as the surface they were moulded on, they were very indistinct. The first panel displayed some sort of big chair or skyscraper with a small star and a little circle near the top. Where the panels had joined a triangular shape straddled the junction between the sections. A snake shape on the photo of panel number two was clearly visible. Joy made clear drawings of what she thought the images would be if the damage were removed.

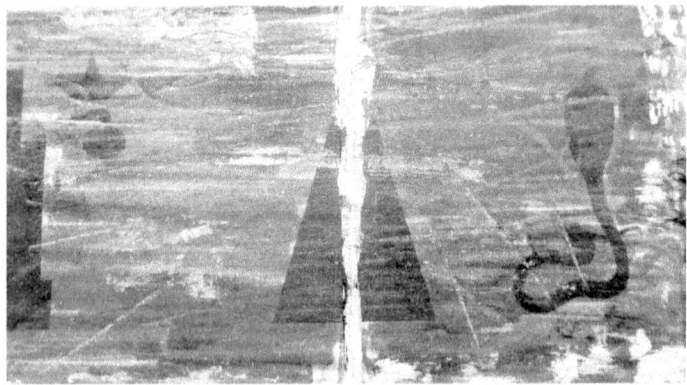

"Wow!! These are fantastic," exclaimed Joy. "I wonder if there is a connection between the shapes. They may symbolise something. I have to admit that I haven't a clue as to what they mean."

"No need to worry about security," said Bert with an audacious smile. "I just downloaded them into a file on my computer and printed them. There is no other record."

Joy was not alone. None of the observers around the table had any idea what the shapes represented. There was a silence as each person searched for some connection, some plausible interpretation of the shapes. Eventually, Chris spoke.

"When I was studying at Exeter University, I met a Professor from the Faculty of History. We did not talk much because it was at a prize giving presentation. It just happened that by chance I was seated next to him. He asked me about my degree course and so I enquired into his specialism. He told me that he specialised in Logographic systems."

"What's that in English?" asked Bert.

"Apparently, a logogram is a written character that represents a word or a phrase. An example could be an arrow shape intended to show direction like a road sign. It could be that the shapes on the panel are some sort of logogram. During our short, but interesting chat, he explained that there were problems with some symbols in that someone viewing them could easily misinterpret them. The arrow could be taken to mean a weapon. His Faculty were researching symbols, their use, their clarity or their ambiguity. I know it is uncertain that he would be of any use in this context, but I am willing to contact him if you think it would be helpful."

Bert was the first to respond. "I think that would be a splendid idea. His area of expertise sounds like it could be just the sort we need. Left to our own devices we could spend months ploughing through books and still get nowhere. You can be sure that our 'friend' Dennis Torrance is doing his best to interpret the symbols. We would be the last people he would tell if he found something. So, if that Professor friend of yours can assist, that may be our best chance to improve our understanding."

"Why don't we make a copy of the shapes by taking a photo of your prints using a mobile, just as a precaution," suggested Joy. "It would be insurance just in case the authorities try to deprive you of the copies. I can just see the headline, **'Burglary at Innyvale Farm – nothing of value taken'**…" At least we will have a secondary record."

"Good thinking. Let's do that now," Chris agreed.

Bert had no objection, so Joy wasted no time taking her shots. After inspecting the results on her mobile Joy looked up and smiled. "These won't win any prizes, but they do give us a backup copy. Chris can attach the photo to his email when he messages his contact at the university".

"I know it may sound over cautious, but I would rather just send him your drawings of the symbols. We can explain where they came from if we get the chance to meet him," said Chris.

Bert and Joy agreed that it would be prudent to be discrete until they could judge the Professor's reaction.

On their way home Chris told Joy that he would try to contact the Professor the next day. He was struggling to remember his name. He was confident that he would recognise it from the names of Faculty members listed on the University website. The Professor was about to receive a very unusual email. Chris wondered how he would react to seeing the symbols and whether it would be best to keep quiet about where they had come from. He convinced himself that it would be expedient to address the UFO issue later when the Professor raised the inevitable question as to the context of where the symbols originated. This was, of course, presuming the Professor would not just dismiss the symbols as of little interest. The wording of the email would need to stimulate his curiosity without appearing to have been sent as a prank! If the Professor invited them to a meeting, that would be ideal. Chris was preoccupied with these issues as Joy drove them back to Grenah Manor. She did not notice the single headlight which had followed them all the way back from the farm.

As a journalist, Chris did not find it difficult to find the Professor he had met whilst a student at Exeter University. It was routine research. Professor Buckle no longer worked at Exeter. Following enquiries through his own contacts at the University he had found that the Professor had moved to take up a post within the History Faculty at Bristol University. As it had been a while since his casual conversation with Professor Buckle, Chris sent him an email which started with the phrase 'You may not remember, but we met at a prize giving presentation in Exeter some years ago.' Chris explained in the email that he and a couple of friends had found symbols on some damaged metal panels recovered from a field. Although he had photographs of the panels, he could not interpret the meaning of the symbols. He attached the symbols that Joy had drawn to the email and asked if it would be possible to meet to discuss the matter more fully as there were unexplained issues surrounding the composition and origins of the panels. It seemed a flimsy request to make to a Professor without him knowing the full story, but much to Chris's surprise, Professor Buckle responded positively, offering to meet with him and his two friends on the Friday of that week. Bert was unable to leave his work at the farm, but Joy was free to travel to Bristol on the Friday and accompanied Chris on the journey.

TWENTY-THREE
PROFESSOR BUCKLE

'Heaven above, Heaven below;
Stars above, Stars below;
All that is over, under shall show.'
Tabula Smaragdina

It turned out to be a cloudy morning with heavy showers punctuating their journey along the A30 and northward along the M5. Bright headlights reflected off the wet surface of the carriageway. They passed convoys of heavy vehicles which threw up clouds of spray, taxing the efforts of the wipers to keep the windscreen clear. It was not pleasant driving with Chris concentrating on their safe passage rather than indulging in conversation. Joy was hoping that their journey would be worthwhile, although she knew the Professor would need to ask them for more details than they had so far disclosed.

Professor Buckle met the couple in his study within the campus of the University. One wall of the study housed a library of books from floor to ceiling. The room was wood panelled and although there were windows on one side it felt a bit gloomy. There was the faint smell of cigar smoke tinging the air. Buckle was a man in his mid-fifties. His desk looked well used with the veneer worn way on the top surface where most of the paperwork passed. On one end a pile of folders balanced precariously, one on top of another. At the other an untidy stack of books. Seated centrally between these towers of paper the Professor peered at them over the top of his spectacles. He was wearing a cream jacket that looked as if it needed ironing. A red handkerchief casually flopped from the top pocket. As he rose to greet them Chris caught a glimpse of red braces with the image of a snake curling upwards. This was a person who had aged since their last encounter at Exeter. Here was a man with a ruddy complexion and rotund physique who looked as though his dietary, drinking and smoking habits needed to be reviewed. Nevertheless, he warmly greeted the couple, kissing Joy on her cheek after Chris introduced her as his partner. Resuming his seat and sliding the images of the symbols that Chris had emailed across the desk, the Professor spoke with a faint West Country accent.

"These symbols pose quite a few questions for us to consider! As you can see, I have had them printed and enlarged to make it easier to compare to shapes in my books. However, the symbols are not those usually displayed on metal panels manufactured in the twenty first century. Where have you been conducting your archaeology as I am curious as to the source?"

Chris looked at Joy with wrinkled brows. He knew that they would have to be honest with the Professor if they were to benefit from his expertise. There was no point prevaricating.

"They are panels that were left amongst the debris after an unidentified aircraft collided with a wind turbine on the edge of Bodmin Moor!"

With his eyebrows raised perceptibly, the Professor's head moved backwards as if confirming incredulity.

"Is that so?" His voice sounded defensive and understandably sceptical. "By unidentified aircraft, are you implying an alien craft?"

It was obvious that the Professor would need to hear the full story if he were to be convinced of their sincerity. Joy took a breath and started to relate the events of the night, all those months ago, when the whole saga started. She avoided reference to the military, Russian spies and Chris's unfortunate experience with the defence people.

The Professor listened politely, occasionally jotting notes on a blank sheet of A4 which lay on the table in front of him. There was a period of silence before he spoke as he absorbed the story. "I don't want to sound patronising, but that must have been a frightening experience for you my dear. When did this incident happen?"

"It was in the spring whilst we were lambing on the farm where I worked."

Joy explained that the site of the collision had been cordoned off and all debris confiscated by the army. "After Chris wrote an article about my experience, we were warned to keep quiet."

"Yes, I do remember reading something about this now I come to think about it." Professor Buckle looked at Joy over his glasses. "So, I presume that any photos you took must have been taken before the army arrived, immediately after the collision."

Joy nodded. If it could be avoided, she had no intension of involving Bert or revealing the circumstances of their struggles with the military.

The Professor turned back towards Chris "Quite a scoop for your newspaper, I should imagine? Have you got any more photographic evidence?"

Chris sighed. "I'm afraid this is the only evidence we have."

"The whole business has caused me a lot of trouble with both my editor and the MOD", Chris sighed. "That's why I think there is a hidden agenda and I am hoping that your expertise might help to throw more light on the origins of the craft."

Professor Buckle examined the prints carefully, like a doctor reviewing a patient's X rays. There was another pause before he spoke. "Do the authorities know that you have these prints?"

"They don't know and we would like to keep it that way. That is one of the reasons why we thought that it would be best to talk to someone we knew and believed we could trust to be discrete," said Chris. He knew that sometimes a bit of subtle flattery could lubricate co-operation. On the other hand, it could also backfire spectacularly. It was a risk that he thought worth taking under the circumstances.

The Professor rubbed his chin as he mulled over the prints. "The authorities always want to control the flow of information. I can see that they would not be happy if these prints suddenly appeared in the press. I think that this implies that they already know more than is common knowledge about the metal panels in your photo. I am wondering that after such a serious collision the entire craft could have crashed nearby. If that is the case, past experience would suggest, the military will have spirited it away somewhere for further examination. I also understand that you need to be cautious as the more people that you involve in your investigations the greater the risk that you will be silenced. You obviously feel that the risk of exposure will be more than compensated for by enhancement of your knowledge and understanding."

The Professor took a sharp intake of breath before continuing. He gave the impression of someone who had serious doubts about becoming involved, but his curiosity was winning against expediency.

"This makes a lot more sense now that you have explained the context in which the symbols are displayed. The last time we met we had a short chat about Logograms if my memory is correct. Since your prints show several symbols, I consider Logographic systems will be relevant to help answer your question about meanings. These systems are really a form of writing where groups of symbols can represent a concept or tell a story. For example, an eye can be used as a symbol to mean observation. A tear shape could mean rain. If you show an eye and then a tear together this usually means sadness. The combination of symbols tells more than just an isolated one. Your prints show what appears to be a seat with a little star shape, a triangle and a snake. These symbols remind me of Egyptian Hieroglyphs. I have to ask myself which hieroglyphs include these symbols."

"I thought they looked like Egyptian hieroglyphs too," said Joy excitedly. She felt annoyed that she had not focussed on the similarity herself. "I can see the connection, but do the shapes translate into anything meaningful?"

"Actually, they are quite revealing," replied the professor. "In ancient Egyptian, the hieroglyph of a serpent means both 'serpent' and 'body'. If the serpent is depicted as a cobra the hieroglyph means both 'serpent' and 'goddess'. The chair hieroglyph depicts a throne commonly associated with the Egyptian Goddess Isis. Triangles are identified with pyramid or obelisk designs linked with phallic symbols. The combination of the symbols could refer to the fertility of the star Goddess Isis. This is interesting because the Goddess Isis is associated with the star Sirius. If I were to extrapolate these symbols into some generic meaning I would guess that they were associated with the 'Dog Star, Sirius in the constellation of Canis Major."

"Is it too big a jump to imagine that because these symbols are engraved on a spacecraft, they identify the origin of the craft as coming from the star Sirius," asked Chris.

The Professor held out his hands and shrugged his shoulders. "If my astronomical memory serves me correctly the brightest star in the night sky is Sirius. Venus and Jupiter are brighter, but they are planets. The reason that Sirius is so bright is because of its size and the fact that it is closer to Earth than other stars. It is an interesting star because it has a white dwarf orbiting it. It is a star duo system."

"Excuse me for interrupting, but what is a white dwarf?" said Chris.

"When stars like our sun get old and exhaust all their nuclear fuel only a hot core remains. They become a white dwarf. This white dwarf is enormously powerful gravitationally and causes Sirius to wobble. As you know stars like our sun are uninhabitable, but sometimes they have planetary systems. As far as I am aware Sirius does not have detectable planets in orbit."

Joy had listened carefully taking in all this information. She did not know anything about astronomy or the star Sirius. What she remembered was the discussion with Chris about life on planets within the habitable zone of stars. Sirius did not sound like a likely source of intelligent life. More intriguing to her was why an alien craft should carry markings so closely resembling Egyptian hieroglyphs. Perplexed and a little confused she spoke to the others in a hushed voice. A frown clouded her face as she spoke. "I am finding it difficult to understand the links between ancient Egypt, an alien spacecraft and the significance of the star Sirius!"

Chris and the Professor looked at each other and it was clear that Chris was also unclear.

"Well I am not surprised you are both unclear because there is a lot to absorb," said the Professor with a smile. "There may not be a link. It could just be the name of the craft. After all we give names to ships don't we? Still it is a bit odd that the symbols should resemble Egyptian hieroglyphs so closely."

Professor Buckle leaned back in his chair as if resigned to giving a long talk to his guests. "I am not an expert on ancient Egyptians, but if we focus on them to start with, maybe something relevant will emerge. I will try to summarise the salient facts as I know them so that we all gain some sort of general perspective."

"That would be really helpful," said Chris and Joy in unison.

Folding his arms, the Professor looked at the ceiling and closed his eyes, giving the impression of someone dredging details from their memory. He spoke slowly in a hushed voice.

"The ancient Egyptians were not the first civilisation. Around 10,000 BC three groups of migrants moved into the Nile Valley. They brought with them religions, Gods and philosophy about man's existence. The annual Nile flood enriched the earth and supplied food for the body. Contemplation of the cosmos gave food to the mind. This alchemy of cultures, geography and astronomy formed the basis of the Egyptian belief systems.

To understand this story, you must remember that the Egyptians believed that there were two states of existence. There was the physical or material state and the spiritual state which connected the soul to the body. The ancient Egyptians believed that the deceased must travel after death through a sort of parallel universe, a Netherworld, where the soul was 'equipped' for the journey to the afterlife. They saw the sky, the patterns of the stars and the constellations as the place where the soul would go into immortality. There was a special place in the sky where the ancient Egyptians thought that the afterlife was located and it was called the Duat. Research shows that at the time of the ancient Egyptians about 2500 years BC, the actual celestial co-ordinates of the Duat were in the eastern part of the sky at the place where Sirius and the stars of Orion were visible just before dawn on the summer solstice – the longest day of the year. At this time of day and at no other season it was believed that the gates to the afterlife would be open to receive the souls of the dead. Remember at the time Sirius was positioned just above the horizon, before the sun rose, during the summer solstice. It was the time of year when they knew that the River Nile flooded and the ground would become fertile. Sirius became linked to the Egyptian Goddess known as Isis, who was recognised as a symbol of love and fertility. The ancient Egyptians were Dualists. They considered that the positions of the stars should be reflected by the buildings on the ground. Construction of the pyramids reflected the patterns and movements of the heavens and these terrestrial photocopies could be used to facilitate the transition from this life to the next. They were built as earthly models where individuals could be prepared to gain foreknowledge of the afterlife. This is why astronomy was so important to them."

Suddenly the Professor stopped talking. He returned to his computer and searched for 'The Great Pyramids of Egypt'. After a couple of minutes, he turned back to his visitors.

"I thought so," he said smiling. "The three pyramids at Gaza are arranged exactly as the three stars of Orion's belt. They have been arranged with such accurate tolerances that the builders must have been expert astronomers. The geometry of the Great Pyramid of Cheops at Gaza is a fascinating example. The King's burial chamber, at the time of construction circa 2500 BC, aligned directly with the brightest star of the three stars of Orion's belt. The Queen's burial chamber aligned directly with Sirius. In 2500 BC when Sirius rose just before the sunrise at the time of the summer solstice it would shine down the shaft into the Queen's burial chamber. The portal to the afterlife would be open and souls of the dead could rise to the stars. Queen Isis could ascend through this portal to the Netherworld."

The Professor fell silent. He opened his desk drawer and took out a bottle of water. He was not exaggerating when he said it would be a long and complicated story!

"Let me get this right," said Chris. "Sirius and Egypt are linked because of religion. Sirius and the goddess Isis are linked because of symbolic fertility?"

"Yes, that's right, although the story of Isis and her husband Osiris has other aspects involving murder, resurrection, and revenge all of which are embedded into the religious beliefs of the Egyptians. The same themes are repeated in the Christian religion."

Chris still felt mystified. "So where did the Gods come from?"

"You have to think of the Gods and their stars as personification of a story. It is like one of those arty dramas where all the characters are fictitious, acting in a play which can be taken at face value, or alternatively, representing some deeper meaning. The Gods have always been viewed as immortals reflecting the human feeling that there is some higher purpose, some meaning above and beyond materialism."

"The Gods could be names given to visitors from space who filled ancient civilisations with such awe that they were turned into deities," Joy suggested. "Even so, I still wonder why the Egyptians should be the particular civilisation important enough to have their hieroglyphics on an alien craft."

"That's an interesting question." There was a scraping sound from his chair as Professor Buckle suddenly stood up. "I have to go to a meeting now and will be away for a couple of hours. If you agree, I can take you across the campus to the library and book you a computer where you will be able to read about matters relevant to your area of interest before we reconvene our meeting."

Chris and Joy exchanged puzzled glances. The Professor laughed as he saw their expressions, "There is a period in history known as the 'Younger Dryas'. I know that you have probably never heard of it before. It is an episode in history that had a big impact on human civilisation. It may help you to get a better idea of how civilisation has evolved. Whether this has been with or without the help of an alien intervention we will all need to take a view!"

Leading them towards the door the Professor smiled, "You are probably hungry. Perhaps, I can point out the student restaurant while we are on the way."

TWENTY-FOUR

CIVILISATIONS

───────

The student restaurant was not the most private place to discuss sensitive issues. It was a self-service counter with tables spread around an open plan room. Chris preferred to eat in discrete, enclosed spaces, where there was less chance of conversation being overheard. They were both hungry and they quickly selected meals from the large menu which hung above the serving counter. Chris decided on burgers and chips while Joy chose lasagne. They found a table near to a window on the perimeter of the restaurant. Meanwhile, students walked past chatting in groups, absorbed in their own world. They seemed oblivious to the couple who sat discussing Egypt over this hasty lunch. After hurriedly satisfying their appetites the couple made their way to the library and were taken to a small room with glass windows on all sides by the assistant librarian, an attractive young woman with an hourglass figure. Chris felt a harsh nudge from Joy as she noticed his gaze lingering too long over the librarian's rear as they followed her to the research room.

"I have reserved a computer for you and have accessed our

resource database regarding 'The Younger Dryas' as instructed by Professor Buckle. The CD is now loaded on your computer. If you need any help, I will be working at the central counter over there," said the librarian pointing towards a circular structure that resembled a large air filter.

"I must say that I have never heard of this historic event!" Chris pronounced, hoping that his indiscretion had been forgiven.

Joy sat down without replying and started to read. The more she read the more she wanted to learn. An hour passed as though it was five minutes.

There was a sudden noise as the door opened. Professor Buckle stood framed in the doorway, his handkerchief hanging precariously from the top pocket of his jacket. He seemed a little agitated. "Just spent two hours talking about budgets and still nothing concrete decided. I hope that you have been more productive working in here. Shall we go back to my study where you can share your thoughts?" he said cheerfully.

Once installed in the office Joy was the first to speak. "When we were in the library, we briefly read about ancient Egyptian belief systems on an internet website. What surprised us most was their knowledge of astronomy, their functional architecture and their ability to make complex calculations."

"Yes. I am always in awe of their achievements," replied the Professor. "It is fair to say that Egyptian culture was tribal until about 3400BC when it suddenly changed to become organised into monarchies. At this time writing started, spectacular architecture and civilised culture appeared. I am saying that all this happened in a comparatively short space of time. In the pre-dynastic period before 3400BC there was no sign of writing. Suddenly, written language appeared which was complex and structured, with hieroglyphs that represented sounds, numbers and concepts. Refined knowledge of mathematics, medicine, astronomy and architecture suddenly became part of the culture. There was no sign of Darwinian evolution in the development of these sciences."

"So how did they suddenly become so advanced?" Joy asked.

"I think that we should concentrate on Sirius as we have an interest in the star gods Isis and her husband Osiris. There are clues relevant to your question to be found in the great temple of Horus at Edfu in Upper Egypt. This temple is a copy of an earlier temple on the same site and has lots of hieroglyphs which are known as the 'Edfu Building Texts'. These texts are recorded as being handed down from an 'early primeval age' when Isis and Osiris were gods and their son was called 'Horus'. This ancient age was known as 'Zep Tepi' or 'first time'. It was a time in which a group known as the 'Builder Gods' were believed to have settled in Egypt. The original Edfu temple was believed to have been built as an earthly copy of a place that existed before the world was created. The texts state that this original place was called the 'Netherworld of the Soul'. As I explained earlier, the astronomical location of the 'Netherworld' was located in the area of the sky where Sirius rose ahead of the sun during the summer solstice."

Joy could not resist the urge to interrupt with a speculative thought that had entered her head. "I know it sounds crazy, but would it be silly to suggest that these 'Builder Gods' were actually visitors from Sirius? After their visit to Egypt the civilisation, knowledge of astronomy and other properties of planet Earth would be quickly imparted to the indigenous population. Over time the stories and myths would become diffused into more modern thinking. Is it reasonable to believe that Egyptian civilisation was not an orthodox evolutionary development, but more a legacy provided by visitors?"

"That is certainly not a theory accepted by mainstream academics," said the professor defensively. "All I can say is that primitive people suddenly found themselves in thriving and wealthy civilisations. The general view suggests that there must have been contact with an earlier advanced donor society. Either the 'Builder Gods' mentioned in the Edfu texts were alien visitors as you suggest, or they could have been Sages from much earlier civilisations."

Chris had been listening to this discourse intently and opened his mouth to speak. He had been silent for so long his voice seemed to have disappeared. He cleared his throat as discretely as possible and spoke clearly, "I can now see why you asked us to read about civilisations."

The Professor lit a small cigar and asked, with a twinkle in his eye, "Can you tell me about what you learned in the library? I hope that you don't mind me having a smoke. The Health and Safety people are off site today at a conference about global warming."

It was more a statement than a request as to whether it would be alright to smoke. An answer was not invited by the question. Mercifully, the Professor was considerate enough to open a window.

"We found the CD quite fascinating," Chris replied, although he sounded a bit hesitant. "There is just so much to take in I don't feel I can give it full justice, but I'll do my best. Try to imagine the world 12800 years ago. People were foraging to survive in hunter gatherer communities. After a period of relatively improving climatic conditions there was a cataclysmic event that plunged the world into an ice age that lasted for about 1200 years. What this event was is subject to some differences of opinion by the scientists. There is compelling evidence showing that this dramatic event was most likely due to an encounter with a disintegrating comet. Chunks of the comet entered the Earth's atmosphere and hit ice covering the whole of Canada and North America. This devastating event resulted in the sudden melting of the ice with cold fresh water pouring into the Atlantic. The Atlantic currents like the Gulf Stream were reversed and debris was thrown up into the atmosphere blocking out the sun."

"I am impressed that you were able to absorb all this so quickly," interrupted Professor Buckle. "It was an example of extreme climate change. The effects lasted for 1200 years between 12800 and 11600 years ago. This is the period known by geologists the 'Younger Dryas.'"

Chris took a sip of water before continuing. "Many animals, like the mammoths went extinct during this time. Our human ancestors suffered greatly too, but there is something interesting that I read here. Not all humans were primitive hunter gatherers. There is evidence of the existence of a higher civilisation, traces of which can be identified today. This evidence is in places of archaeological interest."

Chris shuffled through some brief notes that he had made. "Sorry about this pause. I knew I would have difficulty remembering all the names of the places. Here they are," said Chris, relieved to have located the names within his notes. "Places like Gobekli Tepe in Turkey, Gunung Padang in Indonesia, Giza in Egypt and The Moai statues of Easter island to name a few. The primitive hunter gatherers were used to adapting in order to survive, whereas the enlightened, educated people tended to live in towns where they provided for their needs by visiting markets. After the cataclysmic events of 12800 years ago destroyed the natural order on the planet, more hunter gather communities survived than did the civilised city dwellers."

Looking up from his notepad, Chris checked that the Professor was still listening before continuing.

"Who would best survive a cataclysmic event today, tribes in the Amazon or the inhabitants of the City of London? Some town dwelling survivors representing more advanced civilisation were able to pass on their knowledge. They have left records on inscribed pillars and monumental structures like the pyramids. They trained the hunter gathers so that they could restore human civilisation to its peaks of achievement relatively quickly. What we now read as Sages, Gods, 'The Primeval Ones' and King's Sons for example may well be euphemisms for knowledgeable, enlightened survivors who passed on their knowledge. They were Prophet's from the past."

Through the smoky haze now filling the room the Professor asked Chris. "Are you suggesting that civilisations rise and fall in cycles?"

"Yes. If all the culture and materialistic riches of an old, advanced civilisation were lost and only a few people survived a cataclysmic event, then civilisation would have to start again. In a relatively short time memories would fade. Most survivors would quickly become like children in complete ignorance of what had happened in early times. Stories and myths would develop, but the legacy of knowledge would be carried on by just a few individuals."

"History indicates that civilisations do rise and fall in cycles. There is a repeated theme of world floods which wiped out the whole of civilisations, the story of Noah's Arc is one example, the destruction of Atlantis another and 'The Younger Dyas' yet another," added the Professor. "That being the case it could explain why there is a 'Great Silence' in terms of intergalactic communications," he mused. "Imagine an advanced civilisation capable of communicating with other galaxies. Due to cataclysmic events triggered by something like a collision with a comet, the civilisation is wiped out and must start again. If there is intelligent life elsewhere in the universe, the same cycles probably affect them too. It is unlikely that two advanced civilisations would peak in technical achievements at the same time. We may not be alone, but we will never be in contact. Your proposition that a rapid gain of knowledge by the Egyptians could have been the result of a visit by advanced extra-terrestrial space travellers is a possibility. No definitive proof exists and archaeologists would not acknowledge that theory. However, there are alternative explanations as we have heard and that is why I wanted you to read about the past."

"It does seem a coincidence though," said Chris thoughtfully. "After all, consider the evidence so far? We have panels from an extra-terrestrial craft which contain symbols strongly related to Egyptian hieroglyphs. Not just any old symbols, but ones that refer to a goddess associated with Sirius. The Ancient Egyptians revered Sirius in their belief systems and demonstrated incredible knowledge of astronomy to the extent that they knew almost as much as we do today. Finally, we know that their civilisation developed at a quicker pace than would be expected by the usual evolutionary processes. If I had to speculate as to where the craft that Joy saw that night came from, I would say the Sirius star system."

Joy laughed as she brushed her hand over her hair. "Wow! You sounded like a lawyer summing up a court case. I can't get my head around the fact that a craft came all the way from another star system to land at a farm in Cornwall."

Professor Buckle looked a little alarmed by all this talk of aliens. "I hope that I haven't filled your heads with unfounded ideas. This is an academic institution and the subject of aliens is frowned on by the establishment."

"I thought that universities were places open to new ideas," said Chris.

"It all depends on what the ideas are! Some traditional academics are very entrenched in their own research and find it hard to accept what they think is unsubstantiated pseudo-science," replied the Professor. "We must try to stand back and consider all the theories. Your ideas about visitors from space needs to stand against the other possibilities."

Professor Buckle looked at the faces of the two people sat opposite to him in his study. He could see that they were disappointed that he had not endorsed their theory. It was one of those awkward moments when after a frank exchange of views, all participants realise that the conversation is exhausted.

"Before we leave, we must thank you for sharing your insights with us," said Joy sensing that the Professor wanted to end their meeting. "I get the feeling that our lives are tenuous and could easily be blotted out by something beyond our control. Just a handful of us who survived would not be able to restore the level of civilisation that we had previously lived in. The human race may be more vulnerable than they think."

"Much would depend on who the survivors were. If there were just a few 'special' people who could control the content and dissemination of knowledge it would be possible to collectively write down and communicate knowledge for future generations. I too have often wondered about the status of these 'special people'. Were they Gods, Sages, Wise Men or Aliens? Were 'The Followers of Horus' just wise men who had access to a treasure chest of knowledge from earlier times?" the Professor speculated.

Professor Buckle leaned forward in his chair and stubbed out the butt of his cigar. "You have listened to me for long enough. Before you leave, can I ask if you would mind if I showed your prints to a colleague. It might be helpful to get a second opinion."

It was understandably hard for the Professor, a person who had spent years in research, not to continue his interest in this story. He did not want to cause trouble for anyone, but this matter was too rich in detail just to drop in his pending tray.

Chris hesitated to reply. The room was filled with a pungent fug of cigar smoke which threatened to irritate his throat and seemed to be impeding his thoughts. He was worried that their visit would reach the ears of the Ministry of Defence. He did not want to reawaken the problems he had been having about breaches of secrecy. The Professor only suspected that the army had recovered the downed craft. If he wanted to make his own enquiries that was fine if he did not implicate them.

"I would appreciate you not involving either of us in any consultations that you make. The authorities are sensitive about the subject of the craft that collided with the turbine and we have been warned against discussing the matter. Because of all this I prefer to take the prints home with us." Of course, Chris realised that by showing the prints total security of the information had been compromised. When information is shared the risk of an unauthorised leak vastly increases. Still keeping the prints would be a small precaution.

"I fully understand. Be assured that I will treat the whole matter with discretion. Can you remind me as to what happened to the craft that the panels were ripped away from? You see, whilst I am sceptical about the origins of the craft I am intrigued by its very existence. Now that I have heard your story I am wondering if our Government is hiding bits of crashed alien craft somewhere in a secret location."

There was something a little furtive in the way the Professor spoke which made Chris suspicious.

Joy came to the rescue. "After my encounter on the moor and the subsequent collision with the turbine, the craft shot way at speed and disappeared from my vision. Local people say there was a crash nearby and the military people recovered some wreckage."

"So, it almost certainly did crash! I am not surprised, as the damage was likely to be serious enough to cause it to malfunction," stated the Professor thoughtfully.

Joy just shrugged her shoulders in a gesture of uncertainty. The Professor extracted the red handkerchief from the top pocket of his jacket and blew his noise loudly. It was such a loud blow Chris thought he sensed the window vibrate. If the intension was a ruse to conceal his scepticism of Joy's story it worked. Chris knew that they had aroused the Professor's interest and he had a suspicion that in this case inquisitiveness would override discretion.

"I presume that all the newspaper articles that you write are available to read online. I will ask the librarian to print off copies. Thank you for confiding in me. I have found our meeting today to be very interesting. We must keep in touch to share in any developments."

Looking at Joy, the Professor smiled. "I hope that you don't experience any more close encounters with alien craft!"

Joy looked taken aback. She remembered what had happened to the Russian spies. Seeing her discomfort, the Professor quickly added, "Sorry! That was an inconsiderate comment."

He may have been joking, but it was in bad taste and it preyed on Joy's mind for some time. The phrase 'many a true word is spoken in jest' kept polluting her thoughts. She was glad that the meeting was ending. It would be good to take a breath of fresh air.

They were leaving with a better idea as to where the alien craft could have come from. It was a new insight that could only have been gained by sharing their story with someone with specialist knowledge. If the Professor 'opened Pandora's box' by reigniting public interest in Joy's close encounter, they had to hope that it would not be associated with their visit. Chris realised that there would be a positive element to this. He would be in a good position to write an article for his newspaper. He would be able to justify his writing as a response to a matter of public interest. At least he could use this argument to persuade his editor to authorise the article. The wisdom of such journalism was another matter, but Chris saw a headline in his journalistic eye, 'Travellers from Sirius visit Cornwall' and this made him want to smile.

Even before the couple reached the car park the Professor had been unable to resist the temptation to uncover details about the crashed spacecraft. He had given up a lot of his time today to address this issue and his natural inquisitiveness had taken over. He looked at the pile of unmarked assignments on the edge of his desk and decided that it would be much more interesting to delve further into the Cornish UFO story. He unearthed copies of Chris's articles from newspaper archives stored on the internet. By the end of the afternoon he had checked with the RAF station at Newquay airport to see if they had additional information. Of course, they issued a bland statement indicating that they were unable to comment on security matters. The very nature of the enquiry had the effect of arousing their suspicions and the Professor's name was entered on their 'watch list'. The Professor's naivety about the matters he was now delving into would make him vulnerable to consequences that he could not anticipate.

TWENTY-FIVE
FINAL RECKONING

The journey home took longer than usual. The rain had stopped, but the traffic was heavy. As the sun dropped, autumn dampness descended. Along the length of the carriageway two dry parallel tracks showed where the passage of many tyres had absorbed the surface water. Flurries of golden leaves shuffled skittishly over the road disturbed by the intermittent breeze. The land features looked dark, shadows were long and a silver mist twisted along the low-lying valleys. Joy was glad that the car had an efficient heater as she reflected on events.

She looked across at Chris, who realising that he was being surveyed, turned towards her and smiled. Joy rested her head on Chris's shoulder. "It's been a long day," she said wearily. "Why don't you stay at my place tonight?"

"I would like that," Chris replied. He slipped his left arm around Joy's shoulders and gave the top of her head a little kiss. "I missed you when we were apart and that's when I realised I had been in love with you for quite a while."

"I feel the same," Joy replied. "I was gutted when you were

detained. I should have been focussed on my work, but I couldn't concentrate." She smiled at Chris, but resisted the impulse to kiss him. "Better put both hands on the wheel though, or ours might be the shortest relationship in history!" Reluctantly, Chris complied.

"What do you think Professor Buckle will be doing now?" asked Joy. "I don't think he knew what to make of our story. He probably suspects that there is more to it than what we told him."

Chris had been thinking along the same lines. "I can't imagine that he will just shrug his shoulders and forget the whole matter. He is an academic, used to research. It would not surprise me if he were checking out the details of the story right now. I just hope that he doesn't mention us as the source of his interest."

In her thoughts Joy could imagine the Professor making his enquiries and running into the same wall of secrecy that had plagued their own research. "That devious Dennis Torrance guy that you told me about is going to realise that the photos must have come from us. Who else would have had access to the panels? Sooner or later he is going to confront you or me or Bert or all of us and we need to be prepared."

"You are right", sighed Chris after a few moments reflection. "Maybe we should bow to the inevitable and publish our own article showing the photos and the meaning of the symbols. If we maintain the initiative the likes of Mr. Torrance will remain one step behind. If we keep silent about the events at St Eval, the authorities may just try to pass off the whole story as a hoax. If they get too heavy-handed people will begin to think there is substance to the story."

"Why don't we call in to ask Bert for his opinion?" Joy asked. "He took the photos and we need to tell him what we have found regarding the markings. The farm is on the way home so we only need to make a short detour."

The couple fell silent as the car cruised relentlessly along the A30 dual carriageway. Chris started to reflect on the day at the

University. He glanced over towards Joy. She had fallen asleep in the passenger seat. The day at the University had unsettled Chris. The more he had learned about civilisations, ancient Egyptian belief systems and the Cosmos, the less confident he felt in his understanding. It was stunning to realise the depth of knowledge that existed before the time of Christ. The Egyptians had knowledge of mathematics, astronomy and building techniques sufficient to construct pyramids with esoteric features. Then there were certain recurring themes concerning floods and life-threatening disasters. Not to forget repeated episodes featuring wise men like Noah, Hermes, Quetzalcoatl and Oannes. Sometimes these Builder Gods, Sages, Lords of Light, Watchers, or so-called Shining Ones acted as conduits of wisdom. They were purveyors of ancient knowledge passed on from earlier advanced civilisations which had succumbed to apocalyptic disasters. Were these people mortals? Perhaps they were just intelligent individuals lucky enough to survive disaster and who lived to disseminate their knowledge? It was not impossible that they were visitors from other planets who injected their expertise from time to time. Could it be that they were not mortals and had an interface with some energy force not yet detected by physics?

As the miles passed by, these imponderable matters circulated in Chris's head. He had an uneasy feeling that there was some other force in this equation. Some other unrecognised cosmic energy that had become inseminated into the biology of human beings. This energy within humans could be the force that made the difference between extinction, survival and immortality. His thoughts were suddenly interrupted by a nudge from Joy who had woken up.

"Don't forget we need to turn off here if we are going to see Bert," she said.

"Good job you reminded me," replied Chris. "I wasn't concentrating on the route!"

When they arrived at Innyvale Farm the last light had faded. There was a damp film over the machinery outside the barn. A single light in the downstairs window reflected its yellow glow across the yard.

Bert was pleased to welcome them. "I got your text earlier and I'm eager to hear what you found out," he shouted from the kitchen as he made a pot of tea.

As they sat around the table Bert listened carefully as Chris and Joy related their findings.

"If it turns out that the craft came from the star called Sirius, it would be an incredible discovery," gasped Bert.

The sudden striking of the clock on Bert's mantelpiece reminded Chris of what a long day it had been. His journalistic instincts suddenly returned, activated by the sudden noise from the clock. He felt that they all had a duty to share more generally the events that had happened in their area of Cornwall.

"What if we write the story of what happened to you and Joy that night?" asked Chris. "That piece would need to include your discovery of the panels and an interpretation of the markings."

Bert sighed "It would be a sensational article. I do not think it is wrong to report matters which are in the public interest. However, what you describe goes some way to explaining the pattern that those two Russian bodies were displayed in behind my barn. It chills me to say it, but they were in a star formation. It suggests that it was not just a random dumping, more a symbolic display! I personally do not object if you want to use the photos in an article about all this, but I would steer well clear of any mention of those bodies or that the military people recovered an actual craft. Leave the authorities scope to cast doubt on the integrity of your story. Better to be labelled a crank than end up in jail!"

Joy agreed. "We can write an honest account of what we experienced that night. People can decide for themselves whether the photographs are faked. The links to Sirius would make the article a real exclusive. We don't need to say anything about the spying, the crash or the activities at St Eval."

"I fear that my farm will become a place of pilgrimage for UFO hunters," said Bert sadly.

"Just take them to the heap of manure where you hid the panels. The smell should make their visit a short one," replied Chris flippantly.

The couple left the farm after saying goodbye to Bert who stood and waved farewell as the car pulled away. Before returning inside Bert looked up and saw the myriad of stars adorning the sky. He had never really been interested in astronomy, but after listening to the story his visitors had told he looked up with new interest. As he contemplated the heavens he was reminded of how small and vulnerable human beings are. The moon bathed everything in a silvery, spectral light. He turned to re-enter the farmhouse, but got a strong sense that there was something behind him. He felt the hairs on the back of his neck rise as he stopped and looked back towards the night sky. A large black shape was sending a dark shadow across the moonlit landscape. It was a huge saucer shaped craft, big enough to blot out the stars as it crossed from a north easterly to south westerly direction. The craft moved silently, gliding slowly, but relentlessly across the dark void of the night sky. Bert felt afraid as he rushed indoors to find sanctuary in the house. He had an unnerving sensation that something bad was about to happen. Gathering his thoughts, he took out his mobile. His hands were shaking as he switched to video mode. Rushing back to the front door, which was still open, he could see the rear of the craft which had now passed overhead. It may have been an illusion, but the craft appeared to have lost height. A red laser beam shot earthwards from underneath the saucer before it ascended at astonishing speed and disappeared somewhere in the direction of the Atlantic Ocean. Bert felt his heart beating fast as he fumbled with his phone. He could not shake off an irrational feeling of impending disaster. Then he remembered that Chris and Joy were travelling home. His thoughts returned to the close encounter that he and Joy had experienced in Davidstow woods. He recalled the effect on the Land Rover's electrical system on the road to the wind turbine. He trembled as thoughts returned of the lost time which they had been unable to account for. Then he prayed that they had not encountered the mysterious mothership. He had no way of knowing if all these incidents were connected. Instinctively, he knew that they were. He was glad that he was still alive and had not suffered the same fate as the two Russian spies.

Meanwhile, Chris drove along the narrow country road in the direction of Davidstow airfield. Joy turned on the radio. There was a song playing that she could not remember the name of. She knew the band was 'Queen' but was unsure of the title so she asked if Chris could remember it. Chris did not reply because he was concerned about a malfunction with the car's electrical system. The headlights had dimmed and it was hard to see the road ahead. He decided that he would park at the next layby, but before he could do anything the radio signal faded and a strong vibration shook the vehicle. An unnatural red glow flooded the landscape outside. It was like entering some hellish twilight zone. Without warning the car engine stalled and the steering lock engaged. Out of control and still travelling at speed, the car hit a large tree. There was no time to speak as the violence of impact was followed by the explosion of the airbags. The car collided with the tree so severely that it rebounded onto the road and slid on its side for some distance. There was an awful metallic scraping sound as the metal bodywork was scoured by the surface of the road. A shower of sparks was generated by the friction. Then, for a few seconds, there was an eerie calm silence. One of the wheels slowly continued to rotate. It was the only reminder that the car had been a moving vehicle. Fuel dripped from a ruptured line and the unpleasant smell of petrol vapour enveloped the wreckage. A column of white smoke drifted up from somewhere underneath the twisted metal. Suddenly, the stillness was destroyed by a 'woosh' like a gas burner reacting to a match. The leaking fuel had ignited and the whole vehicle quickly became engulfed in an inferno.

As Joy regained consciousness a warm trickle of blood ran down from her head before dripping off the end of her nose. She managed to unbuckle her seatbelt even though she was in pain from the wound on her head. It was difficult to see and to breathe. Still barely conscious, she crawled out through the space where the windscreen had been as flames licked her clothing. There was no time to pull Chris out of the vehicle. He was trapped in his seat, invisible through the fog of choking smoke. Joy lay at the side of the road inert, her head throbbing, sick with shock. She tried to stand, but immediately collapsed back onto the road. Then everything went black until she woke up in hospital.

It was a sudden and violent end to Chris's physical life. His body was incinerated, but the intangible energy represented by his conscious soul remained in the cosmos, indestructible, spiritually tactile, invisible and now immortal. Everything that he had wondered about was now accessible, everything that he had feared rendered obsolete. Chris journeyed into another dimension leaving behind the physical universe. Above the wreckage, the stars were getting ever more visible, the brightest one of which was shining in the constellation of Canis Major. Slowly, inexorably, the large dark mothership continued its course towards the vacuum of outer space.

The intended article about the UFO experiences was never written. As the flowers left by the roadside at the scene of the accident wilted Joy immersed herself in the family business which became a commercial success. Henry resigned from his job at Precision Castings (Wadebridge) Limited to support the expanding family enterprise. Shocked and saddened by the terrible accident so near to his farm Bert disassociated himself from any further involvement in UFO investigations. He dedicated himself to his work on the farm.

Forever etched in Joy's memory were the events that she experienced during that fateful year. Although heart broken, she retained the warmth that she had felt for Chris and she thought about him often. Especially in those quiet moments when the work of the day was done and the light faded over the lonely expanse of Bodmin Moor.

For exclusive discounts on Matador titles,
sign up to our occasional newsletter at
troubador.co.uk/bookshop

Lightning Source UK Ltd.
Milton Keynes UK
UKHW022154150621
385567UK00009B/236